Praise for Sara

"A sweet, enjoyable second chance at love Regency romance with a strong heroine, a steadfast hero, a dash of suspense, and elegant descriptive prose. I rooted for this well-matched couple from the very first page!"

—Syrie James, author of *The Missing Manuscript of Jane Austen*, for *In the Shelter of Hollythorne House*

"The Regency has found a gifted voice in Sarah Ladd who spins magic from windswept moors and romance from a love separated but not forgotten. *In the Shelter of Hollythorne House* is a beautiful tale of lost love finding its strength again when all hope seems lost. Atmospheric and lush, readers will find themselves swooning in the manner of Jane Austen."

—J'nell Ciesielski, bestselling author of *The Brilliance of Stars* and *The Socialite*

"The swoon-worthy romance of Jane Austen meets the suspense of Charlotte Brontë in Sarah Ladd's enthralling *The Letter from Briarton Park*. As Cassandra navigates the mystery of her own life, it is absolutely clear that family—either of blood or heart—are where she, and we, ultimately find our home."

—Joy Callaway, international bestselling author of *The Fifth Avenue Artists Society* and *The Greenbrier Resort*

"*The Light at Wyndcliff* is a richly atmospheric Regency novel, reminiscent of the works of Victoria Holt and Daphne du Maurier. The storm-swept Cornish coast is a character unto itself, forming the perfect backdrop for an expertly woven tale of secrets, danger, and heartfelt romance. A riveting and deeply emotional read."

—Mimi Matthews, *USA TODAY* bestselling author of the Parish Orphans of Devon series

"[*The Light at Wyndcliff*] expertly deploys elements of gothic mystery . . . The descriptions of the dilapidated property add dark, delicious atmosphere . . . The atmosphere and intrigue keep the pages turning."

—Publishers Weekly

"[Ladd] faithfully depicts the rough Cornish coast of the 1820s, with its rocky coves and windswept moors, the slow-simmering romance between the attractive principals is skillfully done, the suspense is intriguing, and all is brought to a satisfying conclusion . . . This charmingly written, gentle tale of manners and romance hits the right notes."

—HISTORICAL NOVEL SOCIETY FOR *THE LIGHT AT WYNDCLIFF*

"Fans of Julie Klassen will love this."

—PUBLISHERS WEEKLY FOR *THE THIEF OF LANWYN MANOR*

"Cornwall's iconic sea cliffs are on display in *The Thief of Lanwyn Manor*, but it's the lyrical prose, rich historical detail, and layered characters that truly shine on the page. Fans of Regency romance will be instantly drawn in and happily lost within the pages."

—KRISTY CAMBRON, BESTSELLING AUTHOR OF *THE PARIS DRESSMAKER* AND THE LOST CASTLE NOVELS

"*Northanger Abbey* meets *Poldark* against the resplendent and beautifully realized landscape of Cornwall. Ladd shines a spotlight on the limitations of women in an era where they were deprived of agency and instead were commodities in transactions of business and land. The thinking-woman's romance, *The Thief of Lanwyn Manor* is an unputdownable escape."

—RACHEL MCMILLAN, AUTHOR OF *THE LONDON RESTORATION*

"Brimming with dangerous secrets, rich characters, and the hauntingly beautiful descriptions Sarah Ladd handles so well, 1800s Cornwall is brought vividly to life in this well-crafted tale."

—ABIGAIL WILSON, AUTHOR OF *MASQUERADE AT MIDDLECREST ABBEY*, FOR *THE GOVERNESS OF PENWYTHE HALL*

"Lovers of sweet and Christian romance will fall in love with Delia's strength amid the haunting backdrop of her tragic past and the Cornish coast."

—JOSI S. KILPACK, WHITNEY AWARD–WINNING AUTHOR OF THE MAYFIELD FAMILY SERIES, FOR *THE GOVERNESS OF PENWYTHE HALL*

"Absolutely captivating! Once I started reading, I couldn't put down *The Governess of Penwythe Hall*. This blend of *Jane Eyre*, Jane Austen, and *Jamaica Inn* has it all. Intrigue. Danger. Poignant moments. And best of all a sweet, sweet love story. This is by far my favorite Sarah Ladd book."

—MICHELLE GRIEP, CHRISTY AWARD–WINNING AUTHOR
OF THE ONCE UPON A DICKENS CHRISTMAS SERIES

"A strong choice for fans of historical fiction, especially lovers of Elizabeth Gaskell's *North and South*. It will also appeal to admirers of Kristy Cambron and Tracie Peterson."

—LIBRARY JOURNAL FOR THE WEAVER'S DAUGHTER

"A gently unfolding love story set amid the turmoil of the early Industrial Revolution. [*The Weaver's Daughter* is] a story of betrayal, love, and redemption, all beautifully rendered in rural England."

—ELIZABETH CAMDEN, RITA AWARD–WINNING AUTHOR

"With betrayals, murders, and criminal activity disrupting the peace at Fellsworth, Ladd fills the pages with as much intrigue as romance. A well-crafted story for fans of Regency novels."

—PUBLISHERS WEEKLY FOR A STRANGER AT FELLSWORTH

"Ladd's story, with its menace and cast of seedy London characters, feels more like a work of Dickens than a Regency . . . A solid outing."

—PUBLISHERS WEEKLY FOR THE CURIOSITY KEEPER

"A delightful read, rich with period details."

—SARAH M. EDEN, BESTSELLING AUTHOR OF
FOR ELISE, FOR THE CURIOSITY KEEPER

"The premise grabbed my attention from the first lines, and I eagerly returned to its pages. I think my readers will enjoy *The Heiress of Winterwood*."

—JULIE KLASSEN, BESTSELLING, AWARD-WINNING AUTHOR

"If you are a fan of Jane Austen and *Jane Eyre*, you will love Sarah E. Ladd's debut."

—USATODAY.COM FOR THE HEIRESS OF WINTERWOOD

IN THE
SHELTER
of
HOLLYTHORNE
HOUSE

ALSO BY SARAH E. LADD

THE HOUSES OF YORKSHIRE NOVELS

The Letter from Briarton Park

In the Shelter of Hollythorne House

THE CORNWALL NOVELS

The Governess of Penwythe Hall

The Thief of Lanwyn Manor

The Light at Wyndcliff

THE TREASURES OF SURREY NOVELS

The Curiosity Keeper

Dawn at Emberwilde

A Stranger at Fellsworth

THE WHISPERS ON THE MOORS NOVELS

The Heiress of Winterwood

The Headmistress of Rosemere

A Lady at Willowgrove Hall

STAND-ALONE NOVELS

The Weaver's Daughter

IN THE
SHELTER
of
HOLLYTHORNE
HOUSE

SARAH E. LADD

THOMAS NELSON
Since 1798

Published in Nashville, Tennessee, by Thomas Nelson. Thomas Nelson is a registered trademark of HarperCollins Christian Publishing, Inc.

Published in association with Books & Such Literary Management, 52 Mission Circle, Suite 122, PMB 170, Santa Rosa, California 95409-5370, www.booksandsuch.com.

Thomas Nelson titles may be purchased in bulk for educational, business, fundraising, or sales promotional use. For information, please e-mail SpecialMarkets@ThomasNelson.com.

Library of Congress Cataloging-in-Publication Data

Names: Ladd, Sarah E., author.
Title: In the shelter of Hollythorne House / Sarah E. Ladd.
Description: Nashville, Tennessee : Thomas Nelson, [2023] | Summary: "Young widow Charlotte Grey faces an uncertain future . . . until a chance encounter with her first love gives her heart a second chance in this Regency romance set on the Yorkshire Moors"-- Provided by publisher.
Identifiers: LCCN 2023001303 (print) | LCCN 2023001304 (ebook) | ISBN 9780785246817 (paperback) | ISBN 9780785246824 (epub) | ISBN 9780785246831
Subjects: LCGFT: Romance fiction. | Christian fiction. | Novels.
Classification: LCC PS3612.A3565 I6 2023 (print) | LCC PS3612.A3565 (ebook) | DDC 813/.6--dc23/eng/20230130
LC record available at https://lccn.loc.gov/2023001303
LC ebook record available at https://lccn.loc.gov/2023001304

Printed in the United States of America

23 24 25 26 27 LBC 5 4 3 2 1

This novel is dedicated to BM and JS—with gratitude

Prologue

BLIGHT MOOR, YORKSHIRE, ENGLAND
SUMMER 1813

CHARLOTTE GREY SHOULD have been more careful with her heart.

She tightened her grip on the letter and traversed the uneven, rocky path toward Even Tor, refusing to acknowledge the pangs of remorse over her uncharacteristic lack of restraint.

She'd always pitied silly young ladies who freely gave their hearts, who would flirt and open themselves to unnecessary censure and dejection. What was more, she'd never really believed in romantic love—the sort of attachment that intertwined one's mind and soul irrevocably with another's.

Not until she'd first encountered Mr. Anthony Welbourne exactly three months prior.

Charlotte paused in her steps to look once again at Anthony's hastily written note.

Even Tor. Sunset.

She quickened her pace and rounded the bend, and Even Tor crept into view—a gnarled, weathered rock formation towering above the surrounding grassland. Imposing limestone boulders and stones stood as sentinels at the base of the majestic structure, adding to its isolation.

No one would happen upon them here.

All around her, as far as her eyes could see, the vast, waving moor grass emphasized the seclusion. The blooming heather danced in the summer's golden light, and the ever-present wind carried perfumed scents of earth and blooms and mewled a mournful song, as if in melancholic commiseration. This location had been their haven, the private place where they would pass the evening hours away from unapproving eyes. But in mere minutes the amber sun would dip down behind the jagged landscape, taking with it any semblance of warmth and comfort. The day would end, the morrow would dawn, and Anthony would leave for war.

She shaded her eyes with her free hand and squinted at the brilliant setting sun. Anthony was there, just as his note had indicated, clad in the brilliant crimson wool coat and white linen trousers of a regimental soldier.

Anthony Welbourne, with his confident nature and even-tempered disposition, was the physical manifestation of all her girlhood dreams—of all her womanly hopes for romantic love, like her parents had shared, and fantasies of a family and security. She wanted to run to him. Fling her arms around his neck and kiss his familiar lips, as she had so many times since their first meeting, and laugh as if time were limitless and the future was free.

But she refrained.

Tomorrow their worlds would shift. Life would propel them down different paths, and the likelihood that those paths would once again converge was implausible.

He straightened as she approached and lifted a hand in greeting. The sun behind him highlighted the wild curl of his dark hair and the strong cut of his broad shoulders. She'd been planning for this—their final conversation—for days, if not weeks. All along she'd determined to show no emotion. What good could come from tears? After all, it was her own fault her heart was breaking. She'd known the risk all along.

She lifted her pale violet chintz skirt to step over the stones at the tor's base. As she drew nearer, he extended his bare hand to assist her over the crumbling rocks. She accepted it and joined him under the tor's cool shadow, hidden from the outside world.

He smiled his casual, easy grin—the very one that had entranced her during their first encounter on the path near this very spot, when they had happened upon each other and he assisted her when her pony threw a shoe. "I was beginning to fear you wouldn't come."

She pulled her hand from his and reestablished a respectable distance, finding it difficult, almost impossible, to meet his gaze. "How could I not?"

They'd never been uncomfortable in each other's presence before, but in this instance an awkward silence hovered that dared each one to speak first.

A dozen sentiments simmered on the end of her tongue, but every word, every notion, brimmed with danger. If spoken aloud, they might reveal a glimpse into the deepest part of her heart—and that she could not allow. She knew well her own hopes and feelings, but she knew not his. In all their time together, he never once made her a vow. He'd rarely spoken of the future or of the dreams that would come next—after the war.

He broke the silence, his alluring voice raspy and low. "I don't know how to bid you farewell."

She forced her practiced smile, almost grateful for how the incessant wind blew long wisps of her hair in front of her face, disguising her features. "We both knew this was coming. That you were leaving. It was expected."

As silence once again fell, the sickening twinge of panic took hold. How, in such a short span of time, had he become the person who understood her better than anyone else in the world? In all her eighteen years she'd never encountered someone who accepted her and her opinions without judgment and whose attention and mere presence emboldened her. He boasted tenacity where she lacked it, encouraged humor where she needed to develop it, and offered companionship when she craved it most. The time they shared had become her sole focus and inspired every dream and ambition. But the attachment would be ending. A thousand thoughts battled for dominance, yet she could only mutter, "I will think of you often, you know."

He chuckled, but wistfulness tempered his usually cheery tone, and an atypical shadow darkened his cobalt eyes. He reached out and tucked a wisp of hair behind her ear, letting his fingers linger against her cheek. "Ah, Charlotte. You will think of me for a bit. Maybe even miss me. But then your life will go on. You will marry, have a family, and live a long and healthy life. Just as you should."

At the mention of marrying another, she jerked her head down and away from his touch. "Stop. Please."

Did he know how agonizing this was for her? She loved him. She did, and the idea of it was intoxicating—of a love that would challenge time and endure war itself.

But it was not to be. For he'd never declared his love for her.

The sun sank farther, and with every second, the vibrant glow dissolved into the misty dusk of twilight. The back of her throat tightened. Her nose twitched. Her confidence in her ability to conceal emotion was wavering. Every passing second prolonged the inevitable and intensified her anguish.

In that moment if he but asked her to, she'd pledge to wait for him. Her heart longed to hear the words that would validate the feelings that domineered every thought.

She hesitated, giving him the space to declare himself.

But he did not.

After a length of silence, she reached to smooth the golden tassels on the epaulet of his crimson coat. "You should go. Your uncle will be expecting you, and everyone will be gathering to say their farewells. If you do not hurry, you'll be missed." She managed a weak smile. "I'm certain mine is not the only feminine heart to break at your departure."

But he did not join her smile. His blue eyes narrowed. His scent of outdoors and leather encircled her as he drew closer. "Yours is the only one that concerns me."

The touch of his hand on her upper arm burned like fire, perilous and wild.

This had to stop.

Every touch, even every word, heaped torment on an already-tender heart. As it was now, they lived in different worlds. Even if he were not leaving, it did not matter what they wanted. Given the nature of the strained relationship between their families, any true union would be impossible. Her father and his uncle were bitter enemies. Both families would vehemently oppose a match between them.

When she returned home to Hollythorne House, she could indulge in tears. She could—and would—give voice to her broken heart and cry until she could feel nothing else. But now, she refused to allow his last sight of her to be one of her weeping.

"Take care of yourself, Anthony Welbourne."

———————

Anthony allowed his gaze to linger first on the dark chestnut hue of Charlotte's windblown hair, then the gentle slope of her petite nose. Then the full curve of her lips that he knew so well.

She was right. He should return to his uncle's.

Prolonging this farewell would not lessen the torment.

But his boots were fixed to the stone beneath him, heavy and weighted, as if the very moors were holding him captive, demanding that he speak.

The words—the declaration of his adoration—wrestled within him, begging to be uttered.

How could he depart without communicating to her the depth of his affection? If he'd had any inclination that a woman would have such a powerful impact on him, he never would have considered the officer's commission. He might have even been content to work all his days at his uncle's gristmill. But the commission had been purchased, and he was committed to an unalterable path.

And another truth, equally as valid and forceful, refused to be ignored. Even if he were free and had no commitments, Charlotte's father would forbid a connection with a man bearing the surname Welbourne, let alone the fact that his social standing was far inferior to hers.

Despite their differences, she'd been an anchor to him in a time of transition. After nineteen years, his role was changing from dutiful nephew and mill worker to that of a soldier. He knew from the first moment he'd witnessed her struggling with a pony—with her flushed cheeks, wild hair, and dogged determination—that she'd laid claim to the concealed, sentimental parts of his heart. As of yet, she had not released it.

Her father's travels had kept him away for the past several months. Throughout that time she'd easily escaped her ineffective chaperone's lackluster supervision to spend the evening hours with him. During those precious times, she'd challenged him. Encouraged him. Allowed him to truly express himself in an environment that didn't contest his plans for his future.

A relationship that started as curious infatuation had developed into the most important and influential of his being, and yet even when all seemed ideal, he held back his true feelings. At this late point, revealing his love for her would be a selfish act. He might never return from the war in America, and even if he did, asking her to wait for him would cause discord within her family. Just because he longed to say the words didn't mean they were prudent.

The silent moments slipped by, and her chin began to tremble. Her high cheekbones flushed pink.

Every muscle in his body ached to reach out and comfort her, but he refrained. It would not be fair, perhaps even cruel, to give false hope to a situation that must end.

Instead, he leaned forward, indulged in a breath of her scent of lavender, and pressed his lips against her forehead. "Farewell, dearest Charlotte."

Without looking at her, he turned.

He forced one step.

And then took another.

She did not call out to him.

She did not stop him.

And in time his own heart might heal. Then again, it might harden.

Regardless, her life would go on.

Chapter 1

Wolden House, Leeds, Yorkshire

October 1817

ROLAND PRIOR HAD gone too far this time. This was not to be borne.

Charlotte's racing blood boiled and fueled each step down the first floor's opulent corridor to Wolden House's broad main staircase. With each inch traversed she formed her argument. Anticipated Roland's retorts. Sharpened her rationale.

Normally, arguing with Roland would only make a matter worse. When it came to their infant son, Roland demanded complete control. But mere minutes ago she'd been informed of his intention to send Henry to live with his brother for the next six months while Roland traveled to the Continent. The suggestion that Henry would be better off with his uncle enraged her. How dare Roland keep her son away from her, for any length of time! She knew well the possible ramifications of questioning Roland Prior. But for Henry's sake, she would fight.

The soles of her soft kid-leather slippers clipped the wooden steps as she descended the staircase. She ignored the sideways glance from the liveried footman and focused her attention on the heavy oak door to her husband's study at the corridor's end. She lifted her hand and rapped her knuckles against the door.

No answer ensued.

Annoyance flared. She knocked harder. Sharper.

When a response still did not come, she gripped the brass handle and turned it, steeling herself for a battle.

But when she opened the door and stepped inside, the chamber was empty.

She frowned. A freshly built fire roared in the grate, and papers and letters, along with a half-empty glass of brandy, littered his desk. The heavy aubergine velvet curtains were drawn in the chamber's two windows, and the fire's saffron glow reflected off the glass decanters on the side table and the gilded mirror on the opposite wall.

She huffed, disappointed not to be able to give voice that very moment to her frustration. She pivoted to leave, but the toe of a polished black boot on the floor captured her attention.

The sight of it, prostrate and positioned at an odd angle, slowed her blood that just moments ago was racing.

Gooseflesh rose on her arms.

She inched closer, one step at a time, until she could see around the desk's edge. There, on the Persian rug beneath the window, lay Roland in an unnatural position on his back. Unmoving. One arm was tucked awkwardly behind him. Papers were strewn around him. His icy blue eyes stared, unblinking.

Nausea seized her, and her hand flew to her throat.

She screamed.

The footman she'd encountered just moments prior rushed in and pushed past her.

The next events simultaneously slowed and sped up.

Servants streamed in.

Voices and shapes blurred into a mess of noise and chatter.

The butler brushed past her and dropped to his master's side.

Someone opened the curtains, flooding the chamber with morning's harsh, colorless light. An arm wrapped around her waist and pulled her backward. A feminine voice whispered for her to come away, but her feet refused to move.

Roland Prior—formidable, imposing, and polarizing—was dead.

Every element from their three-year marriage flashed before her. The fear. The mistrust. His cold words and violent displays of anger.

She should feel sadness at the loss of life. She should feel grief.

But she perceived only numbness—blinding, debilitating numbness.

Perspiration beaded cold on her brow, and every breath burned, as if the very air she was inhaling had died with Roland. In this single slice of time, it mattered not that no love had existed between husband and wife. The fact that arguments and disagreements had ruled their interactions evaporated into a meaningless void.

What mattered now was their son. At only seven months of age, Henry was now heir to his father's fortune and business holdings—a significant designation for anyone, let alone a baby. She might be free from Roland now, but Henry—dear, innocent

Henry—would be further embroiled in the complicated tangle that was the Prior family.

She'd done her very best since the day he was born to protect him. Now that Roland was dead, her mission began afresh. She would sooner die than see her sweet son become a cruel man like his father. It was now her purpose to make sure that did not happen.

Chapter 2

ANTHONY WELBOURNE LOCKED his gaze on the shadowy figure of man at the end of the alley. He dare not look away, lest he lose sight of his target in the night's murky darkness.

Apprehending this man—this criminal—was his singular task. And he would not fail.

In an abrupt jerk, the man, as if suddenly alerted to Anthony's presence, bolted in the opposite direction.

Like a shot from a cannon, Anthony sprinted after him down the dimly lit, uneven road. Blood surged through his limbs and air whipped through his lungs. In this moment his mind was void of all thoughts except one—his ironclad determination to subdue this perpetrator.

Rain stung his face. His wide-brimmed felt hat flew from his head. His boots smacked the wet cobbled street with each staccato step. The few men lingering on the rain-drenched street inched backward as they approached, melding back into the alleys and ramshackle buildings, not wanting to be seen or involved.

But this sort of chase was what Anthony lived for.

In a subtle motion the perpetrator made his fatal error—he glanced over his shoulder. The action slowed his pace just enough for Anthony to gain ground.

The bulkier man broke to the left and ducked around the corner.

Anthony harnessed every bit of energy, lunged forward, and seized the man's coat in his fist. He spun him up against a rough stone wall.

The man whirled out from the hold and slammed his fist against Anthony's jaw.

Refusing to be bested, Anthony pushed him back against the wall with his forearm and then, once certain he had control, shoved him to the ground and pinned him with his own weight.

Within moments the hectic footsteps of the other watchman echoed behind them. Together, Anthony and his partner overpowered the now-winded man, and then with Anthony gripping one arm and the other watchman gripping the criminal's other arm, they escorted him to the constable's office.

By the time he'd seen the perpetrator secured in the gaol and stopped in at the office of Walstead's Watchmen to log his time and activities, dawn was breaking in familiar streaks of smoky gray and mist. Energy and life were still surging through him, as they did after every successful conquest.

Anthony ran a hand down his jaw and opened and closed his mouth, gauging the damage from the blow, then shook it off. If anything, the injury fanned the fire within him. It was impossible to rid the underbelly of Leeds of all the ne'er-do-wells, but tonight he'd apprehended one. And if it made the woman the scum had accosted sleep better, then it was worth it.

If he was prudent, he'd return to his rented chamber at the boardinghouse to sleep, for the next night would, no doubt, call for equal exertion. But he was far too impassioned for rest. He was due to meet Timmons, his friend and colleague, at the Elk Pub, just as he did most mornings after a shift.

As he walked down the awakening street, he adjusted the brilliant Walstead's Watchmen's blue band around his arm, ignoring how a group of men to the side of the pub door straightened as he approached.

It was not his presence that caused them to adjust their posture and lower their voices.

It was the armband.

The swath of sapphire wool secured about his upper arm was always the first thing anyone noticed about him. It was the outward mark of his profession—a symbol that he was a member of Walstead's Watchmen, one of the most renowned groups of thief-takers in all England. Some respected it. Some feared it. But everyone understood it.

Anthony paused outside the public house door to shake the night's lingering moisture from his greatcoat and his Wellington boots. Overhead, dull morning light filtered through ashen clouds, casting a melancholy hue on Leeds's hectic Warehouse District. The ever-present black smoke that puffed from the stacks lingered in the air, despite the rain attempting to douse it.

He shoved his fingers through his wet hair to dislodge any remaining drops and cast a cautionary glance to the right, then the left. At present the shift at the Prior textile mill had changed, and drably clad men, women, and children bustled to and fro, their muted voices mingling with the sound of rickety wooden carts and the shouts of the boatmen on the nearby river. One always had to be on guard on this street—a lesson he'd learned all too well in the two and a half years since he returned from the war.

The squeak of the public house's ancient hinges announced his arrival. Patrons, some of whom also bore the armband, glanced his direction before continuing with their hushed conversations. Scents of stale woodsmoke and ale wafted toward him as he crossed the threshold, and he blinked, allowing his eyes to adjust to both the shifting shadows and the thick smoke seeping from the fire in the broad hearth. Jonathan Timmons was seated at a corner table, as expected. His wide-brimmed hat was pulled low over his eyes, a pewter tankard clenched tightly in his fist.

Timmons looked up as Anthony approached. "What took so long? Was 'bout to give up on ye."

Anthony pulled out the wooden chair opposite Timmons and sat. "Had to deliver a man to the constable's office and then stop by Walstead's."

"Where's your 'at?"

"Lost it. Again." He scooted the chair in closer to the table.

Timmons pushed a second tankard in Anthony's direction.

He gripped the worn tankard handle, eager for his friend's update. "And what of you? How did you find Bretton?"

Timmons scoffed and propped his elbow on the rough table

and held up his disfigured left hand, displaying the misshapen thumb and only remaining finger. "Constable Bretton said 'e admired my selfless service t' our country, but unfortunately my injuries render me unable to administer t' necessary duties of a constable. As such, they do not require my services."

Anthony's gaze drifted to the scarred purple skin where Timmons's other fingers once had been. Anthony had seen the injury so often he barely noticed it anymore, but as he refocused on the wound, the memory of the battle that caused it—not to mention the battle that inflicted Anthony's own injuries—blazed brightly.

Timmons grunted. "Looks like I'm destined to remain a Walstead's Watchmen, eh?"

"It's not so dire, is it?" Anthony grinned in an uncomfortable attempt to cheer his friend. "Steady work. Excellent colleagues. Never a shortage of excitement. Ideal employment, I reckon."

Timmons snorted. "You're one t' talk. You'll jump ship as soon as you're able."

The statement, and the truth in it, sobered him.

Yes, Anthony did have a sharp eye to the future. A man, especially a man who'd endured injuries such as his own, could not chase after criminals his whole life. But at the moment, the goals Anthony had for his future seemed as far off and unattainable as Timmons's did.

The vision of his deceased uncle's dilapidated, charred mill flashed in his mind. Anthony had visited the site in the days after returning from the United States, and the devastating tragedy that met him there had heaped burning coals atop the traumas he'd experienced at war. One day he'd return to the site, repair the fire damage, and see that the gristmill was once again functional, but many things had to occur for him to do so.

"Aye, that might be true, but the mill's in a grim state. No roof. No waterwheel. Mill's not much use without them. 'Twill take capital, and that I don't have. Not yet, anyway. No sense in dwelling on that now—not when there is naught to be done for it except to keep working and earning money."

Anthony swigged the last of his ale. "Come on. Finish that up. Mulligan told me there's a transport convoy taking a load to Scarborough that requires an escort. With any luck we'll be assigned to it. Good money in that."

"I suppose." Timmons indulged in a drink and wiped his wool sleeve across his mouth. "Did ye hear 'bout the thefts on Lowburn Street? Bricks through t' windows of three houses. Probably more. Rumor is t' residents intend to 'ire Walstead to set things right."

Yes, there was no shortage of crimes for men like Anthony to investigate, and the assignments were far from predictable. The wealthy would pay for all sorts of tasks they could not—or would not—do for themselves. The adventure and challenge of never knowing what obstacle he'd face next was a beacon to Anthony. He craved it. Needed it to feel alive. He was a thief-taker, after all. Victims of all sorts hired him or, rather, William Walstead, to bring about justice or for protection.

After emptying their tankards, Anthony and Timmons stood and exited the dark pub into the budding, misty morning. In the short amount of time he'd been inside, the busy street had flared even more to life with more people, more carts, more noise. Anthony took several steps, when a man clipped his shoulder.

"Have a care," Anthony mumbled, continuing forward.

Then a second man, directly behind the first, clipped his shoulder too.

Once was an accident. Two times was not.

Anthony muttered in annoyance and turned to the two men, who were both as dirty and shabby as one would expect a worker from this corner of Leeds to be. There was a hardness, a directness, in the workmen's stares that set Anthony on his defenses.

"Walstead's Watchmen, are ye?" The taller one motioned toward Anthony's armband and spat on the ground next to the toe of Timmons's boots.

Anthony gave no reaction for several moments as he continued to assess the men. "Something you'd like to say?"

The first man's dingy hair clung in greasy strings to his weathered skin, and he inched closer, slow and determined, in the midst of the street's bustling commotion. "Yea, I do. Ye tell ol' Walstead I got a message for 'im. Tell 'im that ol' Rodden remembers. Tell 'im the only thing that'll make me forget what 'appened at Swendel Bay is t' money 'e owes me, and t' longer 'e keeps me waitin', t' looser me tongue's gonna get."

It was a common occurrence—one that used to be unsettling until Anthony had been on enough jobs to see that many men apprehended by one of Walstead's men held grudges.

"If the message is so important, tell him yourself." Anthony continued walking.

"Listen to you, takin' a tone just like 'im," called the man after him. "Sooner or later, someone'll take ye all down a notch or two and put ye in t' gallows where ye belong."

Anthony slowed his steps, pausing only a moment for Timmons to join him in walking. It was one thing to stand his ground. It was another thing entirely to engage with a man intent on a fight. But as Anthony strode away, the truth of what had been said smacked.

As respected as Walstead was, his methods were, at times, questionable. He was just as comfortable dealing with criminals as with magistrates and judges, but if he got results, no one questioned him.

And neither should Anthony.

He continued on. He'd not spend energy concerning himself with a random stranger. He would do as he always did—put the events behind him and focus on the next chase.

Chapter 3

CHARLOTTE SQUEEZED HER eyes shut and drew several deep breaths. Her chest tightened and her head throbbed with each intake of the morning's stifling air.

Three hours.

Three hours since she had discovered Roland's body.

In that time, her entire life had shifted, a tremulous pivot that still seemed impossible.

She opened her eyes slowly, taking a fresh account of the men gathered in the study to assess the infamous Roland Prior's body. Men from every discipline had converged on the morbid event— magistrates, physicians, the coroner, the vicar, Roland's private secretary. Every single one of these people had something to gain by assisting in the investigation into his death. Roland's influence and power, which at one time had impressed her, seemed to continue even posthumously.

She should not be here, in this chamber. She was a woman and, as such, she was supposed to be too weak-minded and delicate for such talk. She should retire to her private quarters and leave the men to deal with the gruesome details of death.

Yet she did not move.

Their deep, low voices rolled on in a continuous, monotonous hum, adding to her general sense of numbness. She was neither hot nor cold. Neither tired nor alert. Even her movements, her voice, was like that from a sluggish dream, when everything was slightly off-balance and peculiar.

Another man entered the study, drawing her attention from her detached reverie. If it had been anyone else, she probably would not have noticed.

But she noticed Silas Prior.

Everyone did.

Silas was Roland's older brother, and he was the only person in Leeds who was more influential than her husband.

Immediately Silas's austere gaze latched onto her.

Silas was ten years Roland's senior and taller by almost a head, and yet their likeness was uncanny. Same icy, pale blue eyes and oddly pale lashes. Same broad forehead, fair complexion, and white-blond hair. She stiffened as he approached. He gripped her elbow and angled her away from the men. "You should not be here."

Defiance already mounting, she readied herself. Every conversation with this man swelled with potential conflict. Roland's death would not change that. In fact, it might make it worse. "This is my home, Silas. Where else should I be?"

"This *was* your home," he snipped. "Everything will be different now that Roland is dead."

A shiver traversed her, snapping her from her contemplations, like a freezing gust of wind chilling damp skin. She pressed her lips shut as the statement's significance dripped over her. Yes, she *did* know that. Roland had been transparent about his will. She'd be left with very little—certainly nothing to which she'd become accustomed. The fact had been hurled at her as a threat often, as if to make her grateful for the life she led.

"Where's Henry?" he demanded suddenly.

Charlotte hesitated.

Silas had a vested interest in Henry—one that went deeper than the expected relationship between uncle and nephew. The Prior brothers had no other relatives, and Silas never had any children of his own. As a result, Henry was heir to it all—not only Roland's fortune, properties, and businesses but Silas's as well.

She needed to be cautious. "He's with his nurse."

"Pack his things. He will come and stay at Gatham House until this is sorted."

Fire lit beneath her at Silas's finite tone, especially as the news of Roland's intention to send Henry to live with Silas reverberated so fresh in her mind. She'd not allow it. Not under any circumstance. "That's not necessary. He'll remain with me."

Silas scoffed, haughty and cold. "This house will be no place for a child in the coming days. There will be an investigation."

"An investigation?" Alarm pricked. "I thought the coroner said he believed it to be apoplexy."

"Of course, it appears to be, but we all know Roland had enemies, and there's no shortage of poisons whose effects appear to be natural. None of us should rest easily until we have more details of exactly what has transpired."

The thought of such activity sickened her. No, this would be no place for Henry in the coming days. But neither was Gatham House.

She glanced around at the men, perceiving anew the importance of measuring her reactions and behavior with the utmost discernment. Even her facial expressions would be scrutinized by those searching for signs of weakness. The very last thing she needed was a roomful of influential men thinking her hysterical.

Shrewdness was essential.

Silas had always been able to control Roland.

He would not control her.

Since the day they married, Roland had overseen and dictated every aspect of her life. His death, however unexpected and shocking, revived Charlotte's autonomy. Never again would she allow any man such domination over her. And thanks to the specifics of her dowry, she was now a woman of property—her childhood home of Hollythorne House was to return to her in the event of her husband's death. She might not have a great deal of money, but now she had a small opportunity to stand her ground.

Silas continued. "I've arranged for guards to patrol outside—Walstead's Watchmen."

Charlotte frowned. "Whatever for?"

"Word of Roland's death had spread, and there's already chatter that the workers of Prior Mill will riot or attempt some sort of unrest during this transition. I don't know details yet, but these things can get out of hand quickly. It's but another reason Henry will be safer at Gatham, so get him ready."

Silas did not wait for a response before he stepped away, leaving her alone with his words' menacing echo.

Now, as she watched the men meander around her, she knew what she needed to do. For herself. For Henry. For both of their futures.

Hollythorne House.

Feeling oddly—and cautiously—motivated, she raised to her toes to see the room. She'd glimpsed Mr. Sires, Roland's solicitor, a while ago, and now he was the only man who could answer her questions.

Of all the men who had worked with Roland, Mr. Sires was the only one with whom she'd experienced any solidarity. He'd been among the first people she'd met when arriving in Leeds. What was more, he'd borne witness to one of Roland's violent episodes, and as a result, he'd always taken care to inquire after her. There was nothing he could do about Roland's behavior toward her, of course, but just the fact that someone noticed bound them in an implicit way.

She left Roland's study in search of Mr. Sires, then found him in the corridor, engaged in conversation. When she drew nearer, the group of men turned, and their conversation fell quiet. They bowed in her direction.

She would not be timid. "Mr. Sires. A moment, please."

He dismissed himself from the others before extending his gloved hand toward her.

She gave him her hand, and he bowed over it.

Mr. Timothy Sires was a tall, sinewy man, whose wire-rimmed glasses seemed too large for his narrow face and whose graying hair made him appear much older than she suspected he was.

"My dear Mrs. Prior, may I convey my deepest sympathies.

How horrible it must have been for you to make such an appalling discovery."

Her tension eased at the directness of his attention. There were very few people she could trust. Roland permitted her no female friendships, and no man would dare speak with her for fear of angering her husband, but as a trusted adviser, Mr. Sires was different.

She lowered her voice to barely above a whisper. "It was horrifying, to be sure. I do not wish to be indelicate, but in light of the circumstances, I feel it is in Henry's and my best interest to fully understand the state of my situation as soon as possible."

He nodded his agreement, then matched his tone to her somber one. "I daresay there will be no surprises for you. Henry will inherit Roland's entire estate when he comes of age—from his properties to his holdings in the business. Current assets, such as this house, will be sold on a case-by-case basis, and the money placed in a trust for Henry. But as for you, things are murkier. As Henry's mother you are now his sole guardian. Roland provided you an annual sum of one thousand pounds until such time that you marry again. Based on his worth and the life you are accustomed to, it is a small sum, but you'll not be a pauper. I will distribute your annual stipend personally and be involved in the administration of the estate and the trust, but Roland specified that Silas Prior should be the executor of his estate and, as such, be involved in all instances and oversee the distribution of Henry's inheritance."

"So Silas will determine how Henry's money is utilized until Henry comes of age?"

"Precisely. I know that sounds dire, but consider yourself fortunate, for he'd spoken of naming Silas Henry's guardian in the event of his death. Fortunately I was able to convince him otherwise, but no doubt that is the arrangement Silas will be expecting."

The meaning of the words sank in, like teeth clamping into a bite. Freedom from the Prior grip would have been difficult to obtain even under the best of scenarios, but this stipulation made it impossible.

With his rheumy eyes fixed on her, Mr. Sires continued. "As the man who holds the purse strings, Silas Prior will have an active voice in young Henry's rearing. As guardian you will receive a specified sum for his general upbringing, but any purchases beyond that, including fees associated with his education, will require Mr. Prior's explicit approval. You, however, will of course retain possession of your belongings, clothing, and other personal items and the sort, but any items you possess that were part of the estate before your marriage must remain within Wolden House."

Charlotte swallowed hard, determined to display no emotion. "And Hollythorne House?"

"Ah yes. Hollythorne House and its holdings belong to you, per the stipulations your father included in your dowry. As you know, it states that if your husband precedes you in death, the rights revert to you unless you have a child who has reached the age of majority. Since that has not happened, the ownership of it remains in your hands. Furthermore, Hollythorne House cannot be sold for two generations, unless in a bankruptcy situation."

The vision of the antiquated stone home on the rough, open moorland flashed in her mind, both sharp with familiarity and fuzzy from years of absence.

He leaned forward, removed his glasses, and cast a glance around to ensure privacy before he pinned his close-set eyes on her. "You've not asked for my advice, but I'm compelled to give it to you. I anticipate that the next several weeks will be difficult. A sudden death like this is bound to stir anxiety and sow seeds of doubt, even in the most general sense, let alone when a man of your husband's standing is involved. Many will attempt to take advantage. I've already heard reports that several men have left their positions in the mill. That being said, my advice to you, my dear Mrs. Prior, is to leave Leeds. Take Henry. Go to Hollythorne House and establish your household immediately, before Mr. Prior can interfere."

Charlotte frowned at the unexpected recommendation. "But do you think it odd to leave so quickly? I do not wish to draw censure, and I fear all eyes are now on us."

"In the end, what you do is of little consequence. Your husband had a certain reputation about the city, especially with regard to debts, and death and money bring out the worst in people. There will always be interest in the heir to a fortune. And at a time like this, all concern should be only for Henry. Fortunately he is quite young. If his mother were to relocate with him before others can get involved, no one could question it."

The decisions to be made overwhelmed her. How would she even implement such a massive undertaking? Hollythorne House had been empty since her father died more than two years prior.

There were no servants. She had no carriage of her own. No actual money other than what Mr. Sires would give her. Obstacles assailed her, one right after the other, and the realization of how little power she actually possessed threatened to undo her. For being the wife of one of the most prominent men in the entire city, her hands seemed tied.

"I can put you in touch with Mr. Ernest Greenwood, Hollythorne House's current steward, and I can also provide you with the money that Roland has allotted you. As for transportation, I can offer you the use of my private carriage."

She eyed him skeptically. She trusted him, but no one offered help so freely, especially in such a volatile landscape. "That is very generous, Mr. Sires."

He narrowed his gaze and lowered his voice to a whisper. "One last word of caution. If you do decide to make a move, do not be secretive about it. You do not want to appear to be making a fool of Silas Prior. That would not bode well . . . for anyone."

"I understand." She swallowed hard at the warning, and her mind leapt to life with the details of what needed to be done. "If you are in earnest, I will gladly accept your kind offer for the use of your carriage. I see no reason to delay the departure."

"Good. Just send word and my carriage and the money will be here for you at your bidding."

"Is it possible to depart in the morning?"

His brows jumped, then he nodded. "Yes. I agree, the sooner you can leave, the better it will be for the both of you. Have courage, my dear."

She bid him farewell, and after he walked away, her gaze once again fell to Silas, who even now was speaking with the other men in the room. Planning. Working. She would never have him out of her life—not while Henry was under her care. Silas would always be a threat to her, and she dare not let herself think anything else.

Chapter 4

ANTHONY STOOPED IN the uneven, dim corridor to unlock the door to the chamber he shared with Timmons. The rusted lock clicked and gave way, and Anthony pushed open the shoddy wooden door to the place he called home.

He stepped through, closed the door behind him, tucked the key back into his welt pocket in his linen waistcoat, and dropped his satchel on the table.

The hour was still before noon—when the rest of the world was rising from slumber and preparing to embark on the day. Anthony, however, had been awake all night. His jaw throbbed from the blow he'd taken, and his tired muscles longed for rest. He crossed to the low-ceilinged chamber's only window and lifted the threadbare curtain, allowing a single stream of sunlight to filter through the dirty glass, giving life to the dust motes balancing in the stale air.

Shouts and clamoring from the street outside mingled with an infant's crying from the floor beneath him. The constant noise used to irk him, but now those sounds were commonplace. They faded to the background, giving voice to a more menacing sound—the silence in his chamber.

It was one thing to be out of doors during the midnight hours on watch. Often it was quiet, but something always commanded his attention—the wind whipping through the branches, the call of the night birds, the distant chatter of men who frequented public houses, the pound of rain on the cobbles. An empty room such as this—a confined, tight space with no other avenue for thought except self-reflection—was another matter entirely.

He removed the brilliant armband, then shrugged his caped greatcoat from his shoulders. The planked floor groaned in reaction to his every movement, and he paused before he tossed the garment on the bed.

This chamber had been home to both Anthony and Timmons since they returned from the war on the same hospital ship. It was narrow, plain, and boasted little more than two small beds, a table and chairs, a rickety washstand, and two trunks. He required nothing more, and the thought of spending money on better lodgings seemed a waste, when he had to save every farthing he could. He could not be a watchman forever, and he had another life to return to one day—the legacy his uncle had left him.

When he'd come back to England, becoming a thief-taker had been the furthest thing from his mind. Timmons's father had been a respected constable while he was alive, and Timmons had used his connection to get them positions with Mr. Walstead. That opportunity, coupled with the fact that the horrors of war had impacted Anthony's view of justice and dulled his sense of fear, made him seem tailor-made for such a role.

He moved to the washbasin, lifted the jug of water, and poured it into the bowl. After washing his face, he assessed his newly acquired bruise in the mottled looking glass above the basin. He ran his hand over the stubble, noting the need for a shave, but then his fingers grazed a scar.

The scar—his permanent reminder of the brutality he'd endured in the war and a physical reminder that life was fleeting. He looked away from his reflection and back down to the water. He didn't need to see it to know that it ran from the top of his right ear, down his jawline and the side of his neck. But it did not stop there. The piece of shrapnel had cut deeper as it crossed his chest, and his left arm had borne the worst part of the injury. He was fortunate to still have his arm.

He was lucky to still have his life.

It would not do to linger on it. The longer he did, the more pungent the scents became and the more vividly the visions flashed. He defied those memories to take a stronger hold than they already had, for as soon as he laid his head down and found sleep, they would visit again in horrifying detail.

Timmons entered the room, his heavy footfalls and deep voice shattering the silence. "Walstead put out t' call for watchmen for t' houses along Lowburn Street. They want a show of force during t' daylight hours to deter vandals at night. Interested?"

Anthony grabbed a cloth and dried his face. Of course he was in. He was tired, yes, but anything was better than being alone in a room—alone with his thoughts. Alone with his memories. "Sure. And the pay?"

"Not sure. But if it's t' folks on Lowburn Street, they usually compensate well."

"Fine by me. Every bit helps."

Timmons sneered as he removed his damp coat and hung it up to dry. "Ye and that mill. Can't imagine why ye would set thoughts on going to t' moors when life is so fulfilling 'ere. Isn't that what ye tried to convince me of just this mornin'?"

Anthony ignored the unmasked sarcasm in his friend's comment. If anyone had told him five years prior that he'd be saving his hard-earned wages to return to Blight Moor to restore his uncle's mill, he'd have laughed. But his injuries forced him to sell his commission upon returning to England, so his plans of living out his days as a soldier were no longer a possibility. The money from the commission's sale, his wages, and the mill were all he had to his name.

Anthony shrugged and hung the towel on the washbasin. "None of us can do this job forever."

And it was true. It was taxing, physical employment. Whereas the excitement and distraction were more than enough for him now, it was not sustainable. So for the time being he would work hard, earn money, and when he was ready, return to Blight Moor and face the past he had tried so hard to escape from. "What do you think the man meant? 'Rodden remembers'?"

"Who?"

"The men we encountered leaving the pub this morning."

Timmons scoffed. "A daft drunkard, no less. Spewin' nonsense."

Anthony recalled the intensity in the man's harsh eyes. "He seemed pretty lucid to me."

"I wouldn't give it 'nother thought. Naught but a vagabond with a grudge. Mr. Walstead 'as interrupted many a plot."

Unable to let it go, Anthony turned. "You were on the transport to Swendel Bay, weren't you?"

"Not t' Swendel Bay transport but Raunten Bay. A similar job. A week apart."

"Odd that someone would bring that up. That was hundreds of miles from here, wasn't it?"

"Ye think too much." Timmons grinned. "Come on. This job will go t' those who show up first. Smith'll beat us to it if we don't 'urry."

Anthony shrugged and reached once again for his coat and armband. It was a fine line Mr. Walstead walked between the law and criminals. After all, there were two sides to every single case—and always someone who did not want to be caught.

Chapter 5

CHARLOTTE LIFTED HENRY into her arms and adjusted his white linen gown around him, marveling at his rosy cheeks and toothless grin. She nestled her cheek against the top of his soft cottony hair and breathed the sweet scent of him. Despite the turmoil churning on the floor below, she could not resist a smile at the sight of the baby's white-blond curls and bright blue eyes.

He reached up with his chubby fist and grabbed at her lock of hair that had escaped the pins. She laughed as she gently unwound it from his fingers and caught a glimpse of her reflection in her bedchamber's gilded mirror and paused.

She was holding Henry.

It was such a simple thing for a mother to hold her child.

And it was all she'd wanted since the day he was born.

Roland, not to mention Silas, had both believed that indulging Henry with too much affection would weaken his fortitude and that emotional attachments would set him up for failure. As it was, Roland had permitted her to visit Henry in his nursery for but half an hour each evening, and even then a nosy nursemaid or servant girl watched and reported her every interaction.

She had argued with Roland about this arrangement. She'd cried. She'd pleaded.

But he would not be swayed.

Now, things were shifting quickly.

Roland was dead, and a strange current of precarious trepidation surged through Wolden House. The servants whispered and stared. Strangers flowed in and out of the corridors, assessing the situation, murmuring. Watching. Rumors were spreading, and Mr. Sires's counsel was sound. She needed to flee Wolden House as soon as possible.

The moment she'd finished speaking with Mr. Sires, she made her way to Henry's nursery, took him in her arms, and instructed that all his things be moved to her chamber. Now she refused to let him out of her sight for a single moment until they were safe in Hollythorne House. Silas Prior was used to getting his own way, and there was no telling what he would resort to in order to achieve that. The most impactful gift she could give her son was the space and freedom to develop his own character away from the cruel and demanding Prior expectations.

Once Henry was safely in her chamber and under her care, Charlotte instructed her lady's maid, Sutcliffe, to take her jewels into town to sell what she could. Charlotte no longer needed—nor wanted—the pearls Roland had given her upon their marriage, nor the rubies he'd gifted her shortly thereafter, nor any other trinkets she'd amassed. She'd need money far more than the baubles—or the memories.

She turned her attention to packing and began sorting her garments by those suitable for the harsh winter on Blight Moor—wool gowns and pelisses, sturdy walking boots, gloves, and hooded cloaks. Stays and flannel chemises. Blankets and gowns for Henry. With each new task her stomach trembled, and her head throbbed. But she could not pause in her actions—she could give no life to her doubts. Time was of the essence, and every second mattered.

When Sutcliffe returned two hours later, she entered the chamber in a ruffle of obsidian wool. Her cheeks were still pink with the afternoon's chill, and damp strands of blonde hair clung to her face as she pulled at the satin ribbon at her neck to release her cloak from her shoulders.

"Oh, thank goodness you've returned!" Charlotte returned Henry to the cradle. "Did you have success?"

Sutcliffe pulled a small pouch of the remaining jewels from her cape and produced banknotes, her pewter eyes wide and bright. "The first buyer I went to was unwilling to purchase without knowing the origin, but the second was not nearly as scrupulous. I sold only for what I believed a fair price, as you instructed. They did not buy the pearls or the amethyst, but we can try to sell them again later, if you'd like."

Charlotte accepted the banknotes and flipped through them, ignoring the prick of disappointment that all the pieces had not sold.

Sutcliffe hurried to the window and pulled the curtain away from the pane. "Did you see that there are guards outside?"

Charlotte packed the money carefully in her reticule and joined Sutcliffe at the window. Sure enough, two men bearing bright blue armbands over their rough caped greatcoats patrolled at the main entrance.

Sutcliffe clicked her tongue and lifted her straw poke bonnet from her head. "It's a disgusting display of power, if you ask me. I do wish I could be there to see Mr. Prior's reaction when he learns you're leaving Leeds. He'll be furious."

"He'll be furious when he realizes *Henry* is gone." Charlotte turned away from the window. "As much as I would like never to see Silas Prior again, he'll be a permanent fixture in Henry's future. It cannot be helped, and I do not wish to provoke him more than I already am. I'll leave him a letter that explains all, although I daresay one of the servants has already informed him that we are packing."

Sutcliffe lifted the bombazine sleeve of one of the discarded gowns. "You're handling this much better than I would."

"Do I have any other choice?"

The question rang in the otherwise silent chamber before Sutcliffe drew a deep breath and propped her hands on her hips. She glanced around at the valises on the floor, then motioned to the gowns piled on the chaise lounge. "Are those the gowns you intend to take?"

Charlotte nodded as she looked back at the small collection of valises and satchels—the remnants of an entire way of life. It was a small gathering, given the number of possessions she'd acquired since her marriage. But what good would elegant gowns and dainty slippers do her in the solitude and brashness of the moors?

Sutcliffe walked over to Charlotte's jewelry case and returned the pieces she was unable to sell. "Shall I go collect the rest of the jewelry from the strongbox?"

"Let's wait. All the remaining jewels belonged to Roland's

mother and, therefore, are part of the estate. I don't want anyone to accuse me of stealing." Charlotte made her way to her writing desk positioned between the chamber's two windows and motioned to another pile of gowns atop the bed. "I've set aside what I needed, so please, take whichever of the remaining gowns you'd like, and we can alter them to fit you after we arrive. The wind is brutal and damp on the moors, and the house is drafty, so I'd select warm ones."

Charlotte set about writing her letter to Silas while Sutcliffe continued to pack. With each passing second, her nerves, not to mention a strange sense of nervous excitement, were building. She, Henry, and Sutcliffe were embarking on a new life—they were taking a daring step into an unknown future.

She looked around the shadowed room that had been her only domain for the prior three years, fixing it in her memory. Heavy drapes of mauve velvet hung at the windows. Hothouse flowers, now faded, had been elegantly arranged in a cut-glass vase on an ornate polished table in the room's center. The chaise lounge where she'd spent her afternoons reading was now covered in the gowns. She'd never been happy at Wolden House, but she'd been safe and she'd wanted for nothing. Roland might not have been an affectionate or even a loyal husband, but he had provided a measure of security most women would consider the ultimate prize.

Now she had to set her sights on the future, and preparation was key. In addition to packing, her most pressing need was to learn how to care for Henry. She'd never bathed or even fed her own son, and it would likely take weeks to find and install an adequate staff at Hollythorne House. That was time she did not have.

She pivoted at the desk toward Sutcliffe. "Please find the nursemaid. We are going to need her to show us how to care for Henry, and quickly."

Sutcliffe nodded, and as the sound of the maid's boots retreated down the hall, Charlotte turned her gaze once more toward her son. He'd fallen asleep in the low wooden cradle, and his tiny chest rose and fell with each breath. At the sight, feelings of inadequacy bombarded her. What made her think she was capable of such an undertaking? The list of why she would fail as a caretaker seemed to grow with each passing second.

But she had to take thoughts for what they were—mere feelings. Not truth. She could not be afraid. There was no time for such emotions, and for Henry's sake, she would fight for the life she'd dreamed of—for them both.

Chapter 6

AS ANTHONY APPROACHED the Watchman's office later that evening, steady rain tapped down, emphasizing the scents of filth and the acrid smoke from the nearby warehouses. Next to him, Timmons whistled under his breath as they traversed the well-worn, familiar path, his countenance vastly improved from his earlier melancholy musings. It was one thing to arrive for duty at the appointed time each evening, when many of the other watchmen were receiving their assignments as well. It was another thing to be personally summoned by William Walstead for a particular assignment. Not only did these exclusive missions pay well, but they were a feather in the cap of any watchman who successfully undertook them.

They turned onto Hustall Street, a smaller dirt road, and spied the office. No shingle hung outside of the unassuming stone building, yet this office was a constant hub of activity for watchmen and patrons alike. The thick scent of tobacco smoke beset them as they stepped through the door's low threshold. The drab, dimly lit space befit the neighborhood, with darkly paneled walls, heavily beamed low ceilings, and dust and dirt gathered in the corners of the roughly hewn planked floor. A smoking fire in the hearth on the chamber's far wall and a lantern atop the attendant's desk provided the only light sources. Anthony nodded a welcome to a few fellow watchmen before he stepped to the high desk, where Philip Dunston, Mr. Walstead's clerk, was writing in a ledger.

Anthony leaned with his forearm on top of the desk. "Mr. Walstead sent for us."

Dunston did not cease writing for several seconds, then he paused and peered over his spectacles. "He did, and you're late. But you're fortunate. He's engaged at the moment."

Anthony lifted his gaze to the closed door behind the desk. It was always a good idea to be on good terms with Dunston. As Mr. Walstead's right-hand man, he was privy to details that most were not. What was more, he could usually be coaxed for information.

"Any word on the assignment?" asked Timmons.

The notoriously stony clerk paused and lowered his quill.

"Oh, come on," Timmons baited. "Surely ye know why we're 'ere this time. Problems at t' inn again? Or at t' docks?"

Dunston cut his eyes toward Mr. Walstead's office door, leaned forward, then lowered his voice. "I know nothin' for certain. You know Mr. Walstead tells me only bits 'n' pieces, but I got eyes, ain't I? Mr. Silas Prior, the man himself, barged in 'ere, not even an 'our ago, demandin' to speak with Mr. Walstead."

Timmons and Anthony exchanged glances. Everyone in Leeds knew Silas Prior—the owner of two mills and a shipping company, a landlord, and employer of thousands.

"What'd 'e want?" inquired Timmons.

Dunston shrugged his scrawny shoulders. "One can only guess, but you've 'eard his brother died, 'aven't ye? Dropped dead right in 'is own study, so t' story goes."

Anthony nodded. Yes, he'd heard. "I thought Smith and Jenkins were guarding that house tonight."

"No, no. This is another matter entirely. This is—"

The creak of the door behind the clerk silenced Dunston, and Anthony and Timmons both straightened as two watchmen exited the office. Mr. Walstead then took notice of Anthony and Timmons and motioned for them to follow him.

When Anthony entered the office, Mr. Walstead was already standing next to the window behind his desk. He was a short man, much shorter than either Anthony or Timmons, but what he lacked in height he made up for in clever intuition. His tailored worsted-wool black tailcoat and buckled, polished shoes hardly suited the humble environment, but it was that very contradiction that Mr. Walstead thrived on. His story was as famous and fantastic as his exploits.

He motioned to the chairs opposite his cluttered desk. "Sit."

They did as bid without comment.

"You're from up by Blight Moor, aren't you, Welbourne?" He stepped to the sideboard and lifted a decanter of brandy.

Anthony stiffened at the preciseness—and suddenness—of the personal inquiry. "Yes, sir. I am."

"Next to the village of Lamby, correct?"

Anthony had not heard the name spoken out loud in years. "Yes, sir."

"Do you still have family there?" Walstead's questions tumbled forth. "Acquaintances? Friends?"

"No, no family anymore. No acquaintances to speak of. I've been back but once since the war, and only for a day."

Mr. Walstead picked up a glass and poured a drink. "Ever heard of a place called Hollythorne House?"

The name, the precipitous mention of it, struck like a punch in the jaw, and a closed door deep in his memory flew open.

Charlotte Grey's home.

His uncle's adversary's home.

The staunch, stoic structure of blackened stone that dominated the windswept Blight Moor.

His neck grew hot beneath his linen neckcloth. "I've heard of it."

"Good. I've an assignment for you. For the both of you."

Normally the details of a new assignment would fill Anthony with eagerness and purpose. But now his stomach clenched.

Mr. Walstead continued. "You've heard Roland Prior died, I'm sure. I was at Wolden House earlier. Saw the body and spoke with the coroner. He suspects apoplexy, but given Mr. Prior's unconventional practices and dealings, he ordered a full autopsy and will likely call a coroner's inquest. Furthermore, there's unrest at the Prior Mill—the one that had been, up until now, overseen by Roland Prior. I've still to get to the root of exactly what the issues are, but events like this trigger every manner of dissension. Silas Prior has engaged our services to secure Wolden House and temper the mill workers. Furthermore, Roland Prior's widow will be departing Leeds immediately, along with his son and heir. Apparently, she brought Hollythorne House into the marriage and intends to make it her home moving forward."

Anthony remained perfectly still. He'd show no emotion— make no movement.

And yet, it couldn't be.

Charlotte Grey . . . was Mrs. Charlotte Prior?

Anthony struggled to focus on Mr. Walstead's words.

"Mr. Prior has learned from a concerned butler that Mrs. Prior intends to depart in secret and alone in a borrowed carriage, with only her infant and her maid. One can only assume grief has affected her senses, for she's seemingly unaware of the danger she's putting the boy in. Mr. Prior cannot legally prevent her from taking such action, but as overseer to the trust, Mr. Prior does have some power, and as such he's determined that guards should accompany them, at least until the coroner's inquest is completed, the situation settles, and he's confident that there are no unanticipated dangers at Hollythorne House. You two will accompany them, remain with them, and ensure no harm comes to that boy."

Timmons jumped up, his face brighter than Anthony had seen it in months. "Very good, sir. They'll be in good 'ands."

Muddling through his thoughts, Anthony followed suit and stood, but his enthusiasm fizzled. The assignment sparked more questions than provided answers. He'd spent years forcing thoughts of Charlotte Grey to the back of his mind. Leaving her had been the biggest regret of his life. And now he was going to see her? Speak with her? Protect her and her son?

Yet he could not turn down this assignment—his thief-taking career would be ruined.

And he needed these jobs if he was to fund the mill reparations.

He could—and would—save his reservations about seeing Charlotte again and deal with them in private. "When do we depart?"

"On the morrow. Meet at Wolden House at seven. You know where it is, of course. You'll each take a horse from the stable and use it for the duration of the assignment. Again, your priority is to keep the boy safe, so you will do what's necessary without interrupting the family life. Not that I expect it to be that spirited. No doubt a woman in mourning will keep a quiet routine. Questions?"

The conversation flowed with the details of such a case— where they would break their journey, the age of the child, what would be done about servants.

But Anthony found concentrating difficult.

Memories of the intoxicating summer he'd spent with Charlotte, vibrant and nostalgic, clawed for his attention.

He'd thought about her more times than he could count—of her sweetness and vitality, not to mention the sense of belonging and solidarity he'd experienced in her presence. Such ruminations had kept him warm on the battlefield and reminded him that goodness existed, even when he was enduring true evil and destruction. But even in his dreams he never allowed himself to consider seeing her again.

He'd adjust to this.

It was just a shock.

After all, she'd moved on. She'd married, very well in fact. And now had a child.

He merely had to remember that this assignment was nothing outside of his usual roles. He would do it, and do it well, even though his past—the very past he'd so ardently avoided in the name of healing and growth—was colliding with his present. Names he thought he'd never again hear, people he thought he'd never again see, were forced to the forefront of his mind, confusing his normally disciplined and methodical ways.

"Welbourne, since you are familiar with the area, you'll be lead on this." Mr. Walstead stepped out from around the desk. "I'll meet you at the departure and then be out in a few days to Hollythorne House. I don't anticipate this to be a terribly long, or even difficult, assignment, but whatever it takes to keep us on the right side of Silas Prior, that's what we'll do."

Anthony nodded, but every muscle in his neck and back tightened. He'd never retreated from an assignment. The more dangerous the task, the more it intrigued him. Facing death had given him a fresh perspective on life, and he would not waste a moment of it. But this—this assignment—was engaging parts of his mind, his heart, that he kept carefully closed off.

Despite the temptation to open the door to those memories, it had to stay firmly shut. Too much was at stake, and he would take no chances.

Chapter 7

ROLAND HAD NOT been dead a full twenty-four hours, and the ramifications were hitting harder—and faster—than Charlotte had anticipated. A sleepless night had given way to an apprehensive morning, and as she made her final parting preparations, her thoughts raced.

Almost immediately following Charlotte's discovery of Roland's body, many of the servants had abandoned their posts, and those who remained were unsettled. Mill workers lingered on the street outside, for what reason no one would say, and the coroner and his associates had overseen the autopsy during the bleak midnight hours. Eerie shadows of mistrust and suspicion shrouded Wolden House, and as far as Charlotte was concerned, she, Henry, and Sutcliffe could not be free from it soon enough.

"Mr. Sires's carriage is here." Hatbox in hand, Sutcliffe bustled in the bedchamber door.

Charlotte nodded and assessed her bedchamber one last time. She felt no sentimental tie to the items surrounding her. If anything, the stately canopied bed and bold floral paper on the walls seemed impatient to evict her from the chamber's restraining confines. And now, with valises packed and trunks at the ready, there was one thing left to do—retrieve the key to Hollythorne House.

Roland had always kept keys and other important items locked in a strongbox in his study. She'd not been able to access it during the night hours because of the autopsy. Men involved with the coroner's inquest had been all around. But now Roland's body had been moved to the library, and all the men had departed.

As she made her way down the broad staircase, the realization that it had been only the previous morning when she'd flown down this very staircase in a flurry of fury struck her. It seemed a lifetime had transpired since then, and a cautionary chill enveloped her as she turned the corner into Roland's private study. She could sense him—she could smell his scent of tobacco and cognac and almost feel the weight of his capricious gaze on her.

He'd be furious with her and her intentions.

The very last thing he would want was for her to take Henry to Hollythorne House and away from Silas's influence.

She gathered her wits about her, refusing to give voice to the doubts buzzing in her mind.

Roland could control her no more.

After retrieving the key from the desk's top drawer, she moved to the pastoral painting nestled in between two stationary oak bookcases. She swung the heavy, framed canvas outward, like a door, to reveal a strongbox built into the wall, then unlocked the strongbox to reveal yet another set of boxes and papers. She squinted to see in the faint light and sorted through the items until she found what she sought—a small mahogany chest with the name *Grey* carved into the top. There, inside, was the iron key to Hollythorne House. Satisfied, she pulled the key from the box, tucked it in her reticule, and lifted the entire mahogany chest from the strongbox, leaving everything else inside undisturbed.

With the chest in her arms, she hurried back through the main corridor and toward the servants' area, where their belongings were stacked and Sutcliffe was waiting with Henry in her arms. Charlotte placed the mahogany box with the other trunks and spied the carriage outside the window. Fresh energy flowed through her, and she motioned for a footman at the corridor's end to draw near. She removed the letter from her pocket and extended it toward him as he approached. "Please, will you have this delivered to Silas Prior at Gatham House this morning?"

The footman frowned at the missive. "Of course. But Mr. Prior is outside. Would you prefer me to deliver it to him directly now?"

All her excitement, every ounce of nervous anticipation, morphed to a sickening sense of dread. She stepped back to the window and angled herself to see farther. Sure enough, Silas Prior stood atop the cobbles, clad in mourning black from head to toe, making his white cravat ostentatiously bright in the budding morning light.

She did not have time to contemplate why he was here. They were ready to depart, and she would not be swayed. There was no choice but to meet this resolutely—to have her say with Silas and then be free of him.

After instructing Sutcliffe to remain indoors with Henry, she stepped out into the dense fog. A sharp wind blew in from the north, promising rain, yet the sight before her rivaled any storm the weather could bring. For there, just before the carriage, stood not only Silas but the famed William Walstead, whom she'd seen in person on occasion when he visited Roland, accompanied by two more men on horseback.

She stiffened and straightened her shoulders at the oppressive sight.

The cape of Silas's black greatcoat billowed as he approached her, and after he removed his tall beaver hat, the wind tousled his white-blond hair. "I suppose you've an acceptable reason for failing to mention your plans, such as they are, to me."

She pressed her lips together, refusing to wince at the harshness of his tone. "'Tis best to leave quickly and quietly, all things considered."

"'All things considered'? Do you mean with your husband not yet in the grave and questions swirling around the entire family?"

She steeled herself before responding. "This decision is a personal one. I do not require your permission."

"Everything that happens regarding Henry is under my purview." Each word was shot like an arrow to its target. "I've made it abundantly clear. Henry needs to be here, in Leeds. His future is here."

She flicked her gaze to Mr. Walstead and the two shadowy men on horseback, whose presence grew more intimidating with every passing second. She could not falter—not with these men watching her. "There is plenty of time for responsibilities later. For now, it is best for us to leave."

He scoffed sharply. "Need I remind you? Hundreds of people in our employ need confidence that our legacy will remain strong.

'Tis not enough for them to know Henry will one day take charge. They must see it happening. It's the only way."

Charlotte was hardly surprised by his arrogance or assumptions. She lifted her chin. Never would she have believed herself strong enough to stand up to a man like Silas Prior. And yet the events of the past twenty-four hours had challenged her in ways she never thought possible. "And I am Henry's mother, his guardian. And I think differently."

His face reddened, making his clear eyes wilder. Brighter. "I'm sure you've considered the ramifications. Your annual stipend is small for a house of that size and the lifestyle you are accustomed to. And I'm told Hollythorne House is in a devilish state. What of staff? Of servants? You are many things, Charlotte, but you're not selfish. Or stupid."

She refused to be affected by his harsh tone or to engage in a fruitless tit for tat. Instead, she lifted her gaze to Mr. Walstead and the two men on horseback. Something else was going on. "Why are these men here?"

"I cannot control your actions, as foolish as they are, but I can state my concern for the isolated nature of Hollythorne House. You may not consider the risk associated with a ploy such as this, but I will. Henry is a wealthy boy. An alarming number of people would not think twice about kidnapping him for ransom. Have you factored that into your plan? How do you protect yourself in the middle of nowhere? With no servants? No guards?"

Her throat tightened. Yes, she had thought of it. The moors, and their silent isolation, could be frightening at times.

That was what he was attempting to do—scare her.

And it was working.

Days could transpire before a single soul would venture past Hollythorne House. She could scream at the top of her lungs, and no one would hear it.

Silas continued. "If you, in your stubbornness, refuse to listen to reason and insist upon relocating to Hollythorne House, then go. I cannot stop you. But as executor of Henry's trust, I must insist that guards escort you, at least until we understand how the business and Roland's legacy will unfold."

She drew a sharp breath as the current reality sharpened into focus.

These horsemen in their heavy coats and bright blue armbands—they were to go with *her*.

"The security detail will be funded from the trust, and I've instructed Mr. Walstead to engage a reasonable number of servants who have been investigated for safety. These men are set to escort you immediately and to remain until such time as we feel comfortable that Henry is not in peril. The servants will arrive in the next day or so."

She returned her attention to the two dark men on horseback. *Walstead's Watchmen.*

She knew their reputation. Dangerous men who undertook dangerous tasks. The reports of their exploits tripped on the tongues of ladies, gentlemen, and servants alike.

Their presence would be like prison walls to her.

But if their presence would permit her to escape Wolden House and exchange one cage for another of her choosing, then she should accept it.

And the truth was, she did need help—she did need protection.

She hardened her gaze and considered his words. If she agreed to his stipulation, then he would *gain* a measure of control over her. And over Henry. He'd undoubtedly be apprised of her every move. But Silas did have a point. Hollythorne House was positioned on an isolated stretch of road, one known for its history of highwaymen and robberies.

But what were her options? To throw a fit and leave in a huff? Unprotected? And with Silas even angrier with her?

An unsettling panic gripped her as she took notice of the horsemen's satchels and straining saddlebags.

They were already packed. The decision was made.

William Walstead, who had been silently observing, stepped closer. His reputation truly preceded him. Dashing. Daring. He was not a tall man, and yet the intensity of his russet eyes made up for his lack of stature. His voice was surprisingly deep and soothing. "You can rest assured, Mrs. Prior, my men are very astute and discreet. These men would both give their lives to protect your son. Surely that would give you a measure of peace."

He motioned to one of the men on horseback to dismount, and she eyed him skeptically as he did.

But as the man stepped forward and the dawn's faint light illuminated his face, her eyes beheld the familiar shape of the face. No introduction was needed.

No. For she knew this face with its straight nose and square jaw as well as she knew her own.

Anthony Welbourne.

Chapter 8

ANTHONY TIGHTENED HIS grip on his horse's rein as he stepped forward, as Mr. Walstead had bid.

He was about to see Charlotte Grey again. Face-to-face.

He had no idea how she'd react to seeing him, but he did know one thing for certain: two people did not share a romance like theirs and forget a single detail of it, despite what they had moved on to be.

Since arriving at Wolden House almost a quarter of an hour earlier, he'd overheard bits and pieces of the conversation between Mr. Silas Prior and Mr. Walstead. It was not his place—or his business—to get involved. Mostly their words were hushed, but even so, unmasked anger tinged Prior's tone, and he paced like a man with much on his mind. Yet his reputation was hardly one of emotional sentimentality. In all likelihood, his ire had more to do with what was occurring at Roland Prior's mill. The reports of arson and workers leaving their posts were increasing. Several watchmen had already been sent to the mill to keep the peace.

But in this single instance, Anthony did not care about Prior Mill. He did not care about the workers abandoning their posts or whether Silas Prior was upset or not. He only cared how Charlotte would react to seeing him again.

And she now stood before him.

He'd recognize her anywhere—the charming slope of her nose. The slender angles of her face. They were all so familiar, so beautiful, and in an instant, every other thought faded. The unnerving realization that she had been in such proximity for all these years shocked his senses, and the sight of her, and memories he had buried, were released in vibrant detail.

But they were worse than strangers—they were two people who'd shared an affection that had been severed.

Now she was his client—a woman whose son he'd sworn to protect. He had to remain master of his thoughts. He could only assume that after all this time she was not the same person she'd been, and he certainly was not the same man. As she stepped farther into the morning's light, snippets of her conversation with Prior rose above the stomping horse and the gusting wind.

Something was wrong. She did not want them here.

Mr. Walstead had said Mr. Prior had engaged them on her behalf, and Anthony had assumed she would be apprised of the arrangement. It was one thing to be here if she desired assistance. It was quite another to be here if she did not.

As he took another step forward, he removed his hat as casually as possible to not draw the attention of the other men. He deemed it only fair to her that he divulge his identity, even if it was not spoken aloud. He owed that to her, at the very least, and she could respond how she saw fit.

At first she did not notice.

But then she jerked her gaze back to him. Her eyes widened.

Recognition flashed in her topaz eyes.

Yes, she knew exactly who he was.

And now he had to wait for her response.

The breath fled from Charlotte's chest, and in that moment, all thoughts vacated her mind.

She forgot what she was saying. Forgot what they were doing.

Anthony Welbourne.

Surely this apparition was merely the shock of Roland's death playing tricks on her exhausted mind. Or perhaps the prospect of returning to Blight Moor was resurrecting memories and wreaking havoc on her thoughts.

But no.

It *was* him.

Cobalt-blue eyes fringed with black lashes. Wild, dark hair. A new scar on an otherwise familiar jawline.

It was a glimpse into a past that was so far behind her and yet raring and large as life.

Anthony was not dressed as an immaculate soldier as he had been when she'd last seen him. Instead, a bulky caped greatcoat, slick with the morning rain, cloaked his broad shoulders and a beard's shadow altered the angles of his face, but what altered him the most was the subtlety in his countenance, one of time and experience that now trumped the adventurous, boyish expression that used to reside there.

Mr. Walstead's quick, matter-of-fact words snapped her back to the present. "This is Mr. Welbourne, lead watchman on this assignment. He'll be in charge at Hollythorne House in my absence. You'll not find a more capable watchman. You and your son will be in excellent care."

Anthony bowed slightly, stoic and inscrutable, as if seeing her again had no effect on him. No casual grin lit his face as it did in her recollection of him. In fact, he barely met her gaze.

Conversely, she struggled to even speak as memory after memory beset her.

As she regained control, her defiant streak flared.

She did not know why or how he was here, but she did know that nothing good could come of his presence at Hollythorne House, regardless of how much time had passed.

She should demand he be sent away.

But on what grounds?

She'd seem a petty, foolish woman if she told Mr. Walstead about her girlhood heartbreak. And what had her experiences with the Prior family over the past three years taught her? Any sign of emotion would be interpreted as a hysterical response by men.

She had to keep her composure.

And she *would* keep her composure.

Mr. Walstead, seemingly unaware of Anthony's effect on her, continued. "Welbourne here is from Blight Moor, and his particular knowledge of the area will be helpful. Mr. Timmons will also be at your disposal, should you need assistance. Both men were soldiers and are experienced watchmen. What's more, with Mr. Prior's approval I have engaged servants on your behalf, including a housekeeper, a manservant, and a nursemaid. I'm told there are none currently working at Hollythorne House, and if my men are to guard, I prefer to have staff that has been inspected."

Charlotte could only stare at the man as his words tumbled forth.

Servants. Guards. Watchmen.

She dare not shift her gaze to look at Silas, for she knew what she would find there—a smug grin of satisfaction that, despite *her* decision to leave, he was still taking control.

It was all too much—the reappearance of a man she thought she never would see again. The racing emotions of the death of Roland mingled with her fears for her son. And now, all the men were staring at her, waiting for her to decide, and who, no doubt, expected her to succumb to womanly emotions and fanatics.

She would prove them wrong.

For they had no idea to what extent she would go to protect Henry.

All she had to do was survive this moment—keep her composure and determination—for a bit longer, and then she and Henry would be away from here. She could deal with the watchmen and Silas's manipulation another time. But if she did not leave Wolden House now, the opportunity might not come again.

Chapter 9

THE DREARY MOORLAND landscape flashed by Charlotte through the rain-streaked carriage window. To many, the moorland would seem cold and foreboding. But to her, the isolation—and privacy it afforded—offered the unexpected comfort of familiarity in a callous world that no longer seemed recognizable.

She adjusted Henry on her lap and tightened her wool cloak around them both to guard against the chilly gusts permeating the door. After fitful hours of riding in the jolting carriage and a handful of stops along the way, he'd finally fallen asleep.

The ride that should have been relatively short had become a difficult one. A delayed departure, coupled with an onslaught of rain and a broken wheel, conspired to put them hours behind schedule. But if the journey progressed with no other delays, they would be home soon.

Home.

How many times over the past few years had she dreamed of escaping Leeds and returning to the moors of her carefree childhood, when she was free and life was simple? Where no other way of life existed except to be content and bold, of being supported and loved. Yes, she'd always wanted to return, but not like this—a widow surrounded by watchmen with pistols.

And not just any watchman, but Anthony Welbourne.

She could not prevent her wearied mind from turning to thoughts of him. She blamed her lack of mental discipline on sleep deprivation and the consternation of the entire situation, but the truth was, the sight of him awoke a part of her that had long been dormant. How had he gone from the carefree, enthusiastic young soldier to one of Walstead's Watchmen, an ensemble renowned for braving danger and the shadows of night?

She closed her eyes and leaned her head back against the tufted seat and swayed with the carriage's movements. She was not sure how long her eyes were closed, but when she opened them, she spied it, like a veiled dream that had suddenly manifested: Hollythorne House.

Charlotte nudged the sleeping Sutcliffe to alert her to their impending arrival and leaned forward even farther, hungry to see the ancient stone building and slate roof topping it. It was hundreds of years old, constructed of gray gritstone that had blackened over time. A large wall of mullioned, multipaned windows overlooked the gated, cobbled courtyard, and faded ivy vines clung to the facade despite the autumnal wind's tenacious attempts to loosen them from their stronghold.

The carriage paused to allow one of the drivers to open the wrought-iron gate, and then he navigated the conveyance through the narrow opening. Unable to wait, to be free of the carriage, she pushed open the door. And a gust of moorland wind swept in, rich with the familiar aroma of damp earth and heath.

And with it the sudden longing for what had been.

Oh, if only she could be returning to the bosom of her childhood, the gentleness of her mother's embrace, and the warmth of their family home. Here, on this land, she could almost hear her father's booming laughter, laced with joy and good humor.

But it also revived other memories—ones that were equally as tied to this moor—ones of disappointed love and heartbreak.

She drew a deep breath, allowing Blight Moor's pensive aura to brush over her. She would not linger on thoughts of Anthony Welbourne. He was but a piece of her history here at Hollythorne House. An entire life had existed before him, and she would dwell on that. She would remain mistress of her thoughts, of her emotions, for she could not get distracted from her goal—Henry's well-being. Too much was at stake, and this freedom was what she'd wanted for so long.

Eager to see the house that she knew as well as any living creature, she passed Henry to Sutcliffe and adjusted the ribbons securing her wool traveling cloak. Without waiting for assistance, she stepped down. Her sturdy leather half boots sank heavy into the sodden earth, as if the land itself was reclaiming her and, as a result, filling her with confidence. This was not a new environment she had to learn to maneuver, as she had done at Wolden House. This was her home.

With Henry once again in her arms and the iron key in her free hand, she stepped toward the heavy oak door.

"A moment, Mrs. Prior."

She stopped. She need not turn to identify the speaker, for the timbre of Anthony's voice was etched in her memory as deeply as her own.

A part of her wanted to be happy to see him again, but a much larger part of her was far too aware of how her experiences of the past four years had hardened corridors of her heart. Now, uncertainty and the basic need to establish a safe environment for her and her son trumped any emotional inclination.

She turned in response to his request, trying to look both directly at him but also past him.

He continued. "Before you go inside, Timmons and I will inspect the building and the grounds to ensure all is secure and in order."

She shook her head. She'd not traveled all this way to wait outside of her own house. "There's no need. It will be dark soon, and I should like to ensure that we have at least one fire lit before night falls. I needn't tell you how difficult it can be to see anything after the sun sets on this moor."

"Even so, it's protocol to assess the property before we can allow you and your son inside."

She raised her brow at the word *allow*. "I'm sure it is, but as I frankly informed both Mr. Walstead and Mr. Prior, Sutcliffe and I are quite capable of handling this situation on our own. If you feel the need to explore the grounds, then you are more than welcome to do so."

Without giving him the opportunity to respond, she pivoted and cut her way across the muddy, leaf-strewn courtyard to Hollythorne House's entrance. With Henry on her hip and Sutcliffe immediately behind her, she inserted the key in the lock and turned it. The lever gave way with a satisfying *click*, followed by the squeak of the heavy door swinging open on its hinges.

Relief flooded her as she stepped into the low-ceilinged screens passage and then through to the open great hall. Murky darkness and the stodgy aroma of disuse besieged her senses. She lowered her cape's hood and turned a full circle, absorbing every visible portion of the great hall. The gray light of dusk slid through the dirty windowpanes of the southern wall, lending a somber glow to the dirty stone floor beneath her feet and the timber beams crossing the ceiling nearly two stories above her head.

She and Henry were *home*.

But then, in the very next breath, the magnitude of what she'd undertaken engulfed her.

Sutcliffe stepped next to her and placed the lantern from the carriage on the long table anchored in the room's center, the light from which further illuminated the dust-laden surfaces. Charlotte exchanged an uneasy glance with Sutcliffe. Complete darkness would be on them shortly, and the house, such as it was, was unopened. It was up to her to give direction—up to her to decide where to put their efforts first.

Mr. Timmons entered, a welcome relief to her pensive reverie. A trunk was balanced atop his shoulder. "The driver and footman are unloading the carriage now. Where would you like this?"

Charlotte, followed by both Sutcliffe and Mr. Timmons, took up the lantern and led the way to the tenebrous wooden staircase and ascended a few steps before sharply pivoting on the narrow landing to the left. The stairs groaned beneath them and their footfalls echoed from the high ceilings and heavily paneled walls, as if in protest of being awoken from their otherwise undisturbed slumber. At the top of the steep staircase, they reached the railed minstrel's gallery that overlooked the great hall and continued to the corridor leading to her chamber. "My chamber is to the left. Please put all the valises and trunk there for now."

There was much to do, but unable to resist the temptation of spying a room that had been so precious to her, she paused and looked in the bedchamber of her childhood. Here, time had stood still, frozen in a tribute to a bygone era.

White cloths draped over all the furniture, the garnet curtains were pulled tight over the multipaned windows, and darkness met her: dark paneling, dark floor. And yet in this familiar space breathing felt easier. Her shoulders felt lighter. She stepped to the west-facing window that looked out toward Blight Moor, tugged the curtain aside, turned the metal handle, and pushed the creaky window open. A cool gust burst in, as if it had been waiting for an invitation, and swirled into the room's corners, like a large inhale after a deep sleep. She then stepped to the east-facing windows on the opposite wall and pulled back the dusty window coverings to look down.

There, in the courtyard, was Anthony at the drystone wall that separated the courtyard from the main road, securing the black iron gate.

For just a moment she let herself take in the sight of him. To her knowledge, he'd never stepped foot on Hollythorne property before. A property dispute between her father and his uncle led to a bitter feud that resulted in Mr. Welbourne refusing to offer his milling services to her father's tenants. It had been a silly, petty disagreement, but one that had a lasting effect on the community.

She let the curtain slip from her fingertips. Whatever might have been between Anthony and her at one time had ended. She'd bid her final farewell to him years ago in her heart and in her mind, and a new life had emerged. The only thing that mattered was Henry. And there would be no turning back.

Chapter 10

ANTHONY COULD HARDLY blame Charlotte for the cool indifference of her tone when they spoke in the courtyard. He'd been hired to be here, to protect her and Henry, yet he felt like an unwanted intruder, invading a personal matter.

The sentiment dominated his thoughts as he made his way to Hollythorne House's rear courtyard after completing his initial assessment of the property. Out of respect he'd avoided interacting with Charlotte for much of the journey. After all, her husband had just died. She was mourning, and given their history, it would be foolish to think his presence would be welcome. He could not forget he was at Hollythorne House merely to perform a task. Entertaining any thought to the contrary would stir unnecessary unrest.

By the time he reached the rear courtyard, night had fallen, and he stepped to the half wall separating the space from the land beyond. After setting his lantern atop it, he retrieved his pencil and small book to make notes to include in the assignment log that would be shared with Mr. Walstead.

Hollythorne House's property was hemmed in by open moorland on three sides, save for the east-facing wall of the home that overlooked a broad forest. A rectangular cobbled courtyard filled the space between the house and the main road, and next to it to the left stood the modest stone stable and a few smaller outbuildings. Behind the house stretched a rear courtyard and two individual walled gardens connected to each other by a wooden gate, and beyond that another stable, a carriage house, a graveyard, and two more outbuildings. Hollythorne House itself was a secure structure, as there were only a few entrances, but the inside was a maze of passageways and corridors, chambers and halls, each added on or altered by new generations.

The sound of footsteps interrupted his thoughts, and Timmons's words drew his attention. "T' driver and t' footman are settled, along with t' carriage and horses. They're none too 'appy about spendin' the night 'ere, though."

Anthony glanced to the stone carriage house where faint orange light flickered from dirty windowpanes. The original plan for Mr. Sires's driver and footman—deliver the Priors to Hollythorne House, rest the horses, and have them back to Leeds the same night—had been foiled by foul weather and impassable roads. It was an ambitious timeline, not to mention dangerous for the horses.

Anthony leaned his elbows on the drystone wall. "Couldn't be helped. One can't predict what the weather holds."

"No, but we'll make t' most of it." Timmons tugged up the collar of his greatcoat to guard against the misty rain that had started to fall. "Besides, it doesn't really matter what any of us think, does it? All that matters is that this assignment is for Silas Prior 'imself. That can only be good for us."

Anthony would undoubtedly feel the same if he did not have a personal attachment to it. He'd not served on a Prior assignment before, but Timmons had, and it was no secret it had been his most lucrative task to date.

"Should be easy," continued Timmons. "This place is even more isolated than I thought. Anyone not familiar with it will 'ave a devil of a time findin' it, even though it seems a might far-fetched that someone would travel all the way from Leeds to 'arass a widow and baby."

"I don't know. You've seen how the mill workers get when they band together."

Timmons smirked. "Ah, those boys were just lookin' out for themselves. Can't blame a fellow for that, I reckon. I'd probably do t' same thing in their stead."

Anthony glanced up from his writing but did not respond to Timmons's opinionated words. They were friends, yes, but since their return from war, the treatment Timmons had received because of his injury had made him cynical, almost to the point where Anthony wondered which side of the law he was really protecting.

Pushing aside the thoughts on his capricious comrade, Anthony straightened from the wall and adjusted his wide-brimmed hat against the wind. "From here on out we'll each take four-hour shifts and rotate between the house and the outer perimeter. We'll sleep as needed during the daylight hours. There's a bedchamber above the kitchen for us to use."

"Yes, sir." Timmons chortled with mock formality, then

snorted at his own little jest. He sobered, and his eyes scanned the murky landscape. "Are we close to your mill, then?"

Anthony hesitated, unwilling to share his personal past with Timmons. He'd never told him about Charlotte, or really any significant details of his personal life prior to the war, and now that Charlotte had resurfaced, the past suddenly seemed a secret to be guarded, and he would prefer to keep it that way, given the damage that could be done if word of their relationship became public. But there was no harm in answering Timmons's question. "Not exactly. We could ride there and be back in an afternoon, though."

It was a lie.

They were very close. By horseback he could arrive there in a quarter of an hour. He could even walk.

"Surely you'll pay it a visit then."

"Maybe."

"'Maybe'?" Timmons scoffed. "Savin' your money t' repair that mill 'as been your fool'ardy mission since we returned from the United States. Ye say ye *might* visit it? Bah. I don't believe it. You'll be there as soon as ye can sneak away."

Yes, Anthony wanted to go to his mill, but returning would force him to revisit memories he was not ready to face.

His uncle had been vocal about his concern over Anthony following in his father's military footsteps. But it had been his father's last wish, and he'd left enough money for Anthony's commission with the instructions that it be used for that purpose alone. Anthony had given up contemplating what his life would have been like if he had taken his uncle's advice. If he had, he never would have been injured. And who knew, if he'd been home to help fight the fire, his uncle might still be alive and the mill might be intact.

Anthony forced a lighthearted timbre to his tone. "Well, we've too much to do here now. With just the two of us on a property this size, I doubt either of us will see outside these walls anytime soon."

"I'd expect ye to say no less." Timmons grinned. "Not exactly the sentimental sort, are ye?"

Anthony chuckled. "Sentiment is dangerous."

"Aye. But I suppose it would be nice to 'ave somewhere to call 'ome."

A baby's wail echoed from inside the kitchen entrance, and Anthony turned toward it. Yellow light seeped from behind the thin window covering, and a shadow crossed by it.

"That babe's even louder than Roger," Timmons said of the infant son of the keeper of the boardinghouse. "'Opefully this one won't wake the 'ouse at all 'ours like Roger does."

Anthony frowned as Henry's wail cut the night air. The baby had cried a great deal throughout the journey, and he'd been crying on and off for the last hour. No doubt he was tired. Surely Charlotte and her maid were as well. He could only assume that Charlotte was accustomed to a battery of nursemaids and servants, given her husband's social standing. Even the landlady of their ramshackle boardinghouse had assistance with her baby.

It was none of his business. He was here to guard—nothing more. But he was drawn to the situation. When Timmons returned to the carriage house, Anthony headed toward the kitchen door.

Chapter 11

CHARLOTTE DREW A wavering breath.

She blinked away moisture.

No.

She would not cry.

Not on this first full day alone with her son.

But as Henry fussed and screamed, and as the sucking bottle was still as full as it was when she'd first attempted to feed him nearly half an hour prior, tears blurred her vision.

Feeding a child—her child—should not be difficult. And yet Henry writhed and fought against her embrace. His face flushed crimson. His cry reverberated from the low ceiling in sharp, high-pitched wails.

She slid a glance toward Sutcliffe, whose gray eyes were wide with pity. Charlotte would not be pitied, and she would not give up. She drew a fortifying breath and refocused on her child's face.

Henry clearly did not care for something she was doing, but what? The nursemaid at Wolden House had given both Sutcliffe and her detailed instructions on how to feed him. Clean him.

Change him. They had practiced before departing, and she'd successfully fed him earlier. But why not now?

Forcing her voice low and soft, she cooed soft words and offered him the sucking bottle of pap again.

His tight fist batted at it.

He refused to eat.

Charlotte's anger toward Roland flared afresh. She wanted to blame her inability to connect with Henry on him and his decision to limit her interactions with him. But in truth, she was mostly angry with herself. How could she possibly not be able to do this? Did not every mother have an instinct? A maternal inclination?

The door opened, and she jumped at the unexpected interruption.

Anthony's broad shoulders filled the doorway, and embarrassment erupted.

She'd not given much thought to what Anthony must think of her and her current situation, and he'd made no comment, no verbal observation of anything outside of the task he was engaged to perform. She did not want to think of it now, not when her son was inconsolable and shrieking louder with every passing moment.

And yet she would have to get used to this—of Anthony appearing. For he was here, ironically enough, by her permission and agreement.

He took his hat from his head, and his dark hair clung in wet locks to his brow. "My apologies for intruding."

Henry, who had taken no notice of their new visitor, bawled even louder, tattering Charlotte's already-frayed nerves. She tried to adjust the baby in her arms, yet he stiffened and pushed against her.

Anthony said nothing for several moments, but then he shrugged his wet greatcoat from his shoulders and stepped forward. "May I?"

Anthony Welbourne had just offered to hold her son. "That's not necessary."

Henry's piercing bellow intensified, filling the room and drowning her words.

Anthony, his voice calm and his demeanor steady, took another step forward. "My landlord's wife has a baby who cries in much the same way when he's hungry. Either we step in and help her from time to time, or we don't get our meals made."

The stubborn streak in her begged her to refuse. She did not want Anthony—or anyone, for that matter—to regard her as incapable. But the truth was, in this instance, she *was* incapable. And Anthony seemed so composed and collected. She did not want to let the babe go, especially after being forced to do so many times in the past. But how could she not? It would be selfish to continue as things were going simply because she wanted to feed him on her own.

Avoiding eye contact, Charlotte lifted the child. The broadcloth of Anthony's rough sleeve brushed against her as he accepted Henry. He reached for the sucking bottle and turned away from her, bouncing the baby slightly as he stepped toward the window. At first the cries did not stop. But then, after a bit, they softened. Soon, the sound of sucking was barely audible above the fire's crackling and popping.

Charlotte watched the sight, feeling equal parts amazement and incompetence, helpless and sad.

"He's tired out," Anthony exclaimed after a minute or so of peacefulness, and then he moved to an empty chair next to Charlotte and sat. "'Twas a long journey, all that jostling about. It will take days for things to be set to right."

Charlotte watched her son, now serene, as he put his tiny, fair hands next to Anthony's rough one on the sucking bottle. "I wonder why he would drink it for you and not for me."

"You're anxious, I'd expect."

Charlotte stiffened at the personal nature of the comment.

"No harm done, eh? Just angle it like this, see? You don't want any air going in."

Charlotte did not know whether to be impressed or offended. But he was right—she was anxious. Very anxious. How could she not be? But even so, he was speaking as if he were an expert in the matter.

But that had always been his way. Confident and determined.

She had, at one time, considered that attribute attractive.

They all sat in quietude, and for several moments, a feeling similar to peace settled over Charlotte. But then Anthony stood again and stepped toward her.

He was going to hand Henry back.

Inside, she panicked, and every horrible scenario pummeled her. He could cry again. He could scream.

Before she knew what had happened, Anthony lowered Henry to her arms in one seamless transition, suckling bottle and all.

And just like that, Charlotte was feeding her son.

She dare not display the happiness surging through her, for she doubted either Sutcliffe or Anthony would understand it.

Charlotte leaned down and kissed the baby's forehead as he ate.

She could do this.

She *would* do this.

She and Henry would not only survive at Hollythorne House, but they would also thrive. They would build their world and their family, and this was the first step.

Chapter 12

CHARLOTTE STOOD IN the cold, formidable great hall, a rag tied over her plaited hair, an apron over her day gown of puce kerseymere, and a wooden bucket of water in her hand. Colorless light filtered through the hall's front leaded windows, and beyond the wavy glass spread the courtyard and then the moorland, dressed in somber shades of slate and peat. She placed the bucket at her side and lifted a soaking rag from the liquid, wrung out the excess moisture, and pressed it against the pane. Years' worth of dirt smeared and ran, and Charlotte hurried to wipe it before it fell to the stone floor.

Even in this mundane task, Hollythorne House's silence struck her the most.

For the past three years she'd spent nearly every day next to the hustling Leeds streets, where carts and wagons crunched the cobbles at every hour, and harried people shouted and called to one another. It was not only city life that produced a constant hum, for within Wolden House existed an army of servants, always moving. Always watching. The ever-present throb of activity—not to mention the lack of solitude—had become the backdrop to her life. But here, in a house that embodied isolation, she noticed the absence of both. Indeed, at the moment the only sound that met her ears was the house itself as it groaned and danced with the moorland gusts.

The previous day's exhaustion had given way to a night of sleep, for not only her but Henry and Sutcliffe as well. The satisfaction of waking up in her childhood home quickly gave way to realization of the work that was before them.

After her mother's death, Charlotte had helped her father manage the household, but at the time the loyal servants had been with Hollythorne House for so long that the daily routines were effortless. Then when she moved to Wolden House, Roland had been determined and single-minded, and as such he'd left no decision to her. Her clothing, her jewelry, even her daily routine had been subject to his whim.

Now, the knowledge that every decision moving forward was hers to make was invigorating. It was not the time for timidity. The sooner she could prove to Silas that Hollythorne House was an appropriate home for Henry, the sooner they all might have peace.

She returned her attention to the rag in her hand, submerged it in the soapy water, and faced the smudged windows. Roland would have considered this sort of work beneath her and would have been furious to see her engaged in such a task. None of the rules from the past applied now, for she had only two options: wait until her threadbare staff could get to cleaning or do it herself.

Once satisfied the pane was as clean as it could be, she moved to the one directly next to it, trying not to notice how many panes remained. Not only did the windows require cleaning but the furniture needed to be uncovered and dusted. Floors wanted sweeping. There was even a part of the roof that would require repairs. The longer she was at Hollythorne House, the more detailed the list of necessary tasks grew. And that was only the house itself. As owner of Hollythorne House she was now responsible for the tenants and the farmland to the east and south. She could only imagine how her duties would increase after she met with Mr. Greenwood, the steward.

After an hour of working, she wiped her hair from her brow and paused to assess her progress. Through the glass she noticed a figure emerging from the edge of the front stables and crossing into the courtyard.

She studied Anthony Welbourne at this safe distance, unobserved. His presence was not as jarring as it had been the previous day. She was by no means used to being around him again, but she was accepting it. Gone was any semblance of the gangly young man she'd so ardently adored. Before her now was a much more rugged man. His gait exuded a confidence that could only be attributed to experience—of what kind she was not exactly sure. His hair, which had always been cut short, was longer and gathered in a queue at the base of his neck. Even the curl of it conveyed a newfound rebellion.

Every time she'd heard news of the war with the United States, she wondered about him. The reports were highly publicized, gruesome, and bloody, and even if the stories had been only partly true, she could only guess as to what he'd endured.

In a sudden pivot Anthony changed direction and headed

toward the house. He lifted his gaze to the window where she was standing, and their eyes met for a fleeting second.

She withdrew immediately. Heat rushed to her face.

She'd been caught staring at him from a window.

He approached the main door, and it was clear there would be no avoiding him once he stepped across the porch and through to the screens passage.

She snatched off the rag covering her hair and swiped dirt away from the apron. In truth, she shouldn't care that she was pale and her hair hung in her eyes. She had to remember the current state of things. He was a thief-taker—dark and enigmatic. She was a widow and a mother intent on independence and autonomy.

Now, more than ever, she had to be on her guard. Just because romantic feelings had existed between them at one point was no reason why there should be any question of it now. She had a reputation to protect and a child to raise, not to mention she was reinventing her entire existence. And as lovely as her memories of her time with Anthony were, recent events compelled her never to enter back into a romantic attachment of any sort. That chapter of her life was closed—it was a prison to which she refused to return.

The door to the porch scraped open, and then heavy boots fell on the stone floor. The door creaked closed once again, and Anthony appeared in one of the arches separating the screens passage from the great hall.

She'd anticipated the sight that would meet her as he entered the hall, but even so, her breath caught. Deep-blue eyes met hers, as she'd expected, but it was the start of a beard on his chin and jaw that altered his appearance the most. It covered the boyish ruddiness and garnered a more mysterious, if not roguish, appearance. Gone was the gentleness in his expression and the easy smile she remembered so well.

His scar ran from his ear down his jaw and disappeared into his neckcloth. The sight tightened her stomach. She *had* cared about him. Very deeply. The thought of him wounded—and having endured the injury that put such a scar there—ached.

He did not speak for several seconds, as if he was accustomed to the fact that people would notice the scar, and gave her a moment to digest it.

"Mrs. Prior," he greeted casually, swiping his hat from his head and stepping farther into the great hall. "Where is the boy?"

"Henry's with my maid, sleeping, while she settles things upstairs. Is there something you need?"

He looked over his shoulder before refocusing on her. "I think you and I should talk."

Nerves burned through her, each breath firing memories of this man. Of their affection for each other and the sadness of separating from him.

But she had to push that aside. Because, of course, he was right.

If this arrangement was to be successful, they could not carry on as if nothing had transpired between them. Under any other circumstance, she'd refuse to let her guard down or engage any genuine emotion. It was a strategy she'd perfected when married. Such tactics would be insufficient now, for she'd had no respect for her husband. But Anthony was different—he'd once held the key to her heart.

She nodded. "Very well."

His voice was as steady and cool as it had been when they were discussing the grounds the previous day. "I hope my presence here is not an intrusion, given our past acquaintance. I was unaware that *you* were Mrs. Prior until the day of the assignment. If you would rather I not be here, I will request a reassignment."

Silence—along with its crushing expectation for her response—once again reclaimed the room.

How like him the question was. Blunt and succinct. He'd always been a direct person—and certain about his plans. His opinions. His intentions.

She shook her head. "What I think or want in this particular situation does not matter, Mr. Welbourne. This arrangement is my brother-in-law's doing. Not mine."

———

Anthony allowed his gaze to linger on Charlotte longer than he should have. Her thick chestnut hair was gathered in a plait down her back, and she wore a white linen apron over a high-necked, long-sleeved gown. Shadows balanced beneath her red-rimmed topaz eyes, but alertness brightened her expression.

She'd failed to answer his question.

What was more, he did not recall her being so difficult to read.

He refused to let the topic drop. "It *does* matter what you want. This is your home."

"The agreement has been made, Mr. Welbourne. We can only hope that this ordeal will be behind us very soon and each of us can go on about our lives."

Her words were austere, her tone inscrutable.

He suddenly felt foolish for inquiring.

Perhaps the memory of what they had shared weighed heavier on him than on her. Perhaps his recollections of their relationship were far more intense than hers.

In this moment the morning light lingered on the soft angles of her narrow face. How explicitly he recalled each one. There had been a time when the caress of his hand would have been welcome there, when he'd kissed that smooth cheek. Her soft golden eyes, as sharp and vibrant as ever, were fixed on him, but her tightened expression lacked the warmth he remembered. He might still regard her with fondness and even affection, but she clearly did not return the sentiment. Could he blame her? She'd married another, and any nostalgic attitude would not be welcome. What was more, it would be inappropriate.

Her sharp words returned them to conversation. "Perhaps I should pose the option to you. If you're uncomfortable here, given the unique relationship between our families, then I will think nothing of it if you ask to be reassigned."

"This is my profession, Mrs. Prior. Personal circumstances will never affect my judgment."

An awkward quietude hovered in the tall room, as if it were an active participant, daring someone to speak next.

Then Charlotte pressed her lips together. It was a sign he recognized—an expression she used to make when she was uncertain or uncomfortable.

She tilted her head to the side. "I must ask, have you informed Mr. Walstead of our prior acquaintance?"

Then he understood her hesitation. Such a revelation could have far-reaching impact—for them both. "No. Of course not."

She nodded, then her shoulders straightened and her chin lifted. "Is there more we need to discuss?"

Yes, there was more.

Much more.

So much more that it ached in the deepest corners of his soul. But now was not the time. He cleared his throat. "If you wish to leave the property, send word and one of us will escort you. Additionally, if you are expecting guests, please inform us. Timmons will be going to the village to post a letter later today, so he'll take one on your behalf, should you like to send one."

She only nodded, and if one did not know better, one might think her indifferent.

The Charlotte Grey, nay Charlotte Prior, he knew was anything but indifferent.

He cleared his throat again. "The servants Mr. Walstead engaged will arrive today. I was told to expect a housekeeper, a manservant, and a nursemaid who will also serve as a maid. We will notify you upon their arrival."

Anthony gave her a few more instructions, and when their conversation concluded and she left him alone in the great hall, he could only stare at the empty space where she had just been standing.

She seemed to take his very breath with her.

It was a ridiculous sentiment, and sentiment had no business in his line of work. He needed to follow her lead. Her behavior had been perfectly clear. She was a grieving widow, and any affection she might have had for Anthony was dead and buried.

If he were to find peace with this assignment, he would have to accept the fact that her heart had been given to another man. Then he could toss that ridiculous fantasy of reviving their past behind him.

Chapter 13

AFTER LEAVING ANTHONY alone in the great hall, Charlotte's face flamed as she made her way up the uneven wooden staircase and crossed the minstrels' gallery on the floor above.

She was frustrated, but not with Anthony. Nay, she was frustrated with herself and her reaction to this situation.

No one had ever asked her opinion on anything. Not Roland. Not Silas Prior. Not even her father. Yet Anthony had just asked her about whether she was comfortable with his presence at Hollythorne House.

Anthony Welbourne's question was in line with the considerate character of the man she knew. But even so, the warmth she remembered in his tone was gone, as if he was inquiring out of obligation and nothing more.

She should not be feeling conflicted. He should have no effect on her. It had been years since they saw each other, and she was, after all, a widow. But with each encounter, additional memories flared. Happy memories. Safe memories. Memories of a time when she'd felt alive and free.

In all her longing to return to Hollythorne House, she never thought she'd be returning to *him*. She'd walled off that part of her heart, for she'd not been able to even think about the sharp contrasts between Anthony and Roland without pangs of regret. She and Anthony had not parted in anger or the result of a quarrel. He'd done nothing wrong and neither had she. Circumstances had intervened and propelled them down different paths. Now that she knew he was a member of Walstead's Watchmen, a formidable and dangerous picture of him was forming.

But he'd already begun to prove that he was not that man. He'd helped with Henry. He'd offered to leave if she was uncomfortable with his presence. And it was only the first full day of the arrangement.

Her footfalls echoed loudly on the bare wooden steps, giving voice to the anxieties swirling within her, as she turned into the smaller corridor that led to her chamber. Once inside, she found Sutcliffe standing next to the window, intently looking out to the west bank of windows toward Blight Moor. Henry was asleep in his cradle, and all was quiet and still.

Charlotte stepped next to Sutcliffe, expecting to look out to the moorland, but instead she found her lady's maid observing Mr. Timmons as he rode along the drystone wall at the property's edge.

Upon being discovered, Sutcliffe jerked. A flush colored her cheeks, and she whirled away from the window.

Charlotte glanced down at Mr. Timmons, whose stocky, barrel-chested frame was dressed in a heavy greatcoat and wide-brimmed hat, very similar to the one Anthony wore. She supposed most women would scold their lady's maid for such obvious gawking, and she probably should.

But how could she dare say a word to the one person who had remained faithful to her?

Sutcliffe wanted the same things every woman wanted—security in a world where tomorrow was never certain. Family to ensure she never would be alone. A home of her own. Freedom.

"M-My apologies, Mrs. Prior," Sutcliffe stuttered, returning to the bed, where gowns were scattered about. "I was unpacking, and—"

Charlotte held up her hand to quiet her. Sutcliffe was her servant, but she was also her friend. And Charlotte didn't have the inclination—or the energy—to reprimand the young woman, especially as Anthony's sudden appearance had just reminded her of her own escapades. "The scenery is enchanting here, is it not? So different from Leeds."

Sutcliffe sighed, folded her willowy arms over her chest, and stood for several moments. "I've never been on the moors like this before. It's certainly unlike anything I've ever seen."

"It is quite beautiful, especially during a summer sunset. When the evening sun hits the grasses just right, it sets the entire moor afire. It looks like endless ribbons of gold." Their conversation faded and as stillness resumed, gratitude toward her lady's maid fell over her. Not many maids would have consented to embark on a journey to such an isolated, rugged place, especially given the circumstances. "Everything has happened so quickly has it not? I'm curious to know what you think of this new arrangement."

"It's not really for me to have an opinion on it, is it?" Sutcliffe shrugged. "If you're content, then I am too."

It was the perfect answer for a lady's maid to give her mistress, yet Sutcliffe's opinions had to be stronger than she'd indicated. She had shared that she'd once been the member of a prominent family, but her parents' deaths had greatly reduced her circumstances. The skills she developed as a gentleman's daughter made her an excellent candidate for a lady's maid, but the position was just that—she was still a servant, and as such she had little time for romance.

Charlotte's situation was very different, but in truth, neither of them were free. She, at least, was on the cusp of a unique version of independence, but a great deal of work stretched ahead of her. Sutcliffe's only hope for a different life would come through marriage. Charlotte would not dissuade her friend from watching a man who caught her fancy. "Surely you must have thoughts. Hollythorne House is quite different from Wolden House."

Sutcliffe stepped away from the window to the pile of gowns on the bed. "The surroundings may be different, but we're still the same people. Besides, I'm fond of a new situation. I am content."

Charlotte pulled one of the heavy, deep-garnet brocade drapes away from the bed's canopy and secured it with a thick gold cord, just as she remembered her maid doing every morning when she was young. "You're not frightened at all to be here, this far out of the city? Given the concerns about the mill workers?"

"Perhaps a little, but Mr. Walstead has been tasked with keeping us safe, so that provides a measure of confidence. And after speaking with Mr. Timmons earlier this morning, I earnestly believe he takes his position rather seriously. Have you noticed his hand?"

Charlotte shook her head.

"'Tis horribly injured." Sutcliffe's wide-set eyes widened. "Scarred and disfigured. Some of the fingers are missing."

Charlotte stiffened. "Do you know how it happened?"

"He caught me looking at it, and he told me it was injured in the war."

Anthony's scar flashed in her mind.

Sutcliffe continued. "It does make one feel secure, does it not? Knowing someone is watching after things while we sleep and keeping an eye on things during the day?"

The young woman didn't conceal the tone of admiration in her words. Charlotte did feel safer with the watchmen's presence, especially knowing Anthony's character, but Sutcliffe knew nothing of her past with Anthony, and Charlotte wanted to keep it that way.

The women turned their attention to the task of unpacking the trunks. As Charlotte sorted through her belongings, including the box with her jewels and the chest she'd retrieved from Wolden House's strongbox, the importance of understanding her financial situation struck her anew. She'd be receiving money from the will as well as from the estate to see to Henry's care, but she needed funds now to make Hollythorne House livable. The money Mr. Sires provided to her before leaving Wolden House would only last for so long, and she would have to pay servants and see to immediate repairs.

She moved to the small traveling desk atop the writing table opposite the bed and opened it.

"What are you doing?" Sutcliffe lifted her attention from the wool stockings she was sorting.

"I'm writing to Mr. Greenwood. I must speak with him as soon as possible to get an understanding of Hollythorne's finances before things go too far. Mr. Welbourne told me Mr. Timmons is to post a letter in the village today, and I want this to be included."

Sutcliffe lifted the box of jewelry and opened it. "Do you still want to sell some of these? If so, I can return to Leeds after the new staff arrives. If I borrow one of the horses, I can go there and be back within the day."

Charlotte took in her maid's eagerness, and yet she hesitated. It was a risky endeavor. Charlotte trusted Sutcliffe—that was not the issue. She did not, however, trust the jewelers or the sorts of men who would be buying the goods. But what choice did she have? She turned to the locked chest, which was also atop the desk, opened it, and inside were several storage boxes—each piece of jewelry in its own case.

She picked up a leather box and opened it to reveal a ruby pendant. "This is the first piece Roland ever gave me." She touched her fingertip to the ruby's smooth surface and shivered. The beautiful gem—an attempt by Roland to pacify her—propelled an exchange with her husband to the forefront of her thoughts, and the memory of the experience raced through her mind.

"That's the best I can do." Disappointment colored Sutcliffe's tone as she stepped back and assessed her work.

Charlotte, too, turned her face to the looking glass. No amount of powders and creams could conceal the deep purple-and-blue bruising around her eye, nor the crimson gash on her cheek left by Roland's ring.

Her stomach roiled and tears gathered in her eyes. The physical pain would subside, but the knowledge that she was married to the man responsible for her injury terrified her.

Heavy footsteps echoed, and the sound of someone whistling drifted in from the corridor.

Charlotte and Sutcliffe locked gazes.

Roland.

"I don't want to see him," whispered Charlotte, gripping Sutcliffe's hands with desperate strength. She wanted an escape, some sort of shelter, but what could be done? If Roland wanted to see her, there was nothing either she or Sutcliffe could do to stop him.

The door to her chamber flung open. Charlotte winced at the suddenness of it.

"There you are, my darling."

His voice was loud. Booming.

Charlotte caught Sutcliffe's sympathetic gaze before the maid curtsied and withdrew, leaving her alone with her husband.

It had been two days since she'd last seen him—two days since he roared at her in drunken anger and struck her. But now he strolled in, nonchalant and unaffected, his smile and voice uncustomarily bright. "Mrs. Dalton tells me you haven't been eating."

She somehow mustered courage and met his icy blue gaze in the mirror's reflection, but trepidation robbed her of speech.

"You must keep up your strength, my darling." He stepped closer behind her and placed his large, heavy hands on her shoulders, his suffocating scent of tobacco and sandalwood engulfing her. "We can't have you falling ill."

Her gaze dropped slightly from his round face to his right hand and the heavy signet ring on it—the very ring responsible for the gash on her cheek.

"She also tells me you've a headache. A pity." He continued with a click of his tongue that commanded her attention. "How I wanted to show off my beautiful wife at the Rogers' ball tonight. I doubt you'll feel up to attending."

A lump formed in her throat, jagged and dry. Unable to hold his gaze any longer, she looked down to her hands. They were trembling. She tucked them in her dressing gown.

"I know you're disappointed, my love, but here, I have brought something to cheer you." Now his smile beamed with pride, and he pulled a necklace from his coat.

She turned back to her reflection, and he motioned for her to lift her hair away from her collarbone. She obeyed, and he draped the ruby-encrusted adornment about her neck. Her skin crawled as his clammy fingers brushed her skin, followed by a shiver that was almost painful in its intensity.

She dropped her loose hair over her shoulders, and he pressed a kiss to the top of her head.

Her eyes fixed blankly on the piece of jewelry.

"You're awfully quiet." His light brows furrowed, and a shadow passed over his expression. "Do you not care for it?"

She attempted to swallow the lump. "It's very beautiful."

He scoffed. "You're not still upset from the other day, are you?"

She shook her head. "Of course not."

"I should hope not. It was a ridiculous exchange, but I daresay we both learned a lesson in it."

How had she ever thought him kind? Or handsome?

"My beautiful wife," he repeated, his face resuming the relaxed expression. "I really am the most fortunate of men. I will come and see you tonight when I return from the ball, if that suits you. And I will have Boswick make you a tonic for your headache. They always do the trick for me."

He pressed another kiss to the top of her head, and then, as quickly as he entered, he retreated.

Now when Charlotte beheld the ruby pendant, she saw no beauty. She could see only the fear and frustration that had been her marriage's constant companions. Charlotte discarded it on the bed. "It can be sold."

Together they went through the pieces in the case—earrings and necklaces and brooches, until Sutcliffe lifted a small pouch of tan leather and frowned. "I've never seen this before."

Charlotte furrowed her brows as she took the pouch from Sutcliffe.

She opened the drawstring closure and tipped the contents onto her palm. Several emeralds, in varying sizes and stages of refinement, tumbled out. She picked one up and held it to the light. "I've never seen these before. Roland must have put them there."

"But why put them in the chest, of all places?" Sutcliffe stepped closer and picked one up to look at it more closely. "Perhaps he intended to have it made into a necklace for you?"

Charlotte returned the emerald to the others. It was a lovely sentiment, but no. She gave a sardonic laugh. "I'm certain that was not his intention." She closed the drawstring pouch, returned it to the chest, and closed the lid. "There's a loose floorboard beneath the table in that corner of the room. Since we're not familiar with the new servants arriving soon, let's put all the jewels there, just to be careful. We have no idea how trustworthy they will be."

Together the women collected the most valuable pieces, then pushed the table away. As she removed the floorboard, a small parcel wrapped in paper and secured with a blue satin ribbon came into view.

"What's that?" asked Sutcliffe, peering over Charlotte's shoulder.

Anthony's notes.

She blinked at the stack of missives. She'd forgotten how, when caught up in the romantic flurry of budding love, she'd kept the notes he'd left for her in the hollow of an ash tree on the moor's edge. It had been a silly, sentimental thing to do— something that would normally be quite out of her character, even when she was younger. And yet as she held them in her hands again, she could feel the excitement and optimism that had accompanied the receipt of each one. The excitement and opti- mism that had accompanied *him*.

"Merely a childhood trinket." She tucked the parcel behind her, out of Sutcliffe's sight. "Nothing important."

After deflecting Sutcliffe's attention from the letters and then carefully placing her jewelry in the hiding place beneath the floor, she returned to the task of writing the letter to Mr. Greenwood. Time was of the essence, and instead of being distracted by the past, she needed to keep a firm eye on the future.

Anthony was not surprised the new staff was late. The carriage ride from Leeds to Hollythorne, while not a great distance, was difficult, and the slightest bit of rain or fog could make the roads treacherous.

But he was growing impatient.

It was not unusual for Mr. Walstead to hire staff for a client, especially in a protection situation. When danger could come from anyone, having control—and trust in those who were assisting—was key.

Anthony's responsibilities in every case varied greatly, but they all usually had one thing in common: the clients were always strangers. Never had he had a past with any of his clients, especially not a client he had loved.

There had been very few people in his life whom he had loved and who loved him in return. His mother died at his birth, and his father died when he was only seven years of age, leaving him to be raised by his uncle, Robert Welbourne, a confirmed and surly bachelor. Their housekeeper had been the closest thing to a mother figure, and even that was a lukewarm relationship. He'd spent the bulk of his childhood and adolescence counting the years and months until the day he could follow in his father's footsteps. Purchasing a commission and becoming an officer had been the one instruction his father had given him on his deathbed, and nothing would keep him from it, despite his uncle's insistence that Anthony should oversee the mill.

But now he hardly knew what to think about these expectations. Since leaving Blight Moor, he'd formed no real attachments with anyone apart from Timmons, whose friendship had seen him through some of the darkest points of his life. But even that friendship was shifting, and only one thing was certain: in Anthony's line of work, affection for anyone, let alone romantic affection, would interfere with his reactions.

A distant rustling caught his attention, and he turned to see a carriage approaching. A strange relief suffused him. More people, even servants, traipsing about would lower the probability of another uncomfortable interaction with Charlotte. He might desire time with her, but every signal she'd given him clearly communicated that their relationship was in the past.

He glanced up at the carriage. Both Charlotte and her maid were watching the carriage approach as well. He did not like this effect she had on him—the sense that he'd lost something precious that could not be recovered stabbed a hardened part of his heart.

Yes, the sooner this assignment was concluded, the better he—and his heart—would be.

Chapter 14

IT WAS HARD to hand Henry to a stranger, even one who seemed kind and genuine. Yet a knot tightened in Charlotte's stomach and refused to loosen as she watched their new nursemaid, Rebecca, cradle her son.

The servants' arrival should have brought a measure of peace, but instead, uncertainly roiled within her.

Charlotte eyed Rebecca with her plaited nut-brown hair; wide, expressionless brown eyes; and firmly set thin lips, silently studying her every move. After months of fighting for any small moment of peace and solitude with her son, entrusting him to a new nursemaid seemed to go against everything she wanted.

But this was how a household was run.

Mrs. Hargrave, the temporary housekeeper, was a plump woman with faded auburn hair, weathered cheeks, and deep-set blue eyes, who, at the moment, was scurrying about the kitchen, evaluating the kettles and pots, the hearth, and the storage. Her husband, Tom Hargrave, the manservant, had just delivered a crate of vegetables and food supplies and already he was in the courtyard talking with Mr. Timmons.

Charlotte shifted her attention back to Rebecca. She appeared quite young, and it seemed that interacting with Henry was the most natural thing in the world to her—as if she had been taking care of children since she was a child herself.

Still, the truth pricked her. Charlotte had never been fully in charge of servants before. Now her words would rule the daily activities.

And that realization overwhelmed her.

Rebecca bounced Henry playfully as they were seated next to the broad fire, and he giggled. Charlotte's chest tightened, squeezing at her heart. She'd been endeavoring to forge a bond with Henry since their arrival at Hollythorne House, and she was failing miserably.

Charlotte drew a deep breath, determining that the best way to feel comfortable with the arrangement was to learn as much about the new nursemaid as she could. "You appear quite young, Rebecca. How old are you?"

Rebecca shifted cautiously and cast a glance toward Mrs. Hargrave. "Nineteen last month, ma'am."

The number surprised Charlotte, for she would have guessed by her ruddy cheeks and small build that she was much younger.

Rebecca reached for the sucking bottle she'd prepared with pap, offered it to Henry, and he took it eagerly.

Charlotte observed the interaction, still acutely aware of how pitifully she had failed that task. "You seem quite adept."

Rebecca shrugged a slight shoulder, not taking her eyes off Henry. "I've 'ad aplenty practice."

"Do you have children of your own?"

"Me? La. No. But I've 'elped rear many a babe. Me mother was a wet nurse, and we always 'ad other folks' babies 'round our 'ouse. Then soon as I was old enough, I went with her to t' big 'ouses t' work as nursemaid."

Charlotte refused to give in to her feelings of inadequacy. After all, this girl had been doing this her whole life. Charlotte was just beginning. "When you're finished, I will show you to the chamber that will serve as Henry's nursery."

She had to start somewhere. Rather than begrudging this girl's presence, as the wounded parts of her stubbornly desired, she would try to learn from her instead.

Charlotte paced in her bedchamber's solitude as the events of the past several hours left her mind reeling.

Had it really been only two days since Roland's death?

It did not seem possible, yet just yesterday she and Henry had arrived at Hollythorne House, and she'd begun tackling the tasks that lay before her. Now the servants were here. Everything was progressing at a mind-numbing tempo, but she could not slow the pace. Her entire plan could collapse at any time. And she simply would not let that happen.

One day she'd be able to relax and let down her guard. One day she and Henry would be at peace in their own home. But it had only been two days, and she dare not underestimate Silas Prior.

She needed to return to the kitchen to go over the list of items that needed to be purchased in the village, but as she turned to leave the chamber, she spied the bound parcel of Anthony's notes atop her desk.

She debated the wisdom of looking inside.

Opening it would be like opening the door to her past—potentially allowing emotions to rekindle and gain power. Resisting such temptation would be prudent. But the call for comfort and familiarity was too great.

With the bundle in hand she sat on the quilts on her bed. Slowly she released the ribbon, and as the paper fell away, memories sprung to life.

The heather bloom he'd picked and tucked in her hair, now pressed and preserved.

A smooth, small rock that shimmered in the light.

The notes he'd written asking her to meet him.

Even Tor. Sunset.

Even the penmanship of his simple missive boasted a confidence that had not changed.

How different her life could have been if they would have chosen each other. She had no doubt Anthony would have been a kind and gentle husband.

What would it have been like?

She carefully returned the contents to the parcel, retied the ribbon, and tucked it between the mattress tick and the bedstead. As she straightened and turned, her gaze caught her reflection in the small, mottled looking glass that hung on the wall next to her bed. She touched her fingertips to her temple. Then her lips.

How pale she was.

Perhaps it was the high-necked ebony gown of heavy brocade

that brought about her almost ghoulish appearance, but as she pivoted to view her face from a different angle, she noted the hollow of her cheeks. The grim circles beneath her eyes. How different she looked from that wild and free girl Anthony would recall. Then her cheeks had always been pink, her skin had possessed a sunbathed hue, and freckles had kissed the bridge of her nose.

But now she looked like a different person.

What was more, she *felt* like a different person.

How she wished that, even for just a moment, she could recapture that carefree feeling of youth—of excitement and passion, of enthusiastic impatience for life to begin. Now, instead of feeling like the world was at her fingertips, she felt like a meager rowboat at the mercy of stormy seas, being pushed and pulled with their every whim.

She smoothed her hair and coiled it into a chignon and pinned it in place. She pinched her cheeks for color before turning to reach for her shawl. All thoughts of the past had to be kept at bay, especially because she needed to find Anthony and speak with him about arrangements for Sutcliffe to travel to Leeds to attempt to sell the jewels.

After settling her shawl about her shoulders, Charlotte stepped from her chamber. She collected Henry from the nursery and made her way down to the kitchen, where she found Mr. Timmons seated at the table with a bowl of stew before him.

He stood immediately upon her entrance and offered a slight bow.

She'd not interacted with Mr. Timmons much, but after hearing Sutcliffe's opinions, she was curious about the other man who'd been assigned to watch over them. He was not nearly as tall as Anthony, and he boasted thick sandy hair and light chestnut eyes. A deep dimple marked his clean-shaven left cheek, and broad shoulders and a cleft in his chin added to his apparent strength. She could see why Sutcliffe would be drawn to him.

She did not dare allow her gaze to drop to his hand.

"Mrs. Prior," he greeted.

"I need to speak with Mr. Welbourne. Do you know where he is?"

"'E's on t' outdoor patrol. Shall I collect 'im for you?"

She shook her head. "No, that won't be necessary. I'll wait for him to return. Thank you."

Determined to enjoy the day's last rays of sunlight, Charlotte carried Henry out to the gardens behind the house. Silvery clouds were gathering, and the indigo and mauve shades of dusk were intensifying. Night would be here soon. She tightened the Prussian blue shawl about her shoulders and walked to the garden's wooden gate.

As the gate swung open, genuine enthusiasm met her. She and her mother would spend hours here, tending to hollyhocks and dahlias, lavender and verbena. It was all overgrown now, but an eagerness to revive it to its former glory budded within her.

The gardens themselves were large enough for several mature trees and intricate groupings of hawthorn and holly bushes. Ivy, faded by autumn's crispness, nearly obscured the drystone walls, and the brambles and branches grew free. She strolled down the brick path, marveling as fresh memories were unearthed with each step. For the first time since her arrival at Hollythorne House, the tension in her shoulders seemed to ease. She retrieved a wooden rattle from the pocket on the front of her apron and handed it to Henry, who waved it and laughed.

She indulged in a deep breath. She could be happy here. Henry could be happy here.

The gate squeaked on its hinges, interrupting her reverie, and she looked up from her musings to see Anthony approaching.

Four years ago, the very thought of being alone with him in a secluded garden would have set her imagination aflame, but time, with its cruel twists and turns, had unwittingly turned so many tides. She barely knew what to make of the feelings churning within. How she wished this painful pull of attraction to him did not exist, but then again, she'd always been drawn to him, from the very first time she saw him on Blight Moor.

He bowed briefly and then spoke as he approached. "Timmons said you needed to speak with me."

"Yes." She pivoted, Henry still in her arms. "Tomorrow Sutcliffe must travel to Leeds and will require an escort. I was hoping you could make the arrangements."

His expression remained stoic. "Of course. But perhaps Timmons or I could see to the errand on Miss Sutcliffe's behalf."

She shook her head. She could never bring herself to admit to him that she needed to sell her jewelry to raise money. Her pride would not permit it. "The errand is of a personal nature. Sutcliffe is quite capable."

"I've no doubt she is, but she'd be safer here. She might be recognized and, as a result, followed."

Charlotte kept her gaze steady. "I'm not in hiding,

Mr. Welbourne. In fact, I do not believe I am in danger in the least, and I will conduct myself as such. It is my brother-in-law who fears for our safety. Not me."

He looked past her, out to the moors. A thick lock of hair escaped his queue and curled roguishly about his face. The scar on his face was sharp and jagged, yet the curve of his jaw was captivating and as strong and defined as it ever was.

"Very well," he relented. "If you're insistent. Timmons can escort her."

She thought of the flush in her maid's cheeks at the sight of him earlier in the day. "Can Mr. Timmons be trusted? As a gentleman?"

Anthony's dark brow rose. After not seeing so much as a smile on his face since their arrival at Hollythorne House, she thought she detected a hint of amusement flash in his large eyes before he once again sobered. "I've trusted Timmons with my life. I know of no man who is more reliable."

The weighty statement caught her off guard, and she tensed at the confident nature in his voice—the same tone he had always employed: conviction when he spoke of his intention. Of the commission. Of his opinions. Of his birthright. He'd always acted as if once a decision was made, no other option was possible.

At one time such determined self-assurance was comforting.

Now it was disarming.

Henry dropped the rattle he had been holding and it clattered to the brick path beneath them. Immediately Anthony bent down to retrieve it and extended it to her son. The corner of his mouth lifted at the baby's enthusiasm.

Anthony used to smile so easily and frequently. His laugh had been contagious. His manner carefree. What had happened to him to bring about such a change?

Regret for speaking to Anthony so coolly up to this point was beginning to take hold. Perhaps he really was trying to assist her, as he said. For so long she'd been around people who would take advantage of every situation that she forgot any other sort existed. When had she become so jaded that she no longer saw kindness when it was extended toward her?

She would be uneasy with him until she addressed her tone earlier in the day. Just because life seemed cruel did not excuse her. "I owe you an apology, Mr. Welbourne."

His expression did not change. "You owe me nothing, Mrs. Prior."

"But I do. I spoke tersely toward you earlier, both in the court-yard and in the great hall. You asked me how I felt about your presence here, and I see that you were only being considerate. I have no excuse other than I fear I'm not myself at the moment."

"You've just lost your husband. Explanations are not needed."

No doubt he assumed she was grieving.

How would he respond if he knew the truth about her marriage?

Again, without warning, Henry launched the rattle, and it fell over the toe of Anthony's boot. Anthony stooped down to retrieve it, and this time he took a step toward them to return the rattle. With his nearness came his scent of outdoors and an unexpected flutter within her chest.

Henry's eyes widened at the return of the toy, and he batted it with such intensity that Anthony chuckled. "He looks like you."

Charlotte sighed and took in the boy's wispy white hair and vibrant blue eyes. "He looks nothing like me. He looks a Prior through and through."

"His nose has the same slope. It will look just like yours one day."

At the personal nature of the statement, she sobered.

It did not matter how much time had passed or what situations they had endured. An unavoidable intimacy would always exist between them. The secrets they had once shared never could be forgotten, and it was taking only a couple of days with him near for it all to come rushing back.

She stepped back, reestablishing an appropriate distance. If she was to be successful, she could not allow these glimpses into her past to affect her son. "I must get Henry inside. He'll be hungry soon. Good evening, Mr. Welbourne."

It was rude, she knew, to depart so abruptly, but she was finding it difficult to know how to act. He was a hired watchman, but her heart was determined to remember him quite differently.

Chapter 15

ANTHONY WATCHED CHARLOTTE carry Henry from the garden to the house.

The fringe of her long, patterned shawl swayed with each step, dragging through the dried russet leaves and rogue branches.

The wind caught locks of her dark chestnut hair in the same manner as he remembered. How natural Charlotte looked with the child in her arms. It was the very sight he'd imagined often in his thoughts—of how he'd dreamed *their* life would be.

But now, she wasn't holding his baby. The child was another man's.

A gentle rain started to fall, the misty sort that ushered in the bone-chilling cold of autumn that would cover the dormant moorland until spring. He sought and found Timmons in the rear garden doing their evening perimeter check.

"Change of plans." Anthony approached Timmons. "I need you to go on an errand."

"Good." Timmons huffed. "This place is a tomb."

"I thought you liked a Prior assignment?" quipped Anthony.

"Bah. At t' end of t' day, one's pretty much like t' other, innit? I can't believe ye lived out 'ere all those years. Does nothing 'appen 'ere?"

Anthony shrugged and lifted his eyes to the south, where just beyond the road the forest rose. He could see why Timmons would think it a droll locale. But Anthony had lived a whole life here. Loved here. Learned here. "It wasn't terrible."

"I 'ave to say, after my last job for a Prior, I thought this would be a bit more excitin'. That job was for Roland Prior though, not Silas Prior."

Anthony's ear pricked at the mention of Roland, and he took the opportunity to learn more. "I forgot that the Prior job was for Roland Prior and not his brother."

"Aye. Roland Prior were purchasin' some sort o' machinery, very expensive, for t' updates to t' mills. Parts of it were comin' from overseas, so ol' Roland hired an escort to meet it at t' dock in Plymouth t' make sure it made it without any problems. Roland Prior and Mr. Walstead were both present on the assignment, so ye know it was of consequence."

Anthony raised his brow. "Did you see what kind of machinery it was?"

"Nay. It was crated from t' time it came off t' ship 'til we carried it inside an outbuilding at Prior Mill."

Anthony ignored the tinge of shame he felt for prodding information from Timmons without divulging the truth about why he wanted to know. But Timmons was not a discreet man, especially if ale were to become involved. Sharing that Charlotte was part of his past would only open her up to gossip.

Timmons pivoted. "So what o' this change o' plans?"

"Tomorrow Mrs. Prior's maid needs to go to Leeds. You'll escort her."

Timmons leaned with his elbows on the stone wall. "What's t' purpose?"

"Not sure exactly. Mrs. Prior said it was personal. She'll take the carriage. You'll accompany it."

Timmons laughed and adjusted his stance. "We could be goin' to buy ribbons for all I care."

"And while you're in Leeds I'll have you stop by the office. I've a letter for Mr. Walstead." Anthony handed him the paper.

"And if 'e's not in?" Timmons tucked the letter in his coat.

"Leave it for him. And, of course, you'll want to change horses at Walstead's stables."

Timmons's expression darkened, and a sharpness heightened his tone. "Good thing ye told me. Never would 'ave thought t' change the 'orses on me own. But then again, you're clever, aren't ye? After all, Walstead made ye lead watchman."

Anthony felt the full brunt of the sarcasm and masked a wince at the unexpected brashness of the tone. Of course Timmons would know to change the horses—everyone would have. Anthony regretted the careless statement. Timmons had always been sensitive about his rank in the organization. Whereas Anthony seemed to be gaining traction, Timmons was not.

Anthony would not argue with his friend over a trivial slip of the tongue and forced a chuckle. "Yes, and as lead watchman I'm telling you to be a gentleman with the lady's maid."

Timmons snorted and raised a brow. "I can't promise t' lady

won't fall for m' charms, but I'll fend 'er off if need be. No doubt it'll prove the most interestin' part of this assignment."

They parted ways, and Timmons headed to the perimeter while Anthony settled to guard the house. Darkness fell quickly, and as he rounded the house toward the front courtyard, he looked up to the window in Charlotte's chamber. The image of her holding her son flashed again in his mind's eye.

He'd expected to be attracted to her—he had been since the moment he first glimpsed her. But the strength of his emotions and the direction his thoughts were taking had caught him off guard. His initial assumption upon seeing her again was that she was a grieving widow. As such it wouldn't be appropriate to breathe life into any romantic thoughts of her. Yet the longer he was in her presence and the more he learned about the nuances of her situation, he realized he might be misconstruing the facts. Indeed, she was likely grieving, but she also seemed to be fighting for control.

It was possible that just maybe, if her heart had not been fully given to another as he'd assumed, there might be room for him once more.

He drew his hand over his face and rubbed the back of his neck as he looked out toward the moorland. Desolate. Turbulent. Untamed. A strange disappointment dripped over him.

He was not quite the same person he had been, but he had not died. He was still alive. And just as he fought to keep air in his lungs during the war, he would fight for Charlotte.

Chapter 16

CHARLOTTE BOLTED UPRIGHT in bed. Perspiration dampened her hairline. Her chest heaved.

The midnight blackness shrouded everything.

A nightmare.

Roland was there—in the recesses of her slumbering mind.

In these listless musings his death had not happened.

He was alive. And angry. And wanted Henry.

She pushed the curtained canopy away, leapt from her bed, and stumbled across the corridor to push open the nursery's wooden door. Her eyes adjusted to the soft amber glow from the simmering fire, and she spied Henry, asleep in his cradle.

"Is everything alright, Mrs. Prior?"

Charlotte jumped at the voice and whirled. She'd all but forgotten about Rebecca, who'd been sleeping on a cot in the chamber's corner. "I-I was only checking in on Henry."

She turned back to observe Henry's little chest rise and fall with each breath. He was here, in her ancestral home. Safe.

It had been a dream.

No, more than a dream.

She withdrew and returned to her own chamber's east window, turned the handle, and pushed the window open to invite the raw wind to curl into the room.

She blamed her nerves, mostly, for conjuring such vile thoughts.

After all, Roland was dead.

She'd seen his body for herself.

Roland could not hurt her anymore. But Silas Prior could, and the words Roland hurled at her in the dream—an accusation and a threat—refused to be silent.

With the window still open she crawled back beneath her quilt and hoped the night sounds of the windswept moorland would calm her anxious thoughts, for despite the fact they were tucked away at Hollythorne House, she feared her worst nightmare was yet to come.

———————

The next morning, Charlotte stood inside the screens passage as Sutcliffe donned her cloak in preparation to depart for Leeds. In her hand she clutched a satchel containing the pearls and ruby that Roland had given Charlotte.

"Are you certain you're comfortable doing this?" Charlotte asked as Sutcliffe secured her cloak. "If you're not, we can find another way."

"Nonsense." A smile brightened Sutcliffe's round face. "I'm quite confident. I've done this before, remember? I'm not at all distressed about meeting with the jewelers."

"I was referring to traveling alone," Charlotte pitched her voice low to avoid being overheard, "with no one but Mr. Timmons to accompany you."

Sutcliffe shook her head dismissively. "Don't give it another thought. Tom will be driving the carriage. We'll not be alone. I'll be back with money before you know it. And what an adventure it will be! I'll be traveling over the tempestuous moorlands in a lovely carriage transporting secret jewels with a mysterious watchman as my protector. What a story I will have to tell."

Charlotte raised a brow at her friend's enthusiasm and cast a glance through the open door toward Timmons and Anthony, who were checking the carriage horses. Her suspicion was that the lady's maid was more interested in the watchman than the adventure, but her options were limited. If Charlotte thought there was a possibility of not being recognized, she would go herself. But with Silas's colleagues and workers everywhere, being prudent was essential.

Sutcliffe lifted her cloak's thick hood over her fair hair, adjusted it, and leaned to the left to quickly assess her reflection in a looking glass hanging on the wall. "Mr. Timmons has always been polite to me. And I do feel safe. Please, do not worry."

She forced a smile as they stepped into the courtyard. Anthony's words about trusting Mr. Timmons rang in her mind. And she did trust Anthony. More than she cared to admit.

By the time the carriage transporting Sutcliffe to Leeds rumbled from Hollythorne House's mist-laden property, dawn was breaking pink and yellow over the forest to the east. Mr. Timmons rode horseback alongside the vehicle, and after the fog claimed the carriage, Charlotte tightened her shawl against the chilly autumn air and looked back to Hollythorne House's blackened facade. Several slate shingles were missing from the roof, and multiple panes of glass were cracked in the windows overlooking the courtyard. It would take more than the sale of a handful of jewels to return her ancestral home back to its former state.

Silence, save for the squawking of the morning birds dipping down from the evergreen branches, descended once again, making Charlotte acutely aware of how the carriage's departure left Anthony and her alone, with only Henry and the servants milling about to distract her. They'd come to a sort of understanding the previous night in the garden, and now there was no further need for discussions. She gathered her skirt in hand and stepped toward the door.

But his words stopped her. "Are you finding the servants satisfactory, Mrs. Prior?"

She resisted the urge to wince. Such a question felt almost ridiculous—as if she was some pampered gentlewoman instead of what she was—a reduced widow desperate to forge a new life.

In truth, she did not care for their presence at all. She wanted a staff of her own selection. But this was part of the arrangement she had accepted. "I'll admit that it was nice to have a proper cup of tea. I fear that neither Sutcliffe nor I are very skilled in the domestic arts."

"And the nursemaid? Is Master Henry taking to her?"

Charlotte nodded. "Henry likes her, and she seems competent. But I confess I'll be far more comfortable when I'm able to select the nursemaid for myself. Have you worked with any of the servants prior to this?"

"No." He squinted as he looked toward the rising sun. "But it's not unusual. Mr. Walstead has a team he uses whenever situations like this arise."

She lifted her hand to still the dark locks blowing across her face. "And you have been in situations like this often? Guarding widows and sons of powerful mill owners?"

He chuckled, and her uneasiness diminished at the sound.

"No," he said. "No wealthy widows. I usually work guarding transports and apprehending perpetrators. I was selected for this assignment because of my history on Blight Moor. Mr. Walstead thought it might prove useful."

"Perhaps Mr. Walstead underestimated how relatively small Blight Moor is. I wonder that he did not consider that we might be acquainted."

Anthony shrugged a thick shoulder. "Well, you're the owner of an estate, and as you said, the widow of a powerful mill owner. I'm the nephew of a miller, not to mention a soldier's son. One would not naturally connect the two."

Hearing the division of their social classes laid out so plainly stung. "That shouldn't matter."

"That always matters."

She softened. She did not want to argue with him. "I was sorry to hear about your uncle."

He pressed his lips together with a somber nod. "And I was sorry to hear of your father. Imagine what they would think of this current arrangement given their hatred of one another. And yet, here we are. I don't think any of this turned out the way any of us expected."

The reference to her father and his disapproval cut her. She had tried so hard to meet his every expectation, especially at the end of his life when he wanted so badly for her to become Mrs. Roland Prior. She could only imagine what he would think of her and the decisions she was making.

She had not realized she'd been staring at Anthony until he spoke again.

"You needn't look so suspicious of me." He grinned. "I'm the same person I was."

"Are you?"

He adjusted his stance and drew a deep breath, as if considering his response. "I've seen a few more troubling things. Done a few more daunting things. But yes. Essentially the same person."

She eyed him skeptically, weighing his words. "There we are different, it seems. I've experienced some harrowing things as well, but they have indeed changed me. I fear the person I was is gone forever."

Determined to maintain dominion over her emotions, Charlotte managed a smile before turning wordlessly to return to the house.

How easy it would be to fall back into the same sort of easy conversation they'd always enjoyed—recklessly easy. Doing so, in the end, would undoubtedly make this difficult situation even more heartbreaking. She had to remember what was at stake. If she was to come out at the end of this with the rest of her battered heart intact, she had no choice but to keep her sentiments in check.

Chapter 17

CHARLOTTE PROPPED HER hands on her waist and surveyed the neglected downstairs parlor. It had been nearly an hour since Sutcliffe had departed, and Henry was sleeping. Charlotte needed a task—anything that would keep her hands and her mind busy.

She could not let her mind linger on Anthony's words.

His reference to the past—and their relationship—was dangerous, for it was far too easy to read a meaning into the words that wasn't there. It was a lovely idea to think that he was the same person as before he had left and they could somehow be transported back to a simpler time. But she meant what she had said—she no longer recognized any of the pieces of the person she'd been.

She secured her working apron around her waist before removing protective sheets from the table and chairs, and she dusted the two chairs and a straight-backed wooden settee that flanked the broad fire. She replaced the spent tallow candles in the candelabra in the center of the table with fresh ones of beeswax and repositioned the rough rug covering the room's uneven stones. With every item she touched, with every scent she breathed, memories tumbled forth.

She could smell the tobacco from her father's pipe.

She could hear her mother singing in the next chamber.

This was the room where her family would welcome visitors.

In fact, this was where she had first laid eyes on Roland Prior. It had been almost a year exactly after she first encountered Anthony on Blight Moor, and several months after he'd left for war. Her father's health had been failing, and he was eager to see her married and taken care of. The memory of that day harkened back in vibrant detail.

Unusual laughter echoed from the parlor, and Charlotte, fresh from an afternoon walk on the moors, removed her straw summer bonnet and set it on the side table outside the parlor door. Curious as to who could be making her father laugh, she gently rapped her knuckles on the doorframe.

"I heard voices," she said, turning into the chamber, expecting to see one of the tenants or perhaps Jon Turner from the village, but no. There stood one of the most handsome men she'd ever seen, standing at her father's side. Tall. Thick white-blond hair that curled over his coat's high collar, and strong, broad shoulders. He was impeccably dressed in a deep-blue tailcoat of worsted wool, with an emerald waistcoat of patterned silk, fawn buckskin breeches, and polished riding boots. A shiny fob was at his waist, and his intricately tied cravat was snowy white against his fair skin. But it was his eyes that struck her most— icy, wide, and clear, entrancing with their paleness and quite unlike any she'd ever seen.

Sunlight splashed through sparkling windows, and it reflected from the sapphire signet ring on his finger and added warmth to the cozy parlor. Her father smiled, creasing the lines on his weathered face, and extended his hand toward her. "Ah, my dear. Join us."

She did as bid, immediately regretting her decision not to visit her bedchamber to tidy her hair before learning their visitor's identity. She also regretted her choice of day dress, for her primrose muslin gown paled in elegance to their guest, who seemed more suited to a visit to London than the moor.

"This is my daughter, not to mention my pride." Her father beamed. "Miss Charlotte Grey."

Their guest presented a smile that dimpled his freshly shaven cheek. And bowed. "A true pleasure, Miss Grey."

"My dear, this is Mr. Roland Prior, visiting us from Prior Mill in Leeds."

She returned her prettiest smile and extended her hand coyly in greeting. "Welcome to Hollythorne House, Mr. Prior."

"I had no idea I would have such a charming hostess." Their guest's smile grew wider, dazzling and bright, and his gaze was enticingly direct as he accepted her hand. "If I'd known, I'd accepted your father's offer to visit much sooner."

Warmth rushed her face at the obvious flirtation in his tone.

Remembering her manners, she lowered her hand to her side. "I had no idea we were expecting company. What brings you to Hollythorne House, Mr. Prior?"

His clear eyes twinkled in the most becoming manner, and he leaned toward her slightly as if to divulge a very great secret. "Wool."

She almost laughed. "'Tis a far way to travel merely for wool."

"I agree with you, Miss Grey, but I blame my brother entirely." He raised a brow. "He insists that before we sign any supply agreements that we see the scope of the operations for ourselves."

"Agreement?"

Her father stepped in. "Mr. Prior's business buys wool for one of their mills, and he is interested in working with the sheep farmers on our estate."

"My family's business signs supply agreements for large quantities. In this case, if we sign an agreement with your father, we'd agree to purchase all the wool from all the sheep farmers on Hollythorne tenancies."

"Ah, I see. And what do you think of Hollythorne sheep, Mr. Prior?"

He shrugged. "I've yet to see them."

"Mr. Prior will be staying on with us for a bit," explained her father. "We'll call on the tenants in the coming days."

"My apologies, Miss Grey, for the unexpected, sudden intrusion. Your father and I have been corresponding for some time, and I found myself in the neighborhood, so I took the liberty to pay a call. I do hope my assumptive nature will be forgiven."

At the idea of Mr. Prior as a houseguest, Charlotte's stomach leapt. An attractive gentleman. In her home. Suddenly the days that had seemed to stretch so long and gray before her sparkled with opportunity. "It is no trouble at all, sir. You are most welcome here. I only hope our hospitality can live up to what you are used to in Leeds."

The ensuing conversation flowed in easy continuity. Not since Anthony had a man piqued her interest so. Maybe this was how her wounded heart would heal—infatuation would open her mind to the possibility of something new and exciting. A new future. A new love.

Later, as Mr. Prior stood in the courtyard speaking with the groomsman, she admired him from the window in the parlor.

"*I do think our fortunes may be turning,*" her father said, his voice low, as he reentered the room.

She wrapped her arm around her father's affectionately as he stepped to her side. Worries over the tenants had been hard on him. It sounded like this opportunity with Mr. Prior's mill could be an answer to some of the issues facing the estate as of late. "*I hope so. For your sake.*"

He patted her hand. "*For your sake as well. This estate will be part of your dowry, and, with any luck, will continue to be profitable.*"

She did not like talk of dowries and marriage. The thought of leaving Father alone when his health was so poor did not sit well with her.

"*Do you know what I think?*" Her father nodded in Mr. Prior's direction. "*I think that's the sort of man for you.*"

"*Oh, Father.*" She laughed in an effort to conceal her own thoughts. "*I'd be foolish to think so. Besides, a man like him surely will pursue an elegant society lady.*"

"*Do not sell yourself short, my daughter. He's wealthy. Steady. Good-humored. If I knew that you had married a man as established and upstanding as Mr. Prior, I could go to my grave and rest in peace.*"

The mention of her father's eventual death summoned a shadow over her budding optimism. "*Please do not speak of such things. You know I cannot bear it.*"

"*Like it or not, we must speak of it someday. None of us live forever.*" He retrieved his handkerchief and coughed into it before he wiped his mouth and tucked the square of fabric back into his pocket.

She sobered, noticing afresh how he seemed thinner. Paler.

"*Just promise me that you will be receptive if he shows interest. And something tells me he will.*"

Roland proposed a month later.

How could she have possibly known during that first interaction how deceptive their guest had been? How could she know that mere weeks after her marriage, his true nature would emerge?

Her mistake became evident as soon as they returned from their wedding trip. Once they were installed in Wolden House and he was back in his normal environment, his demeanor altered to a point that he was unrecognizable. She'd tried desperately in those early days to recapture the happiness of their courtship, but his aloof manner and his frequent journeys away from home clarified his intentions. Roland Prior had not wanted a wife. She'd been a conquest, and once they were married, she was a fixture in the house, nothing more.

Charlotte retrieved a fresh bucket of water and rag from the kitchen and set about cleaning the grime from the parlor windows, and her last conversation with Roland played in her mind.

It had taken place two days before he died, and their words had been terse, cold. During that same afternoon she'd overheard one of the footmen tell another that Roland had made plans for Lady Maria Descer, his rumored mistress, to travel to London with him.

Charlotte had long known that Roland had another life that did not involve her.

But now he was gone, and there would be no final conversation—no way to make peace with any of it other than to simply accept it.

She focused on the dirty window and scoured it harder, determined to remove every trace of filth, until the brittle glass suddenly cracked and splintered, cutting her hand and shattering to the ground. Blood dripped from the back of her trembling hand and from a large cut on the side of her forefinger.

Tears flooded her eyes, and she spun around to find one of the clean rags to press against the wound. Exasperation flared. How could she have been so careless? Before she had a chance to fully clean the wound, movement in the distance captured her attention.

She frowned as she spied a lone horseman cantering up the path.

Recognition blazed and Charlotte stood, frozen in her spot, resisting the urge to panic.

Silas Prior.

The house was still in shambles.

She was a mess.

Her hand was bleeding.

This hardly seemed the proper household to raise the Prior heir. Charlotte resolved herself. She could not avoid Silas forever. But for now, she would pretend all was well.

Anthony ran his hand down his horse's neck and gave her a pat as he settled her into the stall, bits of hay and dust floating in the morning air. He'd just returned from a ride to check the property's perimeter, and a sudden drop in temperature signaled yet another impending change of the weather.

But Anthony was far too distracted to think on the weather.

What had Charlotte meant when she said that she'd seen harrowing things?

He'd assumed that as Roland Prior's wife her life had been a privileged one, and he'd attributed her general aura of melancholy to grief over her husband's death. But she was right—her demeanor was clearly different from what it had been. And there had to be a reason.

After straightening his dark green waistcoat and brushing straw and debris from his white linen sleeves, he reached for his discarded coat and pushed his arms through the wool sleeves. As he stepped from the stables in the front courtyard, he looked up to Hollythorne House, with its myriad windows and blackened stone, its slate roof and imposing presence, and he sobered. In its prime, Hollythorne House must have been a sight to behold, but it paled in comparison to Wolden House.

Silas Prior wanted both Charlotte and Henry to remain in Leeds for their protection, but she refused to stay. What would compel a woman of her standing to leave a home like Wolden House, abruptly, and come to a place that was currently so obviously beneath the standard to which she was accustomed?

It did not make sense.

When the horse was settled, he closed the stable door and lowered the bar across it. Perhaps he was making too much of the circumstances. It had only been three days since Roland Prior's death. Three days was not much time to accept the reality of the death of a spouse and to make such life-altering decisions. Perhaps she was locked in some strange grief. Or perhaps her actions weren't hasty at all. Reports from the other watchmen about the Prior brothers, at times, had been quite odd. The Priors, both of them, had strange reputations.

The distant sound of hoofbeats on packed earth rumbled, and he looked up. A lone horseman was approaching at a canter through the late-morning fog. Anthony stiffened. Had something gone wrong with Timmons and Miss Sutcliffe's journey? But as the figure drew nearer, the rider boasted one unique identifier—white-blond hair. Silas Prior was paying them a call.

The servant girl was crossing the courtyard, and he called to her. "Go inform Mrs. Prior that Mr. Prior is here. Quickly."

The girl nodded, and Anthony approached the gate, then opened it to allow the rider through. The horse had been ridden hard—mud splattered the owner's otherwise elegantly fashioned Wellington boots and fawn buckskin breeches.

"Horrible roads," Mr. Prior muttered as his feet hit the mud beneath him. His jerky movements and sour expression conveyed more annoyance than any words could, and he stared blankly toward the house. "So this is it, is it? The Hollythorne House my sister-in-law was so resolved on returning to?"

Anthony followed the guest's gaze to the house, struck by the unmasked haughtiness in the man's tone. "It appears so."

Prior's startling eyes fixed on him. His pale brows were drawn, and the tight lines on his face emphasized the hard angles of his high cheekbones. "You're Welbourne?"

"I am."

"You're the one Walstead said is from here."

"Not here, but near."

Silas shifted his gaze toward the western moors before

extending the reins to Anthony. "I can see why you prefer Leeds. Dismal bit of earth. The horse will not need to be unsaddled. I do not intend to stay long. But have your boy water her, will you?"

Anthony accepted the reins. "There's no stable boy, but I'll see to your horse."

"Unbelievable." Silas clicked his tongue in apparent disgust. "Where can I find her? Inside?"

"Yes. I've just sent one of the servants to notify her of your arrival, but I can show you inside."

———

Anthony secured the horse before escorting Mr. Prior into the great hall. Given the last interaction between Charlotte and Mr. Prior, Anthony was curious regarding what to expect.

But he did not have to wait long.

The house itself was anything but quiet. A single breeze or even a footstep would give life to the ancient timbers and wooden floors, so Anthony was not surprised that he could hear her approach before they saw her. Instead of crossing the upstairs gallery and descending the main staircase, she took a smaller staircase near her chamber and emerged from a small corridor just off the parlor.

She'd changed from the cleaning gown he'd seen her in earlier that morning, and now she was dressed in a square-necked mourning gown of inky black, with long sleeves covering her lithe arms and a gauzy black fichu that hugged her neck. Her hair, which had been bound loosely at the base of her neck earlier, was now coiled into a tidy chignon. Not a single wisp escaped. She appeared every bit a lady in proper mourning until he took notice of a white linen bandage secured around her hand. There wasn't time to contemplate how such an injury had occurred, for she swept into the great hall without casting Anthony a glance. Her expression held no warmth, and she fixed her golden eyes on Mr. Prior. "Silas. I'm surprised to see you here."

"Are you?" He fairly spat the words as he assessed the room. "We need to talk. Is there somewhere private we can go where the whole of the house cannot hear us?"

She cast Anthony an empty glance before she stepped back and motioned toward the parlor. "In here."

As he watched them exit, the strange sense that Anthony should not leave them alone engulfed him. It was a ridiculous notion. Silas Prior was paying for her security. She was perfectly safe. But something was not right about the relationship between Charlotte Prior and the rest of the Prior family, and he did not think he would be able to relax until he found out what.

Chapter 18

CHARLOTTE USHERED SILAS from the great hall to the parlor, employing every bit of discipline to quiet the qualms roiling within her. Silas would never trouble himself to come out to visit her without a significant reason. Yet she refused to match her brother-in-law's adversarial energy, for her ability to manage her response and stay calm was her power. She could not control his demands or his expectations, nor the plans he was weaving in his mind. But she could control her responses to them. She'd be rational and well-spoken—she *would* combat the infamous Prior temper with a logical, cool head.

They entered the parlor, and it was just as she'd left it—a cleaning bucket on the table. Rags scattered about. A shattered windowpane. The moment the door closed behind them, Silas's sharp tone sliced the silence. "This pile of stones is the home you could not wait to return to, and Roland not even yet buried?"

She ignored his indignation and stepped closer to the fire, hoping its warmth would help calm the nervous chill racing through her. "I trust there is a reason for this visit, Silas, besides merely to question my rationale."

"There is a reason." He arched one white brow, pulled his leather gloves from his hands, and then dropped them on the table in the center of the room. "The coroner has reached his conclusion."

She stiffened, and the image of Roland's lifeless body flashed. The mere thought that he might have been murdered was a terrifying one. "And what did he find?"

"He found no evidence of malicious activity. Roland's death was from natural causes, namely, his heart."

Dread trickled through her. She had not loved Roland, nor had she trusted him. But she did not wish death on him. Yet this news could have been conveyed in a letter. Silas had to have something else on his mind.

When she did not immediately respond, Silas's words flung forth like an accusation. "You're quiet. No retort?"

She weighed her reply. "It's difficult news to hear."

"Is it?" He challenged swiftly, fixing his aggressive stare on her.

She resisted the urge to be drawn into an argument or heated exchange with him. Instead, she had to focus on facts. "Now that that conclusion has been reached, I suppose you can remove the guards."

Silas's tone sharpened. "There's more you must know."

Charlotte steadied herself for what would come next. Silas was many things, but he was not prone to the dramatic.

He removed his caped greatcoat and draped it over the chair. "There's a great deal of unrest at the mill. Apparently, Roland had other ventures, ones he did not disclose to me, and now there are ramifications. Of a nefarious nature."

She drew a deep breath, but she was hardly surprised. Roland was forever holding secret meetings and going on special trips. "What sort of ventures?"

"It appears he was running another business out of the mill— one that involved shipping and distributing goods. Smuggled goods. He was able to disguise them under the regular shipments."

The fact that Roland dabbled in the illegal was no surprise to her. It did surprise her, however, that he would do so right under Silas's purview. "Is that the cause of the unrest at the mill then?"

Silas reached into his tailcoat for his enameled snuffbox and popped it open. "It seems he employed a great many of his workers either to assist in his efforts or to look the other way, and one very significant problem remains: he never paid these people for their services, and now, in the wake of his death, they are demanding recompense. Of course, I refuse to pay them a farthing. They entered into an illegal arrangement with my brother. Not me. But they are making threats. Against the mill. Against me. Against you. And Henry. We will not bow down to their demands. We must call their bluff and present a unified front."

"'We'?" Charlotte crossed her arms over her chest and shook her head emphatically. "Silas, I've removed myself from the situation. I've never been involved in any of his mill business. There is no reason at all why I should be now."

"Your name is still Prior," he shot back, "and what's more, there's Henry to consider. You're not that far outside of Leeds. Anyone could be here within hours." He pinched the black snuff between his thick fingers and inhaled it through his nose. "Hiding away in your moorland house will not make the rest of the world go away."

Charlotte had to tread carefully. Silas was used to being obeyed without question. But she also knew about his sinister side—his compulsive obsession with legacy. When his own wife, Abigail, had been unable to bear a child, he had her institutionalized, claiming insanity, and nothing could be done to help her. He possessed the uncanny ability to shift a narrative to fit his reasonings, and because of his power and prestige, he was rarely questioned or challenged. She strengthened her tone. "I'm not hiding. I'm creating a different life. Surely you can see the difference."

He scoffed. "You clearly do not understand the power these people wield. They believe they're owed money and will stop at nothing to get it. They care nothing for rules. For order. I loved my brother, but he did make foolhardy decisions. We must give a thought to the future. Henry's future, not to mention that of all Prior enterprises. Your dramatic absence is the talk of every member of society, and it is calling into question the family's stability. You and Henry will come back to Leeds."

"That I cannot do."

"This wilderness is no home for a Prior." He bent down to pick up a piece of glass, making a great display of shifting through the broken pieces. "It is not safe."

She stepped forward, determined to keep the conversation from spiraling to a point from which they could not return. "I have agreed to your stipulation of guards. What more do you need? You have said yourself Henry is not safe in Leeds either."

Silence fell, and once again the only noise was the wind

whistling through broken glass and the fire popping in the grate. He pivoted, and Charlotte's defenses, for the moment, abated somewhat. How pale her brother-in-law looked. The lines around his eyes appeared harsher, and the shadows of his face appeared almost gray.

Silas tossed the piece of glass back to the floor and retrieved a packet from his coat. When he spoke again, his voice was softer. "We all owe it to Henry's future to keep this sort of thing in hand, so if you will not heed reason, I intend to appeal to your sense of motherly affection."

She eyed the large envelope skeptically. "What's that?"

"If you insist on staying in this house, then it must be made respectable." He extended the packet toward her. "This is enough money to see to the proper updates and maintenance for Hollythorne House and to employ a staff to properly run a house of this size. Mr. Walstead's ramshackle retinue will not be here for long. We all must look to the future and all its facets."

She stared at the offering. Had she not been clear? "I cannot accept it."

"Why the devil not?" His face flushed crimson.

"That's not my money. Quite frankly, I do not wish to be indebted to you. I'll not be indebted to anyone."

"How else can you afford to care for this?" he protested, his volume increasing. "This is a gift, one family member to another. This offer will not be extended again."

She fixed her sight on the packet once more. It might very well be a gift in this moment, but there would eventually be conditions. "I'll find another way. I am sorry, Silas, but I will not accept it."

He snapped the envelope out of her reach and returned it to his pocket. "If you're unwilling to accept assistance, given freely and without expectation, then there is nothing to be done."

He stepped to and touched the broken window and moved the shattered glass on the floor with the toe of his boot. "I will be watching you, Charlotte. I'll be watching Henry. Do not force my hand and make me petition the courts for Henry's well-being."

She knew what he meant. If she did not comply with his wishes, he would find a legal way to control Henry.

But she refused to bow to intimidation.

Silas snatched his coat and gloves from where he left them and exited without a word.

Charlotte remained in the parlor after he left. She merely turned to look out the window to the courtyard. She drew a fortifying breath and watched as Anthony escorted him back to his horse.

She had done it. She'd stood her ground and defied Silas Prior, again. She only hoped it would be enough.

Chapter 19

IT HAD BEEN nearly half an hour since Silas Prior left the property when Anthony returned to the great hall.

He'd not intended to overhear the conversation between Charlotte and her guest, but even with the parlor door closed, he'd heard almost everything.

Normally, he would not give such an exchange a second thought. But this was a personal matter.

Charlotte's personal matter.

The manipulative tactics in Prior's tone and words sickened him, but her ability to stand up to such a man spoke volumes about her character. But even so, how long could she, a single woman, withstand the demands of a man as influential as Silas Prior?

He rapped his knuckles on the doorframe as he entered the parlor. Charlotte stood at the west window, and she did not acknowledge his entrance. Her long black gown swung slightly about her legs as she swayed slowly. Henry was asleep in her arms, and Anthony's chest tightened.

How many times had he dreamed of this very sight when

he was alone on the battlefield? The thought of her—a haunting vision of beauty, home, and love he'd tucked close when everything around him spun with death and anguish. During his brief visit back to Blight Moor after he'd returned from war, he heard she had married, but he'd not asked for specifics. Now, as every bit of new detail came to light, he did not like the picture that was forming.

He cleared his throat. "Mr. Prior has departed."

"You heard that conversation, I suppose," she said without turning away from the window. "You forget I was raised in this house. No conversation in this chamber is totally private. I don't think my father ever fully realized that. I know I heard more than my fair share of private conversations."

He stepped next to her and took in the late-morning light over the moorland, unsure of how to respond. The watchman in him knew he should stick to the facts of the case. But the other side of him—the side that would always care for her—could not. "One could not help but overhear."

"Then you heard that Roland died of natural causes. His heart."

Anthony remained quiet, giving her space to say what she needed to.

"And the mill workers are up in arms. Roland had hired them to do illegal work, apparently, and he did not pay them. I wish I could say it was not in Roland's character to make a promise to do something and then not honor it, but that would be a falsehood."

There was a sharpness, a bitterness, in her tone he'd never heard before.

When it was clear she was not going to say anything else, he shifted his attention to her bandaged hand. "What happened to your hand?"

She finally drew her gaze from the moorland and gestured to the other side of the chamber. "I was cleaning that window overlooking the courtyard and broke it."

Sure enough, the pane was shattered. Only shards remained. "Did you make sure there's no glass in the wound?"

"Yes. I cleaned it."

"May I see?"

It was her turn to hesitate.

At length she adjusted Henry in her arms to free her hand and extended it toward him.

He helped her remove the bandage. A long, deep gash ran the length of her forefinger, and several smaller scratches reddened the top. His bare fingers touched hers long enough to angle them toward the light. It was a simple, light touch, and yet the softness of her skin transported him to a time when his touch would have been welcomed.

Her fingers trembled subtly against his, and he forced his thoughts to remain steady. "It's not too deep. I don't see any glass."

"I should have been more careful." She sniffed and withdrew her hand. "It was an error on my part."

"When Timmons returns, we will have him make you some of his salve. He's a genius when it comes to healing."

She attempted to wrap the bandage back around her hand, but with Henry in her arms, she was struggling.

"Let me." Without contacting her skin he rewrapped the

bandage and tied it off, then stepped back to reestablish the space and silence between them.

The east wind rushed against the stone wall, rattling the old panes of glass. The fire in the grate sizzled and snapped, and even though it burned with a fervor, it would never be enough to warm the frigid room.

She pushed a lock of hair away from Henry's face and did not look at Anthony when she spoke. "If you heard the entire conversation, then you must think me a terrible fool for not taking Silas up on his offer to fund the repairs."

Her statement caught him off guard. She'd been closed off about the entire topic since leaving Wolden House, but now her statement made it seem as if she invited his opinion on the matter. Perhaps this was the first crack in her firmly constructed facade.

He considered his response, for he did have a great many thoughts on what he'd heard: Anger at Silas Prior for attempting to manipulate her. Pride in how she held her ground. Regret that he was not by her side.

"I don't think you're a fool." He stared down to the sleeping baby in her arms. Wisps of white-blond hair covered his head. With hair that color there was no denying he was a Prior. "How old is your boy?"

The corner of her mouth lifted as she gazed down at him. "Seven months."

Anthony had always believed Charlotte would be a good mother—the strong, determined sort who would insist her child learn right from wrong and love that child with the fiercest of devotion. "He's a fine boy. If you ask me my opinion, you must do whatever you think is right by him. And if that means refusing the money, then so be it."

"If I accepted my brother-in-law's terms and his offer of money, I'd be at his mercy. Never again will I be at anyone's mercy. Neither will my son. Silas claims to want to guide Henry. To mold him. Yet he did not even ask to see him before he left to return to Leeds."

Anthony could only wonder when she'd been at someone's mercy, but her determined timbre suggested it had been significant indeed. "Well, then, it sounds as if you've made your decision. And I know once your mind is set, it is very difficult to change."

She shot her gaze up at him at the personal reference.

They might have only just reacquainted, but a charge still reverberated between them, the bolt of lightning that had been present from their very first encounter. It surged through him. She had to feel it too.

It had been so long since he'd given himself permission to access the emotions from that day they'd parted. They'd been safely locked away where they could do no further damage. But now they waged a fresh offensive and refused to be defeated. "I have something I need to say to you, and I don't know how long I will be here, so there may not be another opportunity."

Her eyes widened. She shook her head and stepped back, "Mr. Welbourne, I—"

"About that day at Even Tor, the day I left. That is not how things should have ended."

Charlotte stiffened, spurred by the onset of unsettling panic as what he was saying registered in her mind.

He intended to talk to her about *that day*—about what they had been to each other.

Her face grew hot. Her head grew light.

Today had already been difficult, and now she could barely contain the emotions pummeling her, let alone allow herself to open that vault.

Yet Anthony was standing so close.

She could feel his warmth. He was not touching her, yet she knew the feeling of sinking against his chest. Of the comfort that could be found in his arms. The sensation of it replayed with vibrant colors in her mind—tempting her to lower her guard.

"I think it best we do not discuss it," she shot back. "Nothing good could come of it."

"But, I—"

"Stop. Please," she said, much sharper than she intended. "'Tis not a good idea."

A slight wince tightened his face before he concealed it.

She immediately regretted the harshness in her tone. The swiftness of her response. But she would not—could not—relive that day. It would weaken her.

He relented. "Very well. But if you'll permit me to say one thing, I'll not revisit it again."

The blood roared in her ears, and she stared at him, unsure how to respond. She feared the words that would pass his lips. Not afraid that they would injure her, for her heart was already broken. Nay, she feared just the opposite—that they would offer her a sense of peace that she, at this time, did not feel free to take.

"I cannot hear it," she blurted. "The past must stay in the past."

His eyes, unnervingly astute and direct, were fixed intently on her. As if he could read every thought flitting through her mind and sense every feeling. "Wouldn't you rather put it to rest than act as if it never happened?"

Tears threatened to gather. "To what end?"

They were staring at each other—the intimate link of two people who knew each other too well. It was a communication all its own—even more frightening to Charlotte than words.

"So this is how we handle it?" he challenged. "Pretend to be strangers? For I cannot pretend that it is not difficult to see you like this. To see you struggle and in conflict."

"I pretend nothing. I am simply doing the best I can in the wake of my husband's death."

"Then it must be me, alone, who cannot forget those evenings on Even Tor." He stepped even closer, dangerously so, and his scent of wool and the outdoors was intoxicating, the directness of his gaze impairing her. "Have you not thought about that day even once since we've been here? It seems to be all I can think about."

She had to make this stop. It was too painful. Anger was starting to wind its way in, for she didn't know how else to feel. "Do you want to know what I really think about it? Very well. All I can think about is Henry. You cannot imagine the world we have just escaped. My sole existence moving forward is to protect him from Silas Prior and to protect him from becoming a man like Roland. I do not have the luxury of time or indifference. I refuse to let Henry be lost to their world. So you will excuse me if my thoughts are not fixed in the past, for my present is very much a nightmare."

She did not wait for his response. She couldn't—tears of frustration she had held back since Roland's death were threatening, and she refused to let Anthony see them fall.

―――――――――――

Anthony stood alone in the silent parlor—alone with the whistling wind, the crackling fire, and the echo of the words that had just been spoken.

Every interaction with Charlotte revealed another layer of her experiences after he'd left.

His suspicion had been correct. She was not a grieving widow but a frightened one. A threatened one—one who was backed into a corner and ready for a fight.

He found it difficult to leave the parlor, as if by leaving he would be putting an end to this conversation.

In his heart, it was far from over.

When he saw the anguish in her eyes, he'd wanted to grab her and kiss her to shut out the rest of the world until just the two of them remained. Until they were more like the two young people who had been so in love instead of the two strangers they were now. Until the torment they'd both endured faded into hope for a happier future.

It would not take long. At least for him. For he was already there.

But she clearly was not.

He needed to give her time, and he suspected she would need a great deal of it. Whereas he had time since returning from the war to come to terms with thoughts and experiences, her world had only just turned in the last week. In a horrific and traumatic manner.

He would have to be patient and understand that things might be out of reach.

Chapter 20

NIGHT, ALONG WITH a steady rain, had fallen by the time the carriage transporting Miss Sutcliffe finally returned from Leeds. Anthony had been watching for it and met it with lantern in hand. After assisting Miss Sutcliffe down from the vehicle, he then stepped back as Timmons dismounted his horse and joined them. "I was beginning to fear you'd encountered a highwayman."

"Bah, nonsense," blurted Timmons, as energetically and good-naturedly as if he had not just ridden a horse to Leeds and back. "Ye know me—I dare a 'ighwayman t' glance at me sideways. No, a bit of rain that proved more offensive. Miss Sutcliffe preferred t' wait in t' dining room at a traveling inn t' pressing ahead."

"I fear I'm not as accustomed to such traveling." She lowered her hood. "I apologize if I put us terribly behind schedule."

Anthony closed the carriage door behind her. "Not at all, Miss Sutcliffe. I was worried for your safety, 'tis all."

Using his lantern as a guide, Anthony walked her to Hollythorne House's main entrance and then returned to help Timmons stable his horse. The familiar scent of horses and straw met them as they entered the stone structure, and the lantern's light flickered and glowed against the ancient stone walls and timber beams.

"Did you speak with Mr. Walstead?"

"No." Timmons removed his horse's head collar. "But I spoke with Dunston. Walstead was out of town."

Anthony raised a brow. "Did you leave the letter?"

Timmons nodded. "Dunston did say that Mr. Walstead was plannin' t' visit Hollythorne House in t' next day or so."

Anthony kept his voice low as he lifted the saddle from the horse's back. "Silas Prior was here today to call on Mrs. Prior. I heard a bit of the conversation. Sounds like things are a bit messy at the mill there."

Timmons snorted and shook his head. "Did 'e tell ye three men were apprehended attemptin' t' set a fire outside of Wolden House?"

"No, but he said some of the men were awaiting payment on a job."

"I 'eard the same. From what I gathered from Dunston, Roland Prior 'ired this group of men t' collect a shipment of goods, but he never paid them."

"What type of goods?"

"No idea."

Anthony reached for the horse's brush. "And Miss Sutcliffe? How did she handle the journey?"

Timmons gave a slight grin. "She's in love with me. O' course."

Anthony scoffed. "I'm sure she is. And did you learn what this all-important errand was?"

Timmons patted the horse's shoulder as he rounded the stall. "She tried t' 'ide what she was up to, but she's a 'orrible liar. She 'ad me take 'er t' th' milliners, but from there I followed 'er to the jeweler. I stopped in after she left, and t' jeweler said she tried t' sell some jewels and baubles and whatnot, but 'e knew who she was an' wouldn't touch something from t' Prior estate if 'is life depended on it."

Anthony stiffened. He'd wondered about Charlotte's finances. He assumed everything that belonged to Roland would pass to Henry, and such arrangements did not leave a great deal for the widow. And based on the current state of Hollythorne House, he doubted the estate was very profitable. But the thought of her selling personal belongings was sobering.

Timmons glanced over his shoulder as Tom led one of the carriage horses inside. "Sounds like our Mistress Prior may not 'ave access to t' 'efty Prior fortune after all."

Anthony nodded. "I would assume that it was left to the baby."

"You'd think so." Timmons smirked. "Wish someone'd leave me money. But then again, you wouldn't know about that. You inherited a bit o' land and funds for a commission. Yet you continue t' play t' role o' thief-taker."

His words were spoken in jest, and yet a hint of skepticism was hidden therein.

They finished settling the horses in silence, and something about this was not sitting right.

Charlotte jumped from her chair as Sutcliffe appeared in the threshold to her bedchamber. "You're soaked through!"

Sutcliffe hurried into the room and closed the door behind her, her cheeks and nose flushed from cold and her light hair wind-blown about her face. "I'm sorry I am so late returning."

"No, no. Do not be sorry. You must be freezing! Come, remove that cloak and draw closer to the fire." Charlotte ushered Sutcliffe in and helped untie the sodden satin ribbons from beneath her chin and lifted the heavy traveling cloak from her shoulders. "Oh, this must have been a miserable trip for you. You must tell me every-thing that happened."

But instead of nearing the fire, Sutcliffe's brows furrowed. "I am so sorry, Mrs. Prior. The jeweler did not buy a single piece."

Charlotte had expected to hear that not all of them had sold, or that she only got a fraction of what they were worth. But none?

She'd not show Sutcliffe her disappointment—not after the journey the lady's maid had endured on her behalf. Charlotte motioned for her to pivot so she could help her with the tiny fabric-covered buttons of her heavy wool gown. "What happened?"

"I spoke with the jeweler—the very one I spoke with the day of Mr. Prior's death. He said he knew who I was now and wanted nothing to do with anything owned by Roland Prior. It was too dangerous. I asked him what he meant, and he said the millers are out for blood and that he didn't want to get involved. Do you know what he meant?"

Charlotte bit her lower lip and helped Sutcliffe step out of the gown. "Unfortunately I do. Silas was here earlier today while you were gone. I don't know specifics, but apparently there is unrest over the fact that Roland owed workers money, but I don't really know what for."

When Sutcliffe was free of the gown, she quickly changed to a dry flannel chemise and wrapped a heavy knitted shawl about her shoulders. She then produced the satchel and poured the items out onto the bed.

Sure enough, every item that she'd selected to sell was still here.

Charlotte groaned, unsure if she should cry, scream, or throw the jewels against the wall.

She would not give in to frustration.

She would *not*.

She shook her head, as if doing so would jar free fresh determination and optimism. "Well, we'll try again. A different shop. A different city if necessary. We are not helpless or without options. We just must be clever, that's all."

A knock on the door interrupted them, and Charlotte held her finger to her lips. The last thing she needed was for anyone in this house to know she was trying to sell her belongings. She opened the door to reveal Rebecca with a tray of tea.

"Beggin' your pardon, Mrs. Prior. Mrs. 'argrave told me t' bring this up. She said Timmons told her Miss Sutcliffe would need it after t' ride on account of t' rain."

Surprised, Charlotte looked to the steaming pot of tea and teacups. "Mr. Timmons suggested this?"

Rebecca nodded, her light brown eyes wide.

It was a very forward suggestion for a guard, but it would not do to vocalize such thoughts. Charlotte smiled and accepted the extended tray. "Thank you, Rebecca. Give Mrs. Hargrave our gratitude."

Rebecca bobbed a curtsey, and no one spoke until the door was once again closed and Charlotte placed the tray on the table in the center of the room.

"Well." Charlotte straightened the teacup that had shifted during the transfer. "That was a thoughtful gesture."

Sutcliffe stood from the bed, a horrified expression on her now florid face. "But it's so forward. Isn't it?"

"It is nothing to get upset about," soothed Charlotte with a dismissive wave of her hand, as much to calm her own nerves. "He probably was merely aware of how uncomfortable the trip was and was getting something to warm himself as well."

Sutcliffe, cheeks flaming, accepted the cup of tea and sank into the chair next to the table. "I promise I did nothing to encourage his attention."

"I know." Charlotte ignored the uneasiness that wound its way through her and drew a deep breath. "Tell me all about the journey."

Sutcliffe sipped her tea and lowered it back to the table. "Actually, it started off quite pleasant. The rain held off most of the day until we were about an hour from home, and we stopped and waited in the dining room of a traveling inn."

"And Mr. Timmons? Was he a worthy escort?"

Sutcliffe bit her lower lip—a telltale harbinger of the watchman's effect on her. "He was very much a gentleman. He's not nearly as rough as one would assume at first glance."

Charlotte listened in silence as the young woman recounted

the day and was grateful to have someone else to think about instead of worrying about her own situation.

Even so, Sutcliffe's admiration for Mr. Timmons was woven into every word she uttered. Charlotte resisted the urge to comment on the seemingly budding relationship. It was *not* her responsibility to guard her maid's virtues and keep her heart from being broken, but circumstances had blurred the lines between mistress and maid, friend and acquaintance. They needed each other. After what they had endured over the past week, they would never be able to return to the traditional rules that guided a lady and her maid. It would do no good to caution her or attempt to dissuade her. And at the moment, if Sutcliffe was happy, who was she to intervene?

Chapter 21

OVER THE COURSE of the next few days, they settled into a routine, and in the warmest hours of an otherwise blustery day, Charlotte and Henry were spending time in the back garden when Rebecca approached and curtsied. "Mr. Welbourne asked me to come tell ye that Mr. Greenwood's arrived. I've shown 'im into t' parlor, and 'e's waiting for you there. I'll take Master 'enry if ye like."

Even though she had been anticipating Mr. Greenwood's arrival for the better part of the day, Charlotte's nerves tightened. This one conversation would not only give her a much more accurate picture of the estate's current situation, but it would aid her in making future decisions.

Charlotte handed Henry to Rebecca and headed back toward the kitchen entrance. As she made her way down the kitchen corridor to the screens passage, she smoothed her mourning gown and patted her hair into place.

She knew nothing of Mr. Greenwood, other than Roland had hired him after her father died. She'd never even met him. As she stepped from the great hall to the parlor, a tall man with graying black hair she could only presume to be Mr. Greenwood turned to face her.

She stifled a groan at the sight—the condescending pinch of his nose and his stilted smile. He appeared dour and colorless. Expressionless and cold. Mr. Greenwood presented himself just as every other soberly clad, pretentious man Roland surrounded himself with had.

"Mr. Greenwood," she greeted stiffly.

He bowed low. "Mrs. Prior."

"It was good of you to come so quickly."

"Indeed, I apologize that it took me this long to arrive. I was tending to another one of your husband's properties to the south of here. I was sorry to hear of Mr. Prior's death. Very sad news indeed."

She ignored how the calculating expression behind his hooded eyes belied his words. It was as if she were back in Wolden House, weighing every word a man spoke, trying to gauge his level of truthfulness.

"You must not be from Blight Moor, Mr. Greenwood. I grew up here, and I confess your name is not a familiar one."

He shook his head. "No, ma'am. I'm not from the area. I hail from London."

She frowned. "Then how is it you came to oversee this property and its tenants?"

"I managed another property for Mr. Prior. He asked for my assistance."

"I see. I trust by now you are acquainted with the tenants and that you visit them regularly?"

"I visit them quarterly, per our agreements."

"And what do you make of them?"

He shrugged a wiry shoulder and then produced a leather-bound tome from his satchel. "You will see for yourself when you review the ledger. Most of them are behind on their payments. We had to evict two families just last month for default."

"Two families?" Charlotte stiffened. "Which ones?"

"The Swans and the Cullens."

At the mention of the name Cullens, her heart lurched. The older farmer and his family used to sit in the pew behind her own family at church. Mr. Cullen's laugh had been deep and hearty—his gap-toothed smile contagious.

She narrowed her eyes. "And I assume Mr. Prior was aware of this?"

"Of course."

Annoyance at his cavalier nonchalance and arrogant coolness wound its way through her. As a result, she could not control the sharpness tingeing her tone. "And this house? Was Mr. Prior aware of the disgraceful state of it?"

"He was. He visited here just last spring. He told me he wanted to let it, but there has been no interest."

"Surely there has been no interest because of the deplorable condition. It is quite an undertaking as it is! Why have repairs not been made? I assume you inspected the house periodically. There is a gaping hole in the roof in the servants' quarter, for heaven's sake."

"Mr. Prior indicated it was to be repaired by winter," Mr. Greenwood responded flatly. "He did not specify a date."

"Well, winter will shortly be upon us, will it not?" She took the ledger from the man and opened it. The haphazard penmanship looked like foreign writing. The words and numbers made sense to her, but it would take a great deal of time to really understand the full scope of what she beheld.

But she would not admit to that.

Instead, she focused her attention on what she could learn. "I do not recall tenants being evicted when my father managed the estate. How do you account for it now after so many years of success?"

"A very late frost," he mused at last, "the summer before last took out a great deal of the orchards on the Cullen property. As you can see, they had been behind on rent for quite some time."

"There must be more to it than that. Not all the tenants have orchards and crops. There must be other reasons."

Mr. Greenwood shook his head. "You're quite right. About half the farmers raise sheep, and under the arrangement your father made with Mr. Prior, the wool is being shipped to Leeds for processing. The charges are high, but under the agreement between your late father and Prior Mill, they must, as tenants, process their wool and textiles there or face additional charges."

She stiffened as the meaning of what was said sank in. "My father never would have agreed to such strict terms."

"Well, to be fair, the arrangement has been modified since your father's passing. It seems that when your husband gained control of the property, his solicitors adjusted the rental agreements."

The heat of anger consumed her. "Could he do that?"

Mr. Greenwood shrugged. "He who owns the land can do whatever he wants."

The sickening realization that her husband had been taking advantage of the very people she'd grown up with drizzled over her. All the work her father had done, ruined. By Roland. "And the other tenants?"

"The others grow wheat and barley. They are faring better than the sheep farmers, but their profits are down as well."

"Why?"

"A similar situation. An agreement is in place with Clarett Mill, but it is a good way away. The travel to get it there and back adds time and money."

"Is there no closer option?"

"Apparently years ago some of them used to conduct intermittent business at the Welbourne Mill, but unfortunately it is no longer an option."

Anthony's uncle's mill.

She closed the ledger.

She had hoped for good news, but instead of feeling optimistic, she was overwhelmed. "And what are the tenants saying? Are they satisfied with the state of things?"

He scoffed, doing little to hide his pretension. "Would you be satisfied with numbers like this? Some have forfeited their holdings and have moved for jobs in Leeds and other bigger cities. We've not had a single person interested in the available farms, when at one time a queue of people were waiting to get in. Times are hard, not to mention unpredictable."

"Yes, times are difficult, but then again, my father ran this estate for many years and in the midst of other trials. Quite successfully, I might add. The Cullens and the Swans are proud, hardworking people. So I am curious to know what we could have reasonably done to assist them."

She resisted the urge to prove herself further—to fight a one-sided battle and convince him that the estate could be run prosperously. Such an argument would only serve to bolster her pride, for it would likely fall upon deaf ears. There was one final question that needed to be asked—which would determine the future for Henry and her both. "And the estate itself? Does it turn a profit?"

He blinked at her, as if surprised the question was posed so bluntly.

The few times she had asked Roland about the Hollythorne House holdings he silenced her, declaring he was too busy or he did not have the facts before him, all the while claiming that a competent man was overseeing it and that no harm would come to it.

Growing annoyed, she tilted her head to the side. "Is there an income to it? Does the estate have debt? Surely, you can tell me that."

"It enjoys a modest income." He took the ledger from her, flipped through the pages, and pointed to a number. "There are the profits and there are the expenses."

At this revelation, simple as it was, she could finally breathe. The sum was moderate, but at least money was coming in. This amount, combined with what she would get from Roland's will and Henry's trust, would be a step in the right direction.

But there was still a great deal of work to do.

"Leave this with me," she said. "I wish to examine it. And before you go, there are a couple of tasks I would like you to see to for me. My servants are temporary. I will be hiring a staff, and I prefer to engage local workers. Can you spread the word? And I should like you to accumulate a list of the gristmills and wool mills within a reasonable distance. I will not force our tenants to send their goods so far for processing."

He raised his brows, as if entertained that she would have an opinion.

"And another thing, we will need a glazier to repair the windows and a carpenter out for the roof as soon as possible. Hollythorne House must be restored, and if you cannot make the appropriate arrangements, I will have to find someone who can."

She would not be deterred or underestimated, and with her current state of mind, she dared him to challenge her. It was easy to blame the man before her for the ills that had befallen the Hollythorne estate, but in truth, it was not Mr. Greenwood's fault. He was merely following orders. Roland was the one who had lied to her—turned a blind eye to her family's estate and chosen not to enforce a better standard of upkeep.

It had been just one of many deceptions, and she would do whatever was necessary to set it to rights.

Chapter 22

THE PERSISTENT RAIN and lingering fog from the previous day had dissipated, leaving nothing but a few wispy clouds in an otherwise azure sky. The chilliness had, for the moment, passed, and the remaining breeze carried what might very well be the last bit of warmth until spring. Charlotte took Henry out to the garden once more, determined to enjoy the rest of the afternoon, despite the fact that her conversation with Mr. Greenwood weighed heavy on her mind.

It had not even been a week since her arrival, and already she'd been tested and stretched in ways she'd not anticipated. She pressed her fingertips to the iron gate to open it and walked through, intent upon ignoring the frustrations. Instead, she allowed her mind to wander and imagine the picture this garden had painted a decade ago when her mother was still living.

Martha Grey had been so proud of the intricate boxwood paths and the roses that would, at times, cover the entire wall with blooms. Together they would spend countless spring and summer hours in this space to pass the time when Father would visit tenants. With the rich memories bolstering her spirits, she carried her son to the sundial in the garden's center and traced the copper numerals with her finger.

How she wished her mother could have met Henry. She would have adored how his ruddy cheeks were kissed by the moorland breezes and how the wind tousled his soft curls. He laughed at a falling leaf that had blown down and caught on the sleeve of her pelisse, and the sheer wonder and amazement in his reaction filled her.

This was what she was fighting for—she could not forget—the freedom to spend time with her son and let him grow up loved and cherished, just as she had been.

But as she stepped to the garden wall to take in the view of Blight Moor, the enormity of what she was taking on also was not lost on her. Just as she wanted to revive the beauty of her mother's garden, she equally wanted to honor her father's passion for the estate. And that meant finding a solution to the problems the tenants were facing.

After passing an hour in the garden with Henry, she prepared to return to the house but slowed when she spied Anthony walking alongside the property's outer wall.

Their conversation, not to mention the sharpness of her tone, from the previous day in the parlor had stayed with her. His words of the past stirred up emotions she thought long buried. She realized now that she'd never properly come to terms with her feelings regarding his departure all those years ago. But what could be done? As soon as Silas rescinded the order for the watchmen to be here, Mr. Timmons and Anthony would pack their belongings and return to Leeds, and Anthony would, once again, be absent from her life.

Regardless, it was becoming impossible to look on him with the indifference she'd employed when they first arrived. Like it or not, his presence—his appearance and the manner in which he looked at her—was very slowly waking parts of her that had long been asleep.

He shifted direction and began walking toward her.

She needed to speak with him about her plan to attend church services the next day, but such a conversation seemed odd without addressing her curt response to him following Silas Prior's visit.

Why did she seem unable to control her reactions and emotions around Anthony and speak more tersely than intended?

"I was hoping to speak with you," she said as he approached.

He gave no response, just stepped closer to her and stopped. No doubt he was uncertain of the rules presiding over their interactions, given her brusque words in the parlor.

"But before I do, I believe I owe you yet another apology for my behavior to you in the parlor."

His dark eyebrows rose, and he removed his hat from his head.

How fickle he must think her.

Indeed, how fickle she felt. She'd always had such agency over her actions and behavior, but his effect on her was unexpected.

"I was wrong to prevent you from saying what you wanted to say. I fear my emotions had gotten the better of me."

"You were upset. Anyone would have been." The wind caught the folds of his neckcloth and tousled his sable hair. He squinted slightly as the sun emerged from behind the clouds. "You have nothing to apologize to me for, Charlotte."

The use of her Christian name caught her off guard.

It was so personal. So intimate. So reminiscent of another time.

He continued. "In truth, it is I who should apologize. I overstepped my bounds by bringing up a past that is no longer relevant."

No longer relevant.

The statement, surprisingly, stung.

"Well then," she forced a masking smile, "we can agree that this is a situation we never thought we would find ourselves in and give ourselves grace as we navigate it."

But even as she spoke, the words did not feel right. For what was going on in her head did not match what was going on in her heart.

"Is that what you wanted to speak with me about?" he asked bluntly, his expression flat, as he circled the conversation back around.

"No." She refocused her thoughts, taken off her guard at an unexpected twinge of sadness as the conversation switched to a business matter. "Tomorrow is Sunday, and Sutcliffe, Henry, and I will be going to church. You'd asked to be notified if we wish to go anywhere."

"Will you take the carriage, then?"

"We'll walk, if the weather permits it."

"Very well." He shifted and bowed, as if preparing to walk away, but then stopped. "Your meeting with Mr. Greenwood did not last long."

His statement was more of a question, and she hesitated. It

was against her better judgment to discuss personal matters with anyone, let alone someone who unknowingly had such power over her thoughts and sentiments. Yet he knew these people—this land—and he was the only person present who could truly understand her predicament. "The Cullens were evicted. The Swans too. My father would be furious."

"I remember them. They were both good families."

She adjusted Henry in her arm and tucked her hair behind her ear. "I do not trust Mr. Greenwood. As soon as I am able, I shall engage a new steward."

Her words sounded so confident, so determined, and yet the truth was, she had no idea how to go about such a task. She found herself wanting to tell him everything and to seek his counsel. It would be so easy to fall back into a familiar place with Anthony. Who else would understand like he did? Who else would care as much as she did?

"Why do you not trust him?"

Her unmeasured response rushed. "Mr. Greenwood's like every other man who worked for Roland. A puppet. I had no idea what was happening here these past few years, not that there was much I could have done if I did. And now it seems as if everything is crumbling."

His response was as calm as her words were harried. "You must give yourself time to absorb this. In time you'll discover the right course. Bear in mind that this is all new to you. Everything about it, from dealing with your husband's death to returning to a home after being gone so long. I know you want to resolve everything at once, but you must be patient with yourself."

His reassurance was like a balm. He knew her—he knew what she needed to hear. She should not take so much comfort from his presence. Yet it was impossible for her not to.

She flicked her gaze up at him, and the expression she met there simmered—challenging her.

She cleared her throat and swept hair away from her brow. "I should not be monopolizing your time like this. I'm sure you have other things to be tending to."

For several moments his steely stare did not waver, but then he drew a deep breath and looked out to Blight Moor. "Very well. Tomorrow then. I'll escort you to church myself."

Charlotte stood frozen to her spot as he bowed again and retreated down the garden path. *He will escort me to church.* They would be walking together, through Blight Moor—the very paths they used to walk together. The thought jolted her.

Henry grabbed at the ribbon of her fichu and pulled it playfully, and she, happy for the distraction, pressed a kiss to his cheek. If she was to be successful, she had to keep her wits, and her heart, about her.

Chapter 23

CHARLOTTE SHOULD NOT be going to church.

She should not be going anywhere.

She was a widow in mourning, and as such, she should remain indoors, tucked away out of sight.

Such were the rules of polite society.

When Roland's mother died, Charlotte had been forbidden to leave Wolden House for six months and then was in half mourning for another lengthy span of time even though she'd only met the woman twice. Roland, however, had worn a black armband for a few days, and then his life resumed. But mourning expectations were different out in the moorland, and her role was different here. She was a landowner now.

Sutcliffe helped her dress for service in a high-waisted gown of delicate black bombazine and a ruffled chemisette of inky muslin. Long, expertly fitted sleeves with lacy cuffs swathed her arms, and jet roses and vines were embroidered along the neckline and the bodice. There was no large mirror in her bedchamber as there had been at Wolden House, but she knew the elegant figure the gown cut on her. Even though Roland rarely permitted her to leave the house, he'd always insisted on the finest garments. Here, away from the city, the bodice's elegant crepe overlay felt ostentatious, and the crystals adorning the hem added to that sentiment.

Even so, for the first time since her arrival at Hollythorne House, she was not dreading the task that lay before her. During the past week she'd faced so many difficult realizations and discussions that something as familiar and comforting as going to church—an activity she had done nearly every week when she was growing up—beckoned to her.

Many of the villagers, even the vicar, would recognize her.

Whether they would welcome her or not was another matter.

The blue morning light filtered through the southern windows overlooking the main courtyard as she, with Henry in her arms, and Sutcliffe made their way down the creaky stairs. Days ago, this space had been dark and dingy. Cobwebs and dust covered everything, and it seemed an insurmountable endeavor to return it to its former regal state. Many tasks remained, but each time she descended these steps, her optimism increased. She, along with her small staff, was making strides, and she'd not stop until Hollythorne House was once again a place that would have made her parents proud and that anyone would consider suitable for Henry.

She, Henry, Sutcliffe, and Rebecca met Anthony in the back courtyard, where they would take the footpath that cut through Blight Moor and led to the village. He was dressed as he always was: a white linen shirt with a dark waistcoat and high-collared cutaway coat of charcoal wool that emphasized the brawny expanse of his shoulders, but today he wore no greatcoat to protect him from the weather. Fawn buckskin breeches hugged his muscular legs, and high-topped black boots, now wet from the tall grasses and morning dew, completed his attire. A wide-brimmed felt hat covered his sable hair, which, as usual, was bound in a queue. She had yet to see him clean-shaven.

They traversed the path, which had been overgrown with faded milkwort and wild thyme. Anthony walked behind them at a respectable distance. As they rounded a rocky bend, Even Tor appeared in the distance—a majestic, craggy rock formation that jutted into the clear air, rising from the grasses and other large rocks at its base. At the sight heat flushed her face. Her life had changed in this spot four years prior. It was the first—and only—time she'd known romantic affection and the heartache that could result from it. Did Anthony remember it with the same vibrance, or had time dulled his recollection?

They crossed the stone footbridge that separated the open moorland from the main village and the High Street, where modest shops and businesses lined the cobbles. Nerves fluttered in her stomach, and Henry, who was growing tired of being carried, wriggled in her arms. A crisp autumnal breeze swept down from the slate rooftops, pushing dry leaves across the path and bringing a scent that revived memory more acutely than any sight could. Families and small clusters of parishioners made their way to the church, and her heart raced as she began to recognize people—first Mrs. Kinnon. Mr. Onslet. Mrs. Smith—all names and faces she had not thought about in ages.

Charlotte stepped into the coolness of the shadowed church, with its thick stone floors and imposing columns, acutely aware of the curious glances in her direction. Light shone through the stained-glass windows, painting the ancient wooden pews and boxes in shades of auburns and greens and giving the entire vestibule an ethereal glow.

She carried Henry to the family pew in the front and paused but a moment to look at the plaque boasting her family name before she opened the door to the pew box and sat down. Keeping with tradition, Sutcliffe and Rebecca sat in the public pew in the back. The familiar setting unleashed a flood of long-forgotten memories from her childhood. Here, almost as much as at Hollythorne House, she felt her parents' absence keenly.

Whispers met her ears, and although she could not make out the words being uttered, she sensed they were about her. About Henry. About all that had happened. She glanced over her shoulder only once to see two women with their heads bowed in a hushed conversation, eyes fixed on her. She pivoted back and slowly looked forward. She could not control what was said about her or the situation at hand. But she would do her best to prove herself worthy.

When they returned to Hollythorne House after service, Charlotte had not entirely worked out her feelings from church. She had not been welcomed with open arms, but then again, she'd not been shunned. She had recognized familiar faces, and there were many new ones. Reacclimating herself to village life—as well as being accepted by the locals—was a process that would take time. Initiative. Patience.

Instead of lingering on those thoughts, she took advantage of the first full day of true sunshine—one where the sky was blue and the breeze felt more like a promise of spring than the impending winter. When Henry fell asleep for a nap, she decided to face one of the more difficult tasks she'd been avoiding since her arrival.

She made her way around the house, back behind the walled gardens. The family burial plot was outside the rear garden, under a copse of oak trees as ancient as the house itself, on the highest point of the garden, overlooking Blight Moor's expanse. Sobriety cloaked her as she approached the place where so many of her ancestors lay. She was almost afraid to come to this space and face the emotions it might conjure.

She was familiar with her mother's gravestone. Her mother had died of fever when Charlotte was twelve, and she'd often tended her mother's grave herself. But it was her father's gravestone that made her hesitate. He'd been quite ill the few years leading up to his death, and during those last difficult months of his life, nothing had mattered more to him than seeing her settled. The last time she saw him was here at Hollythorne House, six months after her marriage. He'd been in his chamber, clad in a patterned dressing coat, looking frail. Very pale and gray. To cheer him she'd regaled him with stories of how happy she was as mistress of Wolden House.

The stories had been a lie, of course—a lie she'd told to give him peace and comfort in his final days, for he alone had orchestrated her match with Roland. She could not bear for him to know that his efforts—that a man he'd trusted to be good-hearted and attentive—had resulted in misery for his only daughter.

Her chest tightened as she sat on the stone bench next to the gravestones. The lullaby of the winds sweeping over the moor grass kept her company, and the skylarks that made their homes in the brambles and hazel bushes reminded her of the life surrounding her. What would her father think of her actions and her return to Hollythorne House? He'd been such a volatile man, patient with those he cared for and brusque with those he did not. He would be mortified at the state she was in.

But his stalwart blood was flowing through her veins. She'd inherited his practical sensibilities and his dogged determination. He would instruct her to do whatever necessary for stability and peace. And she would do just that.

Chapter 24

WHEN ANTHONY FIRST returned to Blight Moor after the war to learn that his uncle was dead, the mill had burned, and Charlotte was married, he made it his singular goal to forget the small village where he'd spent his adolescence and early adulthood.

Such difficult news on the heels of battle could crumble some men, but Anthony had decided early on that it would not break him. To combat the torment and stinging regret, he'd simply not allowed himself to think on it. Fortuitously, the busyness and danger associated with the life of a thief-taker had been the ideal catalyst to keep his mind free of the past's emotional traps. He'd been largely successful at doing so, but one visit to accompany Charlotte to the church in the village, not to mention seeing familiar faces, threatened to dismantle his carefully curated walls and unleash the intentionally sealed memories.

Now, in the midst of all his activity, one truth haunted him: he'd never forgive himself for not saving his uncle. It did not matter that he'd been hundreds of miles away at the time the fire occurred. He should have been here. He knew that. He'd always known that.

One of their many conversations haunted him, and now even the strongest mental determination could not keep his mind from recounting it.

"I encourage you to really think your plans through, Anthony," Uncle Robert said as they sat at the small, roughly hewn table in the mill cottage's kitchen. "This commission you wish to purchase will exhaust the funds your father left you. You'll be an officer, yes, but you'll have no money."

Anthony shrugged nonchalantly with all the confidence of his eighteen years. "If the time comes and I need money, I can just sell the commission. Sounds simple to me."

"Consider, such a sum of money could set you up for a comfortable life here on Blight Moor," his uncle countered. "When I die this mill will pass you to. You'll have a legacy, spanning generations of Welbournes, to leave to your own children. You could do much worse."

Anthony sniffed and stared out the window into the black night. Why did his uncle always have to find fault with his plans? How could he not see the logic of it? Ultimately, the decision regarding what he wanted to do with his life was his.

The shadows caused by the light from the fire simmering in the broad hearth reflected on the weathered lines of his uncle's full, timeworn face. "Every man, young and old, dreams of adventure. Believe it or not, my first choice of occupation was not to run a mill, but other factors came into play."

"But my father followed his calling," Anthony argued, determined to have his point heard and validated. "He had goals and followed them. I intend to do the same."

Uncle Robert's expression didn't change, and he nodded his graying head frustratingly slowly. "Yes, your father made a choice. But that did not mean he did not have responsibilities he left behind."

Defensiveness bubbled within Anthony's chest. "So you're saying my father turned his back on his responsibilities?"

Uncle Robert stood from the table and crossed the low-ceilinged kitchen to stand next to the broad hearth. He pushed up the sleeves of his linen shirt and tossed another piece of wood on the simmering fire. After several moments of no sound other than the popping fire, he asked, "How much do you know about your father's childhood?"

"Not much."

Uncle Robert straightened from the fire, brushed the wood's debris from his hands, and returned to the table. "Your father was three years older than me. Our father endeavored to teach us both to form a good life on the moors . . . how to respect the land and the people in it. But our great-uncle, you see, had been a soldier and traveled far and wide. Your father idolized him and wanted to be just like him. When our father died, everything he owned passed to your father. As the firstborn, the house, the holdings, the farmland—it all went to him.

"Fortunately for me, my father saw fit to separate the mill from the rest of the Welbourne estate and leave it to me for a living, but within months of our father's death, your father had sold everything our father had left him and moved to London, and I never heard from him again."

As much as Anthony wanted to defend his father, he knew such actions were brazen. And he did not like to admit that his father had made a single misstep.

"I later heard through various sources that he married your mother, *who came with a sizable dowry. I then heard you were born, and then of her death."*

Anthony stiffened at the reference to his mother. He'd never met her. She died in childbirth. His birth.

Suddenly the fire in the grate felt too hot—the conversation too heavy. It was his turn to stand from the table and pace the mill cottage's stone floor. He did not want to have this discussion. It pricked parts of his consciousness that were uncomfortable. He much preferred living with what he imagined the truth to be instead of hearing anything to the contrary.

Uncle Robert continued with his cobalt eyes fixed staunchly on him, undeterred. "Years passed, and I still never heard from your father. I would not have known how to reach him even if I had wanted to. One day I received a letter from your mother's sister. She said that your father had died, and that she could no longer care for you. Then you arrived in a carriage."

Anthony stepped to the window and stared out. Even as a child he'd always felt guilt over the expectation that Uncle Robert would care for him. He'd never really belonged anywhere with his father away with the military.

"Since then I've tried to do my best by you, but I'm a bachelor. I know nothing of children. Was your father brave? Probably. Was he dashing and heroic? I'm sure he was. But those pursuits are temporary, Anthony. One cannot live that life forever. Consider that you are more fortunate than most. You have options, for this mill will pass to you, as the only living Welbourne. If you choose to accept that path, your future could indeed be bright."

Anthony turned from the window, with no idea how to respond.

Uncle Robert had been good to him, yes. But he did not want a life like his uncle's, and he did not like the negligent picture the man was painting of his father. "But what if I don't want this life? What if I don't want the mill?"

The words echoed in the corners of the modest room. Chiding him. Condemning him.

Anthony had thought it would feel good to make that declaration— that it would lift the weight off him to finally give voice to the truth of his opinions.

But the opposite seemed to be true.

The words echoed more sharply than intended, and instead of the sense of freedom he'd anticipated, regret crept in.

His uncle's expression didn't change. "How like your father you are. In many ways. I know you think your father was a hero. But taking care of home and those around you is heroic too."

Anthony lifted his gaze to the weapon hanging above the mantel. The rifle hanging there had been his father's weapon—one of the only things he had that belonged to him. He could not even remember what his father looked like.

And a sense of anger began to build.

All his grief over being alone and being an orphan had been channeled into the desire to be like the father he'd never really known well—as if living a life that would make the man proud would somehow cross the divide that death had created. Uncle Robert was challenging that.

His uncle moved to exit the room. As he passed Anthony, he stopped at his side and rested his hand on his shoulder. "You are young. Your life is ahead of you. You don't believe me now, but one day you'll want a home to rest in. Permanency. Do not discount steadiness and security. You don't

have to go to war to fight to be important. You don't think it, but the work
we do here, now, is important to every farmer we work with."

Anthony hadn't understood how significant that conversation was—how it would stay with him for years, becoming one of the dominant memories of interacting with the man who had essentially raised him when no one else would.

He also hadn't realized how hurtful it probably was to Uncle Robert. What was more, the awareness that Anthony had never really thanked his uncle for taking him in and raising him would forever haunt him.

He never should have been off chasing heroics. He should have been here on the moor where he belonged. Had he been, his uncle, his only relative, might still be alive.

Chapter 25

AS ANTHONY SCANNED Hollythorne House's rear courtyard, he reminded himself of the importance of remaining focused.

Thoughts of Charlotte and their past had been dominant as of late, and that simply could not continue. It was not safe. Complacency and distraction were the enemies of his assignment, and the fact that Mrs. Hargrave had just informed him that she had seen a dark figure in black walking on the far side of the garden wall reinforced that fact.

In all likelihood the figure was Charlotte, but now that the locals and tenants were aware she and Henry were at Hollythorne House, curious visitors might happen by.

He continued on, and sure enough, he spied Charlotte through the back iron gate at the small graveyard. She'd not noticed him, so as soon as he confirmed there was no danger, he slowed his steps to take in the sight at his leisure.

Much had changed since their time together that summer years ago, but there was no denying she was every bit as beautiful as she had ever been. At present, no bonnet covered her hair, and the bright sunlight filtered through the sparse yellow and brown leaves still clinging to the oak branches, dappling her thin shoulders and fair face. Her dark hair had been coiled at the nape of her neck for the earlier church service, but now the autumnal wild winds had freed several long locks, and they fluttered untethered around her narrow face. She was kneeling at a grave, brushing dried leaves and grasses from it.

He strolled closer to the iron gate as she adjusted the black shawl over her shoulders, swiped her hair away from her face, and pressed the bare fingertips of her long white fingers to the stone.

This was a private moment, and he was intruding.

There was no present peril. He should return to Hollythorne House and leave her in peace.

But it was also a moment of solitude in her presence—a rare, precious encounter he was reluctant to quit just yet. While in the United States, he'd always wondered what it would have been like to have just one day more with her.

That day was here. Now.

So he removed his glove and pushed the gate open.

Startled, she jumped to her feet at the noise.

"I am sorry for interrupting," he said.

She quickly reestablished her composure. "You're not."

"Mrs. Hargrave said she saw someone past the garden, and I'm only making sure all is well."

"I should have let someone know I was coming out here." She motioned to a grave marker, a fresh gray one next to one that was much more weathered. "I'd not yet seen my father's gravestone. I was paying a visit."

He stepped closer to read the inscription. "When did he die?"

"About two and a half years ago."

He caught the tinge of sadness reflected in her voice, and he stooped to lift a small stick that had fallen near the stone and tossed it toward the moor. "I know you respected him."

"I did. Although I know he and your family did not exactly see eye to eye."

Anthony nodded in agreement. "No, they did not."

They stood in silence, as if to allow the restorative moorland winds to brush away the tension that circumstances had constructed and to serve as a balm to heal the wounds time could not.

She broke the silence and looked toward him. "It is such a shame that your uncle and my father were so against one another."

He sobered. Who knows what could have happened if they'd never fought over land boundaries? If they'd ever come to some sort of understanding, he and Charlotte might have had a different story. "I fear saying they were merely 'against one another' might be an understatement. It's hard to say which one was more stubborn."

Reticence again descended, and the wind, with its persistence and patience, urged them to continue, as if the moor itself were eager for their reconciliation—to restore a union so natural it felt like part of nature itself.

"Do you ever miss it here?" she asked suddenly.

He shifted his gaze out to the grassy expanse. "I do think of it from time to time. The mill and the land were left to me after Uncle Robert's death, and I do intend to return to it one day, but . . ."

His voice faded away as he found it difficult to succinctly explain his opinions on the matter.

"It's uncanny, isn't it," she mused, "how we both made a decision that took us away from this place, but it never really let go of us? It's pulling us back to it."

Us.

Such a small word, but a powerful one.

He'd just told her in the parlor that he would not bring up the day they had parted. And he wouldn't. But he'd not promised not to make inquiries about her and her past. "May I ask you something?"

She arched her delicate brows and hesitated, as if preparing to decline, but then softened.

"How did you come to be *Mrs. Roland Prior?*"

Her topaz eyes grew wide, almost indignant.

It was likely a topic she did not wish to discuss. It was a private matter, and the day he left he'd given up his right to know such things. But he would never know if he did not inquire after it. And he desperately wanted to know.

At first he thought she'd refuse to answer, but then she spoke. "Actually it was quite a simple arrangement. My father's health was failing, and he was desperate to see all aspects of his life settled. At the time he'd been in talks with the Prior Mill about working together to cut costs by selling all the wool for our tenants together. Roland was often a guest at Hollythorne House, and he took an interest in me. He and my father worked out an agreement, and we were married shortly after that."

"It was a marriage of convenience then?" he asked with a strange hope that she would affirm it.

"No. It was not." She smiled, as one attempting to sweeten

unpleasant news. "At one time Roland was kind and charming. And handsome."

"And were you happy?"

Her smile faded. "That is a very personal question to ask."

"Is it?" he countered, unwilling to let the topic pass. "I think it a very natural question for one friend to ask another."

She drew a deep breath, as if carefully selecting words. "The only thing that matters to me now is Henry and his future."

"So the answer is no, you were not happy."

The corner of her mouth twitched.

He stepped closer. "Henry is a fortunate lad to have such a dedicated mother. But in all this, I do hope you intend to carve out happiness for yourself."

Eyes wide and unblinking, she inched backward, reestablishing the distance between them. "You speak of my happiness as if you knew all about what Henry and I have endured, but you forget how long it has been. If we are speaking in full honesty, then I could suggest the same thing to you. I remember you to be a carefree lad, and yet the man I see before me is anything but that."

She was turning the tides of the conversation—another tactic of hers he remembered so well for when the situation grew too uncomfortable.

"That's a fair observation, but if you have a question about me, then all you need to do is ask. I will tell you whatever you want to know."

He thought he saw moisture gather in her eyes. It could be the sting of the breeze or the dust in the air. Or she could be remembering or yearning for what had been. Yet with their every interaction there was a softening of her shield—when one crack would form, allowing him a glimpse into not only the young woman he had known but also the woman she had become.

"Very well." She lifted her chin confidently. "You told me earlier your uncle left you the mill. Are you truly earnest about returning to open it?"

He settled his disrupted neckcloth and took his hat from his head. "Very much so. But it takes capital. And that is what I am working for. But I confess the thought of returning home without my uncle, without . . . others, is a lonely prospect."

She said nothing in response to his statement but only held his gaze briefly before looking back to the house. "I should head back. Henry will wake soon, and Mrs. Hargrave and I are going to open the Blue Bedroom today."

"I'll escort you."

As they walked together back through the garden's brambles and vines, Anthony's mind was alive with all the things he yearned to say. He was not sure exactly how to proceed with her, but the earth beneath him was shifting, and he would have to shift with it.

At length she broke the silence accompanying them. "Do you recall any of my father's tenants who grew wheat? Or rye?"

"Do you mean *your* tenants that grow wheat or rye?"

She smiled sheepishly and tucked a loose strand of hair behind her ear. "Yes. *My* tenants."

He chuckled. It felt good to tease her again, even if subtly. "I never worked with them, of course, but I'm fairly familiar with what was grown and where it was grown."

She clicked her tongue and wrapped her arms around her waist as they walked. "I fear the farmers are in a difficult situation."

"How so?"

"I've spent a little time with the ledger Mr. Greenwood left, and it appears almost impossible for them to make any profit. As I mentioned, Father originally made an agreement with Prior Mill for the wool, but after my father died Roland made a similar arrangement for the farmers. Apparently they must take their grains all the way to Clarett for milling. Such a long distance, and the transportation expenses are exorbitant. I might have trouble getting us out of the agreements with Prior Mill. But I can definitely work to get us out of the Clarett one."

"Clarett, eh? I know him. He's a good man, but you're right. It's a great distance."

"If you have any advice on how to handle the mills, I'd be grateful for it. Perhaps you could look at the ledger. I fear I don't know how to handle this situation. This was my father's world, not mine."

He glanced down at her as they traversed the path, and the glimmer of trust he sensed there struck him. "Aye, I'll take a look at the ledger. But do not sell yourself short, Charlotte. You know more than you think you do."

She shook her head vehemently. "I know nothing about the mills."

"You grew up in this world. Did you not tell me you overheard more conversations in the parlor than you cared to admit? You lived this life, and it is part of you."

She slowed her steps and lifted her gaze to the house rising before them. "My father would be furious if he knew this was how it turned out, with Hollythorne House in this condition."

"No, no. I don't agree. Your father would be proud."

"But you never met my father."

"I know his reputation. I know how he interacted with my uncle—or, rather, *didn't*. Hollythorne is just a house. Made of stone and slate, timber and rock. He would be more concerned with you. He would not want you to flounder or find fault with yourself. No man would want that for his daughter. He'd want you to fight. He'd *expect* you to fight. And if you need help to get there, then ask for it. But do not let anyone think, for a single moment, that you can't do this. For the Charlotte Grey I know was fearless."

"Fearless, eh?" She laughed, and the sound, the goodness, the gentleness, the memories in it lit a fire in his soul. She stopped and turned to him, raising a playful brow. "You said you would help me if you can. If you really want to do that, find a way to open your mill and not turn away my tenants." She gave a little laugh, as if her comment was an offhanded one. "Or if you have not the inclination, allow someone else to."

To this, he could not respond.

He'd been avoiding it for so long—but now it was clear he could avoid it no longer.

What was he waiting on?

Perhaps he'd been waiting on this moment: the moment he would find true purpose in it—find the reason to leave the life of thief-taking behind and strive for a new sort of justice.

And now she was looking up at him with her wide, expectant eyes. He'd never been able to deny her. He cleared his throat in an attempt to gather his thoughts. "I've not seen the site in a couple of years, but when I did see it last, the roof was completely gone, as was the wooden waterwheel. The stone and bricks seemed intact, but with fire you never know. The mortar could be crumbling or have other structural issues. It will take a great deal of money to make it fit for its purpose again."

"But you know how to run it." An eagerness he'd not heard since their arrival brightened her voice. "You know how to build it."

"Yes, I suppose."

But he stopped there, reluctant to say more. He'd not admit that it rekindled memories he did not want to deal with. After pausing to consider his response, he said, "How about this? I promise that I will visit the mill site and assess it and see what needs to be done."

Her smile was a reward for the commitment he'd just made. But now that the words had been spoken, he could not take them back—even if he wanted to.

Chapter 26

THE NEXT MORNING as Anthony was completing his morning rounds, a wagon wheeled up the road. Mr. Greenwood had sent word that workmen would arrive to see to various necessary repairs, so Anthony crossed the courtyard to intercept the wagon.

The wagon drew closer and the driver came into focus, and a smile spread on the driver's face as he lifted a hand to wave. As the vehicle halted it was clear that an introduction would not be needed. "'O, there! I 'eard you were back. Didn't believe it though."

"Benjamin Spencer," Anthony announced with a grin as the man climbed down from the wooden bench.

Spencer thrust his hand out in greeting and clapped his other hand on Anthony's shoulder. "Never thought we'd see ye 'ere again. Thought you'd gone to Leeds for good."

Anthony shook the hand of the man he had counted a friend in the years before the war. "I'm here on assignment."

"I 'eard. Walstead's Watchmen, if I'm not mistaken. Ye don't think you'd come back to the moor and none would be the wiser, did ye?" Spencer laughed heartily and squinted in the morning light as he looked up to the slate roof. "Mr. Greenwood sent me and me boys out to look at the roof and the back stairway. Says it's in need of repair. Remember me boys? Thomas and Daniel."

Anthony looked up to the two identical auburn-haired youths and was struck. He remembered them as little boys before his departure, and now they appeared adolescent.

"There's another one at home, a baby toddlin' about, but m' wife says 'e's too young for work," quipped Spencer. "I say it's never too early for a man t' start learnin' 'ow to use 'is 'ands, but she won."

Anthony chuckled at the exaggeration. "You're a fortunate man. They're fine boys."

"That I am. Word has it that you own your uncle's gristmill now, or what's left of it," continued Spencer. "'Orrible fire."

Anthony stiffened. He'd not really spoken to anyone in detail about the actual fire. In fact, the only information he had about it was when he returned and found it in the charred state and subsequently spoke with the vicar in the village. His shock at the time had limited his interest in the details. Now curiosity was taking hold. "I was told lightning was the cause."

"Aye. I remember t' storm." Spencer crossed his brawny arms over his barrel chest. "I daresay everyone livin' on t' moor remembers t' storm. Not much rain, but t' lightnin' was fierce and lit up t' sky for 'ours. Best we could guess t' lightnin' struck one of t' trees next to t' mill, and it fell against it."

Anthony's interest piqued with each detail the man shared. "You were there?"

"Oh, aye. I was there. Not initially, of course. But me and lots of other folks came from all around to try an' put it out on account of t' black smoke. By t' time I got there, it was mostly out. And a good man was lost in it. A sad day. Always thought one day you'd come back and open t' mill back up. It's not destroyed, just in need of repair. 'Ave ye seen it?"

Spencer's question echoed the thoughts that seemed to be at the forefront of Anthony's mind as of late. "I saw it briefly a couple of years ago. I intend to visit it again before I return to Leeds."

"So you know the state of it then. I 'elped assess it myself right after the fire. The roof's gone and the beams, if I remember right. The fire was worst on the east wall, and the mortar's crumbled from t' heat and flames. But that was a while ago." He paused. "If you want me t' look and see what all would be involved in repairing it, let me know. T' farmers here could use a closer mill. But I'm sure ye know all of that."

Anthony saw his opportunity and inquired after some of the farmers in the area. Each new piece of information emphasized the dire situation the local farmers were facing. As owner of the estate, Charlotte certainly had her work cut out for her.

But it was not empathy for her plight that caused Anthony's chest to tighten. Because like it or not, he had a role to play in this situation as well. He owned the solution to a big part of the problem.

As he led Spencer and his boys to the areas in need of repair, the haunting realization stole over him: He thought he'd return to Blight Moor, do his assignment, and escape back to his life in Leeds—untouched and unchanged. Charlotte was right—they might have both left Blight Moor for different reasons, but they had been called back.

Now that he was here, it was clear that the hold over him was stronger than it had ever been, and it would not release him until he made peace with the demons that had kept him away for so long.

Night was falling. The bone-chilling rain had subsided, leaving in its wake a thick, damp fog that hugged the rugged landscape. Charlotte knew what it would feel like to be outside on an evening such as this—the gusts would sweep down from the frost-laden moors, ushering in a frigid, relentless bite. As uncomfortable as such a clime could be, she oddly was finding comfort and familiarity in it.

They had been at Hollythorne House nearly two weeks, and in that time she'd endeavored to ensure that not a single hour was wasted. Other than the time she spent with Henry, every spare second, from dawn to dusk, had been dedicated to making Hollythorne House a worthy home once more. She was not sure when the transformation had happened, but somehow, in the undeniably difficult and emotional days of sweeping and washing, scrubbing and dusting, the tasks she'd undertaken to occupy her time had also calmed her mind.

Now, in this twilight hour, she found herself sitting in the comfort of the modest kitchen feeding Henry. Rebecca sat next to her, a needle in her hand and a basket of sewing at her feet. A robust fire roared in the hearth, shedding amber light on the kitchen's occupants and ushering warmth on a scene so very different from her views at Wolden House had been.

Henry shifted in her arms and cooed as he gripped the ruffle on her sleeve. With a smile she guided his attention back to his bottle. Even her ability to feed him had improved. He no longer wailed in protest at her attempts. She'd been worried that it was too late to form the sort of bond she wanted with him, but each day proved that nothing could be further from the truth. If there was one cause for celebration in this entire experience, it was that there were no limits on the time she could spend with her son—no nosy nursemaids observing and reporting to Roland her every interaction. For the first time in his seven months, she was getting to know and understand her child, and she truly loved the little person he was.

Movement outside the kitchen in the direction of the screens passage captured her attention, and she leaned forward in her chair to look through the shadowed corridor. A whisper and a giggle met her. Concerned over the suspicious sound, she stood, Henry still in her arms, and stepped just far enough in the screens passage to spy Sutcliffe in the shadows of the great hall and Mr. Timmons in the corridor.

She should intervene in their flirting.

It was not proper.

What sort of mistress would she be if she knowingly allowed a romance to blossom under her roof? Her father had once discovered a liaison between the groom and one of the kitchen maids, and he'd wasted no time in sending them both packing. He'd always stated that one should expect the same level of decorum and integrity from everyone attached to a household, not just the immediate family members. As mistress of Hollythorne House, she should continue this sort of discipline.

But Sutcliffe was happy.

Charlotte could intimately recall those intense feelings that accompanied blissful stolen moments. For her, it had been with Anthony during the evening hours at Even Tor. Despite everything, she would not trade a single memory.

She withdrew from the screens passage back to the kitchen, just as Mrs. Hargrave was opening the door from the back courtyard and stepping inside from the chilly night. "The menfolk'll be taking their meals soon. I saw Mr. Welbourne comin' in from back by t' garden gate. I imagine 'e'll be 'ere soon enough for somethin' t' fill his belly." The housekeeper wiped her chapped red hands on her linen apron. "Will you eat 'ere before they come in?"

Charlotte looked to the long table that had been anchored in the center of the chamber for as long as she could remember. Since their arrival, she'd taken to eating her meals in the kitchen. The dining room had not been adequately cleaned yet, and her bedchamber felt unnecessarily lonely. She opened her mouth to respond, but Mr. Hargrave appeared in the doorway, his graying hair whipping about his weathered face and his coat slick with rain. He paused, stooped to pick up something, and stepped inside.

"What's that?" asked his wife.

"Letter. On the door stoop." He looked at it briefly before extending it to Charlotte.

Charlotte's heart thudded as she accepted it. She angled it toward the light.

Mrs. Roland Prior.

Gooseflesh prickled on her arms as the reality of what was in her hand registered. All correspondence was to go through the watchmen. "Where did you say you found this?"

"Right out here, on t' step, propped against t' wall."

Determined to gain more information, Charlotte stepped to the door and opened it. The wind rushed her and rain pelted her face and clung to her eyelashes. She looked down at the step, and upon seeing nothing out of place, she lifted her gaze to the black night. Trees swayed and bent, and the wind whistled through the branches, but she saw nothing.

She returned her attention to the letter pinched in her hand. She handed Henry to Rebecca, who had joined her at the door, took up a lantern, and hurried into the corridor. She slid her trembling finger, now wet from the rain, beneath the wax seal, popped it open, unfolded the letter, and angled it toward the light.

You have what we want. We will get it. We will be in touch.

She blinked and then stared at the strong, bold strokes. The jarring words were so blunt, so blaring, that it seemed as if they were being shouted at her instead of delivered to her in a missive.

All had been so quiet since their arrival, and she'd been lulled into a false sense of security. But this changed everything.

The only thing she had that anyone wanted now was *Henry.*

As the realization trickled through her being, her head swam, dizzy and light.

With every limb trembling she hastened through to the great

hall, expecting to encounter Mr. Timmons where she'd spied him but minutes prior. But he and Sutcliffe were no longer there. Blinking to adjust to the large chamber's darkness, she jogged to the front windows and peered out to the courtyard. There was Timmons, clad in a heavy greatcoat with a lantern in his hand, heading toward the front stable. She hurried to the main door and opened it.

"Mrs. Prior." Timmons turned as she exited, his round face creasing in concern. "Is everything alright?"

Mindless of the rain, she stepped into the courtyard and closed the space between them. "I need to speak with Anthony—that is to say, Mr. Welbourne. It is quite urgent. Do you know where he is?"

"I do not." He frowned in the night's darkness, his eyes not visible beneath the shadow of his hat's brim. "Is there something I can do?"

She eyed him. She'd already had her suspicions about him, given his behavior with Sutcliffe. As it was, she rarely spoke with Mr. Timmons, and somehow it felt safer to share this with Anthony. "If you see Mr. Welbourne, will you please inform him I need to speak with him? As soon as possible, please."

"I will."

She nodded and turned back toward Hollythorne House.

Charlotte would be embarrassed later for slipping and saying Anthony's Christian name. For now she had to inform him of what had happened. She had to make sure she and Henry were safe. After all, that was the entire reason why they were here.

Chapter 27

PERHAPS IT WAS Charlotte's nearness and the memories it evoked.

Perhaps it was being in such proximity to the mill and where he had spent so many years with his uncle.

Perhaps it was pausing long enough to allow his mind to contemplate the emotions associated with each.

Anthony was not sure what the reason was, but this job was unlike any other he'd done as a thief-taker. With every other assignment he'd been able to turn off all emotion beyond the desire to bring about justice. But now his personal feelings were interfering with his responsibilities, and that had to change, for it was his ability to act with his head and not his heart that made him so successful in his profession.

Anthony lowered his hat against the drizzle as he turned his horse away from Hollythorne House's outer perimeter. He'd just completed the evening check of the grounds, and now he adjusted the thick collar of his caped greatcoat as he made his way toward the stable, but as he did he quickly took notice of how a lantern light appeared in the back courtyard and slowly moved in his direction.

Assuming it to be Timmons or Tom, Anthony steered his horse toward it. But as he drew closer, Charlotte's slight, feminine figure came into view. The wind billowed the skirts of her gown and caught her uncovered hair as she cut through the courtyard. Once he reached her he dismounted, looped the reins over the horse's head, and held them in his gloved hand.

At this close distance he noticed the pallor of her skin was made even whiter by the contrast against the deepening dark of dusk. The muscles around her lips were tight and her brow furrowed.

"What is it?" he asked. "What's wrong?"

She extended a piece of paper toward him. "This was left on the kitchen doorstop. Tom found it."

He pulled his glove from his hand, accepted it, and angled it toward the light from her lantern. The words sobered him, and the unmistakable prick of failure stung.

His sole reason for being here at Hollythorne House was to protect the Priors from the outside world and from anyone who might mean them harm. And yet this letter had been delivered, unobserved and unprevented, by them all. It was what he had feared—that his distraction would lead to him missing something important.

Her words tumbled forth, each syllable increasing with intensity and each word faster than the last. "It must mean Henry. Someone must want to get to him, like Silas said. A kidnapping for a ransom. What else do I possibly have that anyone would want? Silas said the mill workers had made threats against us. It must—"

He reached out to touch her arm—as much to comfort her as to calm her racing words.

Her lips pressed shut at the touch, and she fixed her expectant eyes on him.

"You and Henry are safe." He refused to break her eye contact. He stepped closer. "This letter—the brevity of it and the manner it was left—is surely meant only to frighten you."

"Well, they're succeeding." She pulled away from his touch and wrapped her arm around her waist.

The rain, cold and intense, started to fall in stronger sheets, and Anthony motioned toward the back stable. Once they were inside the dark structure, he put his horse in a stall and returned his attention to her. The scent of damp hay and ancient wood and stone surrounded them, like a safe canopy of protection, shielding them from the outside world.

She placed her lantern on a half wall, and its yellow light splayed on the stone walls and wooden beams. She then paced the quiet space. "What could Roland possibly have done to anger someone to this extent? Henry is just a baby! I wonder whether someone has approached Silas. I wonder if . . ."

She was spiraling.

He stepped nearer and put his hands on her narrow shoulders, to silence her with the directness of touch. She was trembling. Her teeth were chattering. She wore no cloak over her thick wool gown, and the rain pasted the fabric to her arms and adhered her hair to her brow and cheeks.

He resisted the urge to smooth away the lock of hair hugging the side of her face and stooped his head slightly to look her straight in the eyes. "I know it's difficult, but you must stay calm. It's the only way to think clearly, and you *must* think clearly."

At length she lowered her eyes and spoke again, her voice low and barely audible above the wind whistling through the stable's rafters. "Henry's all I have. He's truly the only thing that matters—not Hollythorne House, not the Priors . . ."

Her voice faded, and he smoothed his thumb over her shoulder in a show of comfort. "Then we will protect him. Charlotte, trust me."

A tear slipped over her lower lashes and slid down her pale cheek. "After all that has transpired, it is difficult for me to trust anyone."

"Then let me prove to you that you can trust me again. Where is Henry now?"

"With Rebecca." She sniffed. "She and Mrs. Hargrave are both with him in the kitchen."

He nodded. "Did you tell anyone what was in this letter?"

"Not yet. I wanted to tell you first." She rubbed her arm and sniffed again. A flash of vulnerability darkened her face. Even with all the hard realities she'd faced since her arrival at Hollythorne House, he had not seen that expression. And it broke him. He wanted to fix everything—to erase that pain and return her—return them both—to that place of peace.

"You're not alone here, Charlotte. Timmons and I are both here to keep you and Henry safe. We will let nothing happen to either one of you."

At the mention of Timmons, she wiped moisture from her cheek and looked to him again. "You said earlier that you trusted Mr. Timmons with your life. What did you mean?"

He'd not expected to talk about the war, here, under these circumstances. Yet if he wanted her to trust him, really trust him, transparency was needed.

He dropped his hands from her shoulders. "Timmons and I were both injured at the Battle of New Orleans—one of the last battles of the war. We first met each other while recovering in the field hospital and were transported home on the same hospital ship. On the voyage home I fell ill. Very ill. Most of the ship did. There were not nearly enough nurses or physicians aboard, and many of those who were there fell ill from fever as well. Through the voyage Timmons kept me alive when so many others did not live. And then, when we returned, he used his connections to get us both positions, which, considering how many other soldiers were returning from war, was quite a feat. I trust him, not to mention I *owe* him, a great deal. He can be trusted."

The tension in her face eased, and her shoulders lowered. She looked up at his face, but she was not looking at his eyes. Her gaze lingered on his scar. "How were you injured?"

Instinctively, he ran his hand over his face—the side-whiskers. The start of a beard. The scar. "An explosion. I was cut by shrapnel, or so I've been told. I've no recollection of the incident, but it hit here." He pointed from his temple and then down across his chest, like a sash. "My arm took the brunt of it."

"I heard the reports of that battle." She tucked damp locks behind her ears. "Absolutely horrible."

"I can assure you that whatever you read, the truth was exponentially worse."

Silence fell over them. Now she was mere inches from him. They had somehow been pulled together, drawn by some force as they had when they were younger. Her next statement was barely above a whisper. "I did wonder about you, and what happened to you."

Her vulnerable, subdued words struck like lightning in an open field, their very meaning inciting a fire deep in him. He should seize this moment and declare the words he'd been unable to say when they had parted years ago. But he refrained. He could not forget that she was frightened. Skittish. Instead, he matched the timbre of her words with his own whisper. "And I thought about you. Daily."

The conversation, simple as it was, answered a host of questions that had been his companions for so long. She *had* thought of him. She *had* missed him.

In that moment he knew what he wanted—he wanted her, and he wanted to reverse time to a point where his touch would be welcome and her smile would be only for him. When the future spread before them would be bright and optimistic.

Yes, his heart was ready for that, but he was not sure if hers was.

But that did not mean he would stop trying. "Come on. Let's go inside and get to the bottom of this. I will notify Mr. Walstead, and we'll—"

But movement at the door silenced him. They both turned to see a man in a hat. Coat.

Timmons.

Anthony immediately stepped back. He knew he was standing too close. His head was bent too low. They had been whispering. Alone. Intimately. In the dark solitude of the shadows.

He felt like a boy caught stealing a kiss.

"Been lookin' for ye," announced Timmons, his tone flat, his face not visible in the darkness.

To play off the uncomfortable discovery, Anthony stepped toward Timmons and extended the letter toward him. "Looks like we have a little trouble."

Timmons took the letter, but he did not look at it. Instead, his dark brow rose and he glanced from Anthony to Charlotte and back to Anthony. "Trouble indeed."

Growing impatient, Anthony blurted, "Just read it."

Timmons angled it toward the lantern's amber light and did as bid. A frown darkened his already-suspicious expression. "Where's this from?"

Charlotte stepped forward. "It was found a short while ago outside the kitchen in the back courtyard."

But as Timmons's gaze flicked from the letter to Charlotte, his expression confirmed the last thing that Anthony wanted: his friend was discovering the secret they had guarded since the day he arrived.

Chapter 28

EVERY NERVE STOOD on high alert as Charlotte adjusted Henry on her hip and stepped back to allow Anthony to enter her bedchamber with the cradle hoisted on his shoulder. Out of an abundance of caution, Anthony had suggested that Charlotte and Henry share the same chamber, which would make it easier to guard them both during the midnight hours.

As their situation was shifting around her, noisy thoughts and formidable emotions battled for dominance.

Fear for her son.

Nervousness and uncertainty with Anthony's nearness.

Continued anger at Roland.

Lack of confidence in herself.

"Where do you want it?" Anthony turned toward her once he reached the middle of her bedchamber.

She pointed to an empty space between the tall, canopied bed and the paneled wall. "There."

He placed it in the indicated spot and then adjusted the blanket that had shifted within.

They should not be alone in her bedchamber. In truth it would not matter who he was—any man in her personal space was shocking. But what about the past fortnight had not been shocking? All the rules that had so strictly governed her every action just weeks ago no longer seemed to apply. She felt adrift in a world where nothing made sense anymore.

She looked toward the little bed and reached down to run her finger over the vines carved on the canopy. She needed to add another blanket before she could lay Henry down. "Would you hold him for a moment?"

Anthony did not hesitate but stepped closer and lifted him from her arms. Henry giggled and batted his arms, then reached up and touched Anthony's face. His coat.

The sight of her son in Anthony's arms tightened her chest.

She could not recall Roland holding Henry. Not a single time.

How different Anthony's pleasant countenance was from Roland's haughty one. Even now a grin formed on Anthony's face as he beheld the baby. Despite his rugged exterior, there was a kindness, a gentleness, that no number of scars or stubble could hide.

The planks beneath his heavy boots creaked with each step as Anthony paced the floor with Henry in his arms. When the creaking stopped, Charlotte lifted her gaze from her task of arranging the bed to see Anthony staring out the window.

Alarmed that he saw something dangerous, she stiffened. "What? What is it?"

He shrugged and turned from the window with a smirk. "Oh, nothing. It only seems that my colleague has taken a fancy to your maid."

Slightly annoyed at such an observation during such a serious time, she abandoned her task and joined him at the window. Sure enough, Sutcliffe was there near the drystone wall, and Timmons was on the other side of the half wall. Their figures were mere shadows in the darkness, but the intentions were obvious.

She drew a sharp breath. "I thought you said Timmons could be trusted."

"He can." Anthony, as if sensing her discomfort, shifted to face her. "I'll speak with Timmons about Miss Sutcliffe tonight. Besides, I need to talk to him about what he saw when he interrupted us, or thinks he saw . . ." His voice faded.

Anthony rarely was at a loss for words. And yet she knew exactly what he meant. It seemed foolish to tiptoe around formalities. Her initial attempts to avoid him and the past were failing. "Does he know that you and I . . . ?"

"He knows I'm from these moorlands. But he knows no details. About you. And me. The only thing he knows about is the mill."

She stared down to her hands, trying to mask her concern with a light tone. "What will you tell him?"

"The truth, but as little of it as necessary. I owe him that much. But if you would rather I didn't, I—"

She shook her head vehemently. "I am certainly in no position to tell you what to do or say. If you are concerned about my reputation, then do not be. I was Roland Prior's wife, don't forget. Nothing could happen to my reputation more damning than that."

The light from the fireplace flickered on the angles of his jaw and lips as he sobered. "Have you told your maid about the letter?"

"Yes. I told her after I came back inside."

"She seems very loyal to you."

"Yes. She is. And I do consider her a friend. She's the only one—" Charlotte paused. She was getting ready to reveal more of her life to him. How easy it was to fall back into that place where there were no secrets, no boundaries. "Sutcliffe has stood by my side through this entire ordeal. She's very trustworthy."

His voice lowered further, and his gaze was uncomfortably direct. "And does she know about me? About our history?"

Charlotte shook her head. "No. She became my maid two days before I married Roland. She has only ever known me as Mrs. Prior. She knows very little of my life before that."

Charlotte said nothing else and looked back down to the courtyard. Sutcliffe was walking back toward the house with slow, reluctant steps. Charlotte reached for Henry, seeking a change of topic. "He's tired. I should put him to bed."

Anthony bounced the boy playfully before he handed him back to her. "I'll leave you to it, then, but one of us will have an eye on this chamber door, and the other will be watching the grounds."

His gaze locked with hers, intentionally, if not flirtatiously. The blueness of his eyes jolted her as they had when she was young, and that giddy, girlish feeling flared unexpectedly. And for the first time since returning to Hollythorne House, she did not want to squelch it. In fact, she could not deny it: She wanted him to stay. She yearned for it.

But as he turned toward the door and exited the room, she reminded herself of all that was at stake and the seriousness of the threat they'd received. It would not do to take her eyes off her goal now. Her heart and personal desires should be the least of her concerns. Right now, Henry's safety was all that mattered. There might be time to allow her mind to engage in dreams at a later date, but for now she had to remain steadfast.

———————

Anthony would have to face the situation sooner or later.

Theoretically, he owed Timmons no explanation, but they'd experienced the worst aspects of humanity together—war. Injury. Crime. What was more, they trusted each other. Therefore, the respect between them required Anthony to address what Timmons had witnessed. So with a lantern in hand, Anthony sought Timmons out as the man sat on his horse at the perimeter.

Even in the darkness Timmons's expression was sober. Any trace of his good-natured humor had fled. Anthony was not entirely surprised, for his friend had been displaying a somber countenance as of late. Only this time, his censure and disapproval were leveled at Anthony.

Timmons slid from his horse's back and spoke first. "That was a rather interestin' sight to walk into t' stable and see. My friend, a confirmed bachelor, wooin' a woman. And not just any woman but our very recently widowed client."

Initially Anthony said nothing in response and fell into step next to Timmons as they walked toward the stable. He'd learned a long time ago that it was best to gather all the facts and find out what the suspect knew before speaking, because many times people wanted to say their piece. He suspected that, in this instance, Timmons was no different.

After several moments Timmons scoffed and stopped abruptly,

turning to face Anthony directly. "T' oddest thing 'appened earlier, before I sought ye in t' stables. Mrs. Prior was lookin' for ye, and she called ye *Anthony*. No one ever calls ye that. Now, why would a well-bred woman such as Mrs. Prior address ye as such? Normally, I'd figure it a mistake. A slip of t' tongue or t' like. Then I started to put things together. Ye used to live 'ere. Her family's owned this property for who knows 'ow long."

Anthony looked past Timmons into the murky night, taking in his friend's argument and wishing he didn't have to respond.

Timmons tilted his head to the side. "'Tis funny, 'ow friendships go. We've seen each other on our deathbeds. We've chased criminals and fought side by side. I know what brandy ye take and what weapons ye prefer, but at t' end of t' day, I know nothin' about ye. Not really."

Anthony inhaled the moor's mossy scent as he considered his options. Timmons had put the pieces together, and Anthony was faced with a decision: He could deny it. Or he could tell the truth.

"I know what you're thinkin'. You're thinkin' 'tis none o' me business. But ye made it me business when ye brought your secrets into an assignment that we're workin' on together, makin' me the fool."

Timmons adjusted his stance, leaned closer, and lowered his voice. "I see you're goin' to be quiet on the matter, so I'll tell ye what I think. Ye know this family and did long before we came out 'ere. Ye know 'er."

Anthony considered each word carefully. "Yes, I know Charlotte Prior, only I knew her as Charlotte Grey. And I knew her very well."

Timmons muttered a slew of curses as he resumed lumbering toward the outbuildings. "Does Walstead know?"

"No one knows. Except now you, of course."

Timmons stopped again, suddenly, and pivoted to face Anthony, an incredulous expression beclouding his features. "Ye lied to Mr. Walstead?"

Anthony nodded. "At the time it didn't seem important."

Timmons's sudden sarcastic laughter bellowed. "Mr. Walstead will find out. And when 'e does, 'e'll assume I knew, too, and did not tell 'im."

"He won't find out."

"*Why?*" Timmons flung his hand out in frustration. "Because ye excel at concealin' truths? If ye believe that, then I suggest ye and Mrs. Prior avoid whisperin' alone in darkened stables and avoid referrin' to each other by Christian names."

Anthony had no response. He had been caught in his deception.

Timmons propped his elbow on the horse's back and paused for several seconds before fixing his eyes on Anthony. "Ye really didn't think to tell me?"

Anthony adjusted his stance. "I didn't want to put you in a situation where you had to lie to Mr. Walstead."

"Ye think me a fool then? That I wouldn't notice?"

"No. Quite the opposite."

"Ye an' Mrs. Prior are playin' a dangerous game. Your omission of t' truth is a lie to Mr. Walstead, whether ye choose t' think so or not." The cynicism in Timmons's voice reverberated. "My advice? Tell Walstead. Ask for reassignment. No good can come of this little arrangement of yours. Don't ruin this—for either of us."

Chapter 29

CHARLOTTE HESITATED OUTSIDE of the Gold Room.

As mistress of Hollythorne House, no area of the property was forbidden to her, including this room that had been her mother's private chamber, yet Charlotte paused before crossing its threshold. As she stood there with Henry in her arms, she could hear her father's words echoing in her mind.

"Stay out and leave it as is. There is nothing you need in here."

Even now that she was an adult, the words stayed with her.

As an adolescent Charlotte would sneak in here when her father was away and admire the round gowns in the wardrobe and try on her mother's dancing slippers. When she had turned eighteen, her father permitted her to select some of her mother's jewelry, but other than that, the space had always been treated as a shrine. Now it felt like a distorted glimpse into her memory.

With Henry on her hip she stepped farther into the room. Everything was as she remembered—from the gold curtains on the heavy mahogany bed to the embroidered shawl strewn on the back of the settee. She stepped to the windows and pulled back the thick curtains of ochre brocade. The white afternoon light flooded the sparse space, giving new life to the room and illuminating the dust motes hovering in the stale air.

The Gold Room was on Hollythorne's northwest corner. Instead of looking out over the front courtyard and main road as her bedchamber did, this one overlooked her mother's beloved garden and the moorland beyond. She dropped the curtain from her fingertips and pivoted to assess the chamber with a fresh eye.

Haphazardly shelved tomes lined the mantel shelf, and a thick layer of dust covered the mahogany dressing table. She lifted a gilded hand mirror on it and turned it to gaze at her reflection. Henry reached out, and she smiled as he grabbed hold of it and giggled and babbled at the likeness that met him there.

A fresh cloak of melancholy settled over Charlotte. At the moment Hollythorne House was not feeling like the safe haven she had hoped it would be. She'd longed for a place of reprieve and shelter, but now with the suspicious letter, it felt as if every moment offered a new threat. She had hoped that by visiting this chamber she would feel a sense of closeness to her past and belonging, but instead it emphasized her loneliness.

"Here you are!"

Charlotte turned at the sound of approaching footsteps in the corridor. Sutcliffe propped her hands on her hips as she entered and lifted her eyes to survey the room. "What a lovely chamber this is."

"This was my mother's chamber," Charlotte responded absently, allowing her gaze to linger on the yellow-and-green floral paper lining the walls. "Did you need something?"

"Ah yes. Mr. Timmons sent me to fetch you." She reached for Henry. "There's a young woman here to see you."

"Is she here about the housekeeping position?"

Sutcliffe shook her head as Henry came to her and settled on her hip. "No, ma'am. She said she is one of your tenants."

Relief and anxiety intermingled. Charlotte knew she would meet her tenants at one point, but she'd hoped to have a better grip on the realities of the estate before she did. But if the woman was here, there was no time like the present to meet her. "Is she in the parlor?"

"Yes," she responded. "And I already asked Mrs. Hargrave to prepare tea."

After giving Henry a kiss on the cheek, Charlotte made her way down the creaking staircase, pivoted at the landing, and crossed through the great hall until she was at the parlor. Inside was a petite woman with long auburn hair; dark, wide-set eyes; and an abundance of freckles across her cheeks and the bridge of her nose. She curtsied awkwardly as Charlotte entered.

"Welcome to Hollythorne House."

"Thank you." The woman's white-knuckled grip on her reticule was matched only by the nervousness tightening her expression. "My name's Molly Mayer. I live at Thresh Cottage on t' moor's edge."

"It is a pleasure to meet you." Charlotte smiled, attempting to allay the woman's anxieties. "But you'll have to forgive me. I am not familiar with your name."

"Mayer is my married name," she rushed. "My father's name was Jerome Simmons, ma'am."

Faint recollection glimmered, and Charlotte lifted her head. "Ah yes. I remember now. What brings you to Hollythorne House, Mrs. Mayer?"

"I came t' pay m' respects. An' offer a gift."

"Oh." Charlotte's gaze fell to the bundle at the woman's feet. "A gift is not necessary."

The young woman ignored Charlotte's protest and knelt to lift the bundle of vibrant blue broadcloth and extended it toward her. "It's a shawl, made from t' wool of our own sheep, spun in the 'ouse by 'and."

Charlotte accepted the beautiful piece, immediately struck by its softness. Such a piece would likely cost the young woman greatly. "This is far too much."

The woman's expression dimmed. "Then if you will not accept it as a gift, perhaps you will accept it as a form of payment."

Charlotte sobered as the reality of the situation was taking hold.

"Mr. Greenwood was by, and since it is just me and my mother, we haven't t' money to pay t' rent quite yet."

Charlotte kept her tone steady. "You mentioned you were married, Mrs. Mayer. Is your husband not at your farm?"

Her face colored, and she stared down at the toes of her scuffed boots. "He left for Leeds, been gone a month now, t' get more work."

Charlotte had heard of this happening—of farmers and country laborers leaving their farms for the lure of steadier and more predictable factory work.

Their conversation was interrupted when Rebecca appeared

with a tray of tea and placed it on the carved table in the parlor's center. Once Rebecca retreated and all was once again quiet, Charlotte poured the girl a cup and extended it to her.

"Oh no." Mrs. Mayer shook her head. "I couldn't accept that."

"Of course you can. I insist."

Once the tea had been accepted and Charlotte poured herself her own cup, she motioned for Mrs. Mayer to be seated in one of the wingback chairs and then settled herself in the one opposite her guest. "Tell me of your farm, Mrs. Mayer. I've been away for so long that there's a great deal for me to catch up on."

Charlotte listened as the young woman told of her sheep and the recent harvest, of the orchard and outbuildings. As she spoke Charlotte's gaze fell to the calluses on the woman's palms, her ruddy, wind-burned cheeks, and the patched holes of her gown. Charlotte was struck in that moment of how fortunate she was, how fortunate she'd always been, to have confidence in always having a roof over her head and food to eat. Life could be uncertain for a single woman—widowed or otherwise.

When the tea was gone and they were nearing the end of their chat, Charlotte stood. "Excuse me for a moment, Mrs. Mayer. I'll be right back."

She left the young woman in the parlor and hurried up the smaller staircase to her chamber. Ensuring she was alone, she moved to the floorboard where she kept her valuables, pushed the table aside, and pulled out a small pouch of coins. She selected a few, folded them in her palm, returned her chamber to its original condition, and hurried back down to her guest.

Mrs. Mayer stood as she entered.

Charlotte approached her. "I would like to pay you for the lovely shawl."

The woman shook her head adamantly. "Oh no, ma'am. If anything, that was meant by way of rent. I couldn't—"

Charlotte took the worn hand in hers and folded the coins in it. "This is for the shawl. It is lovely and I shall wear it proudly. As for the rent, we will address it when the next payment is due. Trust me when I say I am figuring all this out, and we *will* figure it out. Together."

Chapter 30

ANTHONY WAS RARELY nervous or trepidatious, yet as Walstead and two other men thundered toward Hollythorne House atop their horses, both sensations accosted him. His conversation with Timmons was heavy on his mind, and now that Timmons knew of his past with Charlotte, he would essentially be lying for him. And that made Anthony uneasy.

Even so, another part of him was equally relieved that Walstead finally was arriving. Initially he was supposed to visit a few days after their arrival to assess the situation and provide them with a more substantial update, but days had stretched to a fortnight, and they were all eager for updated news.

Anthony met the new arrivals at the gate and opened it to allow the horsemen through, then closed and secured it. Walstead immediately dismounted and approached. His blue wool coat with wide lapels and fabric-covered buttons was a bright contrast to the courtyard's drab grays and withered browns, and it made his sharp eyes appear even darker against the bleak landscape. The tall black beaver hat atop his head added several inches to his otherwise unimpressive height, but Mr. Walstead's mannerisms, his pretentious comportment, made him seem as if he lorded his position above all around him.

"I received the missive about the note Mrs. Prior received," he said, forgoing any kind of greeting. "Has there been anything else?"

Anthony looked up to the two watchmen bearing bright blue armbands who were accompanying Mr. Walstead—neither of whom he recognized—before extending the letter in his direction. "No. Here it is."

Mr. Walstead snatched the letter and quickly read it before he folded it and tucked it in his coat. "And where was this found?"

"The back courtyard. I'll show you the spot."

"Not necessary." Mr. Walstead motioned abruptly to the two men behind him. "I'm increasing the security detail here. These men are Ames and Broadstreet. They'll report to you. I expect you to show them what to do." The sense of detached aloofness echoed in his tone, and he looked back to the house. "So this is the Hollythorne House I've heard so much about, eh? Where's Mrs. Prior?"

The desire to protect her and Henry pulsed strongly through Anthony afresh. "She and her son are both in one of the upstairs chambers."

"I should like to speak with her. Is there anything else I should be aware of before I talk with her?"

Timmons's warning rang in Anthony's head. If he was going to be honest about his attachment with Charlotte, this was the ideal opportunity. Yet he could not make himself do it. His vow to help her was much stronger than his allegiance to William Walstead. He had to think of Charlotte's future, Henry's future, and his own future. And he could not risk being reassigned. Not when he could help her. Not when she was softening toward him.

"No, sir. Nothing else of consequence."

Charlotte heard the horsemen before she saw them.

At the sudden ruckus she dropped the gown she was helping to resize for Sutcliffe and hurried to her bedchamber window. Ever since the discovery of the letter, every sound, every movement set her nerves afire. She'd not ventured far from the upstairs chambers, and she'd only let Henry from her sight if he was with Sutcliffe or Rebecca. Charlotte had expected to feel relief at Mr. Walstead's arrival, but the sight of the two additional watchmen with their bright blue armbands incited more anxiety than peace.

"It's Mr. Walstead, and it appears he's brought more watchmen," she called over to Sutcliffe, who was sewing next to the opposite window to take advantage of the light. "Hurry, please help me dress into the best mourning gown I have."

Together they selected a gown of black bombazine, with black lace netting high on the bodice and the neckline, long sleeves, and a Vandyke hem along the bottom. Her hair, thick and still damp from a washing earlier that morning, was plaited and woven into a hasty yet tidy chignon and secured with jet pins.

The sound of the men entering the great hall echoed from the wood paneling outside of her chamber, and her stomach fluttered. Charlotte tried not to jump to conclusions regarding any news he might bring. She swept from the room, down the parlor staircase to the great hall, where several of the men gathered.

She refused to be intimidated by their presence.

"Mrs. Prior." Mr. Walstead met her at the foot of the staircase, bowed, and reached for her hand to assist her. "I've heard there has been a frustrating development."

"Yes. A most concerning note."

"I've informed your brother-in-law about this, and he agrees that security should be increased." Mr. Walstead motioned behind him. "Mr. Broadstreet and Mr. Ames here will be assisting Mr. Welbourne and Mr. Timmons until this matter is settled. I do have updates to share with you. I was hoping we could speak in a more private setting."

She let her gaze linger on the other two men. Mr. Ames was of average height with a stocky build, a hardened face, and strong, wooden features. She was certain she'd never seen him before. But something was familiar about the other man, Mr. Broadstreet. He boasted an unusual shade of deep-auburn hair—one not easily forgotten. In all likelihood he'd worked for Roland at some point, for where else would she have seen him? She turned her attention back to Mr. Walstead. "Of course. Before we do, would your men care for refreshment?"

"No, I thank you. First, I think it most important to get them familiar with our surroundings." He turned to face the men. "Timmons, you show Ames and Broadstreet the property. Welbourne, you stay with us."

Once the other watchmen were gone, Charlotte led the way

to the parlor and closed the door behind them. "We can speak privately here."

She clutched her hands nervously before her as Mr. Walstead and Anthony filed into the room, and she forced her anxiety in abeyance. The last time she spoke with Mr. Walstead she'd been angry and frightened. She was still those things, but every day at Hollythorne House had ushered in a new measure of confidence that bolstered her tenacity.

Mr. Walstead removed his hat, smoothed his slick black hair into place, stepped to the window, and assessed the landscape, then turned back to her. "I've been working with your brother-in-law to discover the nature of the mill workers' unrest. I'd hoped the problem would be easy to rectify, but the more we dig into your husband's finances and correspondence, the clearer it is that he was in quite a bit of trouble in the months before his death. Were you aware?"

She could sense Anthony's gaze on her, but she dare not look in his direction. "I know no specifics, Mr. Walstead. As I told you before, my husband shared none of his business practices with me."

Mr. Walstead stepped farther into the room, his wet, polished boots squeaking as he traversed the stone floor. "We've uncovered certain details, and I hesitate to share them with you because they're far from delicate, but Mr. Prior assured me that you're quite stoic when it comes to such things."

"If you are concerned for my sensibilities, please, do not be. I fear very little shocks me."

He nodded and fixed his intense gaze on her. "You may

be surprised to learn that your husband had been involved in smuggling some goods from Spain. According to my source, he promised some of his mill workers that he would compensate them in exchange for assistance with the smuggling transport. The run was successful, but apparently the items disappeared shortly after their arrival in Leeds. Your husband accused the mill workers of theft and then refused to pay any of them until the items were returned. Now the workers are demanding payment for services rendered, but without a delivered parcel, there is no evidence of a job done."

Charlotte blinked. The answer seemed so simple. "Surely there is enough money in Roland's estate to pay these men what they are owed. The amount can't be that significant. Why not compensate them and be done with it?"

"Well, that brings me to another point. Your husband had invested in unsuccessful overseas endeavors, and his estate's worth was reduced to such a state that Roland could be considered a ruined man. As you can imagine, the news has angered Silas Prior and he will not authorize any payments to these men at all."

The reality of what he'd said struck her.

Henry's inheritance.

She forced the shock of Roland's alleged destitution and the implications thereof to the back of her mind and refocused her attention back to the matter at hand. "Do you know what he was transporting?"

"A great many things, I've been led to believe. He'd made a large purchase from a Spanish estate, but the most valuable piece

SARAH E. LADD

of the missing import is a set of jewels known as the King's Prize. Does that mean anything to you?"

"'King's Prize'?" She frowned as she searched her memory. "No. I've never heard of it."

"It is a collection of emeralds. All from an Egyptian mine. They are all large and in various stages of refinement."

At the mention of emeralds, heat coursed through her.

The emeralds in my case.

The urge to panic seized her, and a wave of gooseflesh prickled her arms.

She'd assumed the letter had been about Henry. But could the item referenced be the collection of emeralds and not Henry at all?

She should tell Mr. Walstead everything—immediately.

She should go to her chamber, retrieve the pouch, and hand them over and get them out of her possession once and for all. She wanted nothing to do with them, and she would do whatever necessary to remove the threats against her.

But just as she had made up her mind to relinquish them, something within her urged caution. Something *felt* off, and she was not exactly sure what it was. If there was one thing she had learned, it was that she could not trust the men who worked for the Priors.

She needed clarity. She needed to think.

"Mr. Prior has engaged me to get to the bottom of the unrest with the mill workers and to find the emeralds and discern how it affects the amount of money in the estate. My men are conducting a thorough search of Wolden House and Roland's mill offices, and if that proves unfruitful, we will move on to his other holdings.

Furthermore, I want to emphasize the danger I believe you and Henry are in. It is more imperative than ever that you remain steadfast. It is my hope that this will be resolved soon, but until then, please remain vigilant."

Chapter 31

ANTHONY FELL INTO step with William Walstead as they walked along the drystone wall that separated Hollythorne House from Blight Moor beyond. Since arriving here, it had been his favorite stretch of the property, but today uneasiness snaked through him.

"Have you worked with Ames or Broadstreet before?" Mr. Walstead adjusted his beaver hat, which seemed almost foppish out in the wild moorland air.

Anthony glanced toward the other men gathered in the front courtyard. "No."

"They're good men. Both of them. They'll be an asset to you."

"Any idea who might be behind that letter?" asked Anthony now that they were away from Charlotte.

"My instincts tell me that at least some of the mill men are behind the disappearance of the King's Prize and that the letter is tied to that in some way, but without all the facts, I can't be entirely sure. But regarding the danger, I'll be blunt. I think it is significant. I'll admit that initially I thought sending men out to guard one woman and one child excessive. But the mill men have been talking, and news has spread far and wide. Now every thief and treasure hunter will be searching for the King's Prize, and there's no telling what lengths some would go to find it."

"Who's your source?"

"Last week we interviewed Roland Prior's private secretary, who agreed to talk in exchange for anonymity and indemnity. He claims to have witnessed the entire ordeal. According to him, Roland knew he was in dire financial straits and only made it look like the King's Prize was stolen. But he, in fact, took it and hid it. He did not want to pay the men at all, and this was his way out of doing just that."

Mr. Walstead halted his steps and turned to face Anthony. "I want you to watch Mrs. Prior very closely. In my experience a wife always knows more than she lets on. It's rumored that she and her husband did not get on. In fact, I can't recall ever once seeing her accompany him to a social event. But even so, it's possible she knows something, and like everyone else, she could have something to gain from this. We already know she wants independence from the Prior name, and if she had access to such valuable jewels, she could seek to use that to her advantage. What's more, Timmons told Dunston that Mrs. Prior's maid was attempting to sell jewels to a jeweler. One would expect that she would not be so foolish as to attempt to sell hidden jewels in the very city in which she lives, but you never can tell."

Anthony stiffened. Even the thought of Charlotte being involved in such a heist made him sick. "So far I've seen no indication of involvement."

"Aha! You missed it then." A twinkle glimmered in

Mr. Walstead's eyes. "Did you see her response when I mentioned the emeralds? She knows about them. Her eyes widened, her face flushed, and she looked to the floor. She could not bring herself to look me in the eye for that instant."

There was no doubting William Walstead's ability to read people.

"She's a clever one. I will grant her that." Mr. Walstead turned back to continue his walk along the wall, pausing to brush a bit of dried mud from his sleeve. "Women like that are dangerous. Do you believe that a wife would not know about such happenings under her own roof? Bah. She knows something. And she *will* let it slip."

"I'll keep an eye out," Anthony muttered in response.

Mr. Walstead clapped him on the shoulder. "Good man."

As they walked back in silence to Hollythorne House, Anthony attempted to digest all he'd heard. That, combined with the knowledge that Charlotte's maid had tried to sell some jewels, left him with a knot in his stomach.

Each new development was a step toward finding the truth, but at what cost?

———

Charlotte watched Mr. Walstead leave the courtyard atop his horse, just as she'd seen him arrive.

Her heart ached as her mind relived what she had learned.

The King's Prize.

Roland's depleted estate.

His deceptions—not just to her but to many other people.

It was all too much, and yet none of it was a surprise.

And now there were two more men watching over Henry and her, which should make her feel secure. An undercurrent of doubt robbed her of that feeling however, and she now knew why.

The emeralds that she and Sutcliffe had hidden beneath her floorboards.

Perhaps she should have told Mr. Walstead about them when the opportunity presented itself, but the sensation that something was amiss had reared its head. Since Roland's death she'd been learning to trust her instincts. She was learning to stand up for herself and her son, making difficult decisions and enduring adversity—traits she thought she'd lost when she married Roland Prior.

Eager for a rest and for quiet to contemplate all that had occurred that day, she retrieved Henry from the kitchen, where he'd been in Rebecca's care, and carried him up to her bedchamber. But once she was in her room, she paused.

She glanced around her, from the floor to the bed to the desk.

The rug covering the rough wooden floor was rumpled. Henry's rattle was on the desk, not on the small table next to his cradle. The trunk at the foot of her bed was ajar. She had not written a letter, and yet the quill was atop her desk instead of in the drawer.

The sickening suspicion of being watched settled over her like a cloak—as if someone could see her every move.

Footsteps pattered outside the door, and Charlotte stepped to the corridor to find Rebecca on her way to the nursery. Charlotte kept her voice low. "Were you and Henry in this chamber all day when Mr. Walstead was here?"

Rebecca's light brown eyes were wide. "For a bit, but I fed 'im in t' kitchen with Mrs. 'argrave, and then I 'elped 'er prepare the meal for t' watchmen."

"And Henry was with you?"

"I ne'er let 'im out of me sight."

Charlotte nodded both to keep her nerves steady and to comprehend what she was hearing. "And Sutcliffe? Do you know where she is?"

"The last I saw 'er she was 'elping t' prepare one of the extra bedchambers so t' new watchmen would 'ave somewhere t' sleep."

"I see," Charlotte said, forcing a smile. The last thing she wanted to do was alarm the girl, who might say something to the other servants and start their tongues wagging. "Do you know whether anyone else has come in my chamber? Anyone at all?"

"No, ma'am. No one that I've seen."

"That will be all. Thank you."

Rebecca bobbed a curtsey and continued back to the nursery, and Charlotte returned to the solitude of her chamber and closed the door.

The new watchmen had been in her house when she was speaking with Mr. Walstead. Surely the strangers would not go through her things.

Would they?

The thought burned hot, as if touching a poker left in the fire. She placed Henry in his cradle and hurried to the corner where she knew the emeralds to be. She pushed the table away and pulled out the long box she'd hidden there. Everything was still there—even the emeralds.

Only now they had a name: the King's Prize.

She returned the table to its original position to hide the odd floorboard.

Determined to find Sutcliffe, Charlotte picked up Henry once more, left him with Rebecca in the nursery, and made her way through the gallery in the direction of the main staircase, but the sight that met her in the small study was the very one she had feared. Locked in a passionate embrace, Sutcliffe's slender form was pulled tight against Mr. Timmons.

This had gone too far—she had to put a stop to it.

Too many other people were in the house—too many observing eyes. If she saw them, who else would as well? Charlotte had to protect Sutcliffe's reputation. After all, what else did a young woman truly possess?

Charlotte's kid boots fell more heavily than normal against the uneven planked floor as she announced her presence, and that, accompanied with an intentional clearing of her throat, caused the couple to step away from each other.

Charlotte ensured her voice was firm. Direct. "Sutcliffe, Mrs. Hargrave is waiting for you in the kitchen. Please go to her and see what assistance she needs."

Sutcliffe, red-faced and flustered, hurried past her without making eye contact, and when the lady's maid was out of earshot, Charlotte took a step in Mr. Timmons's direction. "I will speak with Mr. Welbourne about this."

Timmons stared at her for several seconds. "Are you sure that is a good idea, Mrs. Prior?"

At first she thought the words, spoken hushed and low, were almost a jest. But then she met his gaze. A hardness smoldered there—a message hidden in his austere glare.

It was a threat—not a question.

He did not blink, nor did he look away. Instead, he closed the space between them with fierce determination. "Ye could tell 'im, if ye wanted. There's none t' stop ye. But don't forget, there's those who know about your escapades. Mr. Walstead already is suspicious. Imagine what 'e would think—not t' mention Silas Prior—of such a newly widowed woman involved with t' watchman 'ired t' protect her boy. That would not bode well for t' reputation of the new mistress of 'ollythorne 'ouse."

Charlotte pressed her lips together, summoning strength as she refused to break her gaze with the much larger man. "I'm not exactly sure what authority you believe you have here, but I assure you there is very little you can do to intimidate me. I've nothing to hide. But exposing my past means exposing truths about Mr. Welbourne. I'm told you two are friends. Are you prepared to do that?"

He gave a little laugh, as if amused at the antics of a child. "Is that a challenge?"

Charlotte would not argue with this man. She took hold of her skirt in her fist and prepared to return to her chamber. Before she did, she fixed her gaze on him. "Mr. Welbourne and Sutcliffe may trust you, but I don't. And I know you think you have some sort of power here, Mr. Timmons, but I assure you, I will be watching you. One misstep and I will have you thrown from this property."

Chapter 32

THE MOONLIT NIGHT descended heavy and crisp over Blight Moor, casting long gray shadows in Charlotte's bedchamber. Outside the wind howled, and inside the fire popped and simmered. Henry slumbered tranquilly in his cradle, and a watchman was outside her door. But for Charlotte, the night was anything but peaceful.

At one time this room, with its low-beamed ceiling, white plaster walls, and wide-planked floors had been such a solace to her. But now her noisy fears refused to settle, even just a little, to allow her to sleep.

Questions that had no easy answers assailed her.

Apprehensions that took on a life of their own mocked her.

She told herself that ever since Roland's death she'd made the best decisions possible with the information she had. But what if she'd miscalculated the situation? The possible consequences of such an error raced through her mind, and each scenario ended in yet another tragedy.

How she wished for guidance. Initially she had turned to Sutcliffe for advice and reassurance, but even she was changing.

With each passing day her normally affable lady's maid seemed more guarded, and Charlotte could only assume her growing attachment to Mr. Timmons had something to do with it. Too much was at stake for misplaced trust.

She wanted to talk with Anthony and share what had transpired. But if her trust was misplaced in Sutcliffe, could it be misplaced in Anthony as well?

Unable to sleep or even to sit still, Charlotte lit a candle from the fire and pushed the table away in the dark of night, removed the loose floorboard, and retrieved her jewelry chest and set it on her bed. She drew a candle close, took out the emeralds, and assessed them, one by one.

They were enchantingly beautiful, even if they were a physical manifestation of the danger in which she and Henry now found themselves. The light caught the hard, polished facets, projecting slivers of jade and chartreuse glimmers onto surfaces nearby.

She tucked them back in the pouch, uneasy with the knowledge that something so valuable was cached in her bedchamber. That quiet, small voice that guided so many of her actions was now screaming at her, urging—nay, demanding—caution. She'd be elated to be rid of them and never again lay eyes on them, but deciding whom to trust and how to proceed proved precarious.

She would not return the emeralds to below the floorboard where she had been keeping them. Instead, she would keep them on her person. If someone had been searching her chamber, it would not take long before they noticed the floorboard that was slightly discolored from the others. Whether she liked it or not, she was involved in this heist, for now she was the one keeping a secret.

And her stomach knotted at the thought.

That same quiet voice was urging her to do something her heart had been arduously guarding against. Until this point she'd relied on her own strength and abilities, but the situation was intensifying and the threats around her were multiplying. She needed help. Even though she had tried desperately to deny it, deep down she trusted Anthony's integrity. His candor. And he understood this world that she had no knowledge of: the inner workings of this world of ne'er-do-wells and thieves.

With the small pouch clutched in her hand, she climbed atop her bed and curled up in the mountain of blankets she'd added for warmth. Sleep came in a mixture of filmy nightmares and vexing thoughts, and that space between sleep and consciousness was where her mind passed a wearisome night.

The next morning, Charlotte rose and dressed early, and as soon as Henry was safely in Rebecca's care, she located Anthony in the great hall. Once she was in his presence there was no need for pretense. She cast a glance in both directions to make sure no one observed them. "May I speak with you? Privately?"

Under any other circumstance, the thought of Charlotte inviting him to the privacy of a secluded chamber would be most welcome.

But today something was different.

Dark circles like he had not seen since their first day at

Hollythorne House shadowed her eyes, and her fingers wrapped around the candlestick with such intensity that her knuckles glared white. He nodded his agreement to her request, then wordlessly followed her into the darkened library—a narrow chamber off the back staircase that was rarely used, with but one small window and very little opportunity to be discovered.

Desperation marked her expression as she lowered the candle to the table. When she let go, her hand was trembling.

"What is it?" he asked, barely above a whisper. "What's happened?"

"I need help, Anthony. I don't know what to do."

His chest tightened at her uncharacteristic vulnerability. "Tell me."

She shook her head, as if dislodging thoughts. "Yesterday, after Mr. Walstead departed, I returned to my chamber. It was obvious that someone had been in there. Someone had gone through my belongings."

He jerked and his dark brows furrowed. "Why did you not say something earlier?"

"I-I wasn't sure if I imagined it, but now I'm certain. I think one of the new watchmen searched my chamber." She pulled a small leather pouch from the pocket in her gown and extended it toward him. "And I suspect this is what they were looking for."

Anthony took the pouch from her, opened it, and turned the contents into his work-worn hand.

The King's Prize.

The implications of the jewels in his hand hit hard and fast. "Where did you get these?"

"I didn't know I had them. Before we left Wolden House, I retrieved my jewelry chest from Roland's strongbox. I rarely used anything in there, and I did not bother checking the contents before we left. When Sutcliffe and I opened the box once we got here, these were in it. I just assumed Roland put them in the wrong place. I did not think anything of them until Mr. Walstead told me about the King's Prize. These are those emeralds, right?"

Anthony shifted his fingers, and the gems caught the yellow candlelight. "I'd say so."

His mind raced and his allegiance was torn. Under normal circumstances, he'd inform Mr. Walstead of this sort of development without hesitation. Time was precious in these investigations, and this was a significant discovery that could advance the investigation by leaps and bounds.

Yet he'd not betray something Charlotte told him in confidence. He just had to find the point where this all intersected—not to mention he had to understand her reasoning. "Why did you not tell Mr. Walstead when he asked about them?"

She shrugged her thin shoulders. "I suppose it was the shock of it. When Mr. Walstead told us of them, I panicked. He's a stranger—one I'm not sure I can trust."

"But if you trusted Mr. Walstead enough to care for you and Henry, then why not trust him with this?"

"Because his care was a condition of Silas permitting me to

go to Hollythorne House without much resistance. Remember, I didn't hire Mr. Walstead. Silas did."

The reminder stung. It was easy to forget that she had not wanted him here in the first place—that she would prefer solitude. But she needed protection—he believed that now more than ever. "Does anyone know you have these?"

"Only Sutcliffe. No one else."

"Will she say anything to anyone?"

Charlotte hesitated.

She was hiding something.

"Charlotte, it's important. There is no doubt a great number of people are searching for these. You must tell me."

She clasped her hands in front of her. "Sutcliffe and Mr. Timmons have grown quite close. I encountered them yesterday in an embrace, and I fear their relationship is quite advanced. If she trusts him, she might tell him."

Anthony exhaled and pressed his lips together. At one time he would have trusted Timmons completely, but everything was shifting.

She fixed her hazel eyes on him. "What should I do?"

Charlotte Grey always had her mind fixed, firm, and resolute, and was seldom influenced. This was a side of her he'd rarely seen. For the first time since their reunion a fortnight prior, she looked small. Even frightened.

His arms ached to reach out to her—to reassure her in a way words could not. He stepped toward her, with the hope that she might follow suit and close the space between them, but she remained steadfast. He desired to draw her close, to feel the warmth of her body against his own after years of her absence. But he knew the truth: She would never be able to give her heart to him again—not when her heart was rightfully focused on her son and she was endeavoring to free herself from the briars of the Prior family. Just because he yearned for her did not mean this was the right time for such declarations. What mattered now was solving the task at hand.

He did not take her into his embrace, but he did place a reassuring hand on her upper arm. "Let's consider the facts. You have the King's Prize, and besides Sutcliffe, we are the only ones who are aware of its location. We also know that Roland Prior had amassed a great deal of debt, and the people he owed are searching for the emeralds."

She nodded. "It makes sense to notify Mr. Walstead, and I know you trust him, but I know the Priors too well. Something *feels* awry. Silas is a proud, determined man and would do absolutely anything for the sake of the Prior name. If he thought for a moment that I knew anything about the King's Prize, he would be pounding on my door demanding answers, not sending someone else to do it, especially if the health of Roland's estate depended on it. And I think that Mr. Broadstreet fellow used to work for Roland. I don't trust him. I don't trust any of them."

"But you trust me. Don't you? I know this world, Charlotte. I will help you connect the pieces."

She looked to the window. Moisture glistened in her eyes. On her dark lashes.

He'd rarely seen Charlotte cry, and the sight ripped at him. He could not turn away from her. In that moment he knew he was committed—not to Walstead. Not to the assignment. He was committed to *her*.

The lines of propriety that governed their interactions were blurring and changing again.

He inched toward her.

She peered up at him with the same bewitching expression that had had the ability to stop him in his tracks for as long as he could remember.

He took another step. His gaze fell to the fullness of her parted lips. The smoothness of her porcelain skin.

He would not push her, but neither would he hold her at arm's length. Not if she needed him.

After several silent seconds she swayed toward him, and the intoxicating scent of lavender met him first. How easily he could get lost in the memories it evoked. But he wanted to be here. Now.

Not once since leaving her at Even Tor did he dare to dream he would be back in this place with her. And the fact that she trusted him . . .

He reached out to set his hand on her shoulder, and she melted against him.

The sense of freedom and home overwhelmed him as he wrapped his arms around her. For the first time in years, it seemed as if he was right at the place he was supposed to be.

He stroked the glossy locks of her hair as they stood alone in the morning stillness and then let his hand fall to the small of her back. When she let her head rest fully against his chest, he rested his chin atop it, just as he used to. He could feel her breath and her warmth, but he could also feel her tension and fear.

"I will not leave you to face this by yourself," he whispered. "Do you believe me?"

They stood there in silence for several ethereal moments until she nodded and stepped back.

In that single moment, she was aligning herself with him.

His pulse raced with the significance of what was happening between them. And his heart was soaring.

Chapter 33

CONFLICT RAGED WITHIN Anthony.

Never had he felt so vivacious and alive. The very thought that Charlotte might be a part of his life set his soul ablaze.

Yet a thread of uneasiness coiled.

He'd pledged obedience to Mr. Walstead's instructions. He was a man hired to do an assignment—to keep Henry and Charlotte safe, whatever the cost. He was fulfilling that obligation, but now the priorities were shifting. In order to continue to keep them safe, the King's Prize must be dealt with.

Anthony found Timmons in the stables between shifts. This budding relationship between his friend and the lady's maid would likely amount to nothing, but if Timmons did indeed know about the King's Prize, then Anthony would have to factor that in to his plans moving forward.

"We need to talk about Miss Sutcliffe," Anthony announced bluntly as he stepped into the privacy of the stone structure.

"Miss Sutcliffe?" scoffed Timmons dryly, looking up from the horse he was brushing. He slowed his action and leaned with his elbow on the horse's back. "Ah, so your sweetheart's tattlin' on me, is she?"

"Don't be ridiculous. I'm concerned, that's all."

"Ah, I forgot. You're in charge." Timmons resumed the task and dragged the brush over the animal's flank. "I must remember t' mind me manners. Funny how ye never really cared about what I did or didn't do before."

Anthony's patience with Timmons's cavalier attitude was growing thin. "I don't know what is bothering you lately, and honestly, it's not my business. Just don't do anything reckless."

"I could tell ye the same thing," Timmons jeered. "Doesn't really matter what t' outcome is, does it? Whether we keep 'er safe or don't keep 'er safe. Whether Walstead finds the King's Prize or doesn't find the King's Prize."

Anthony's ears pricked at the reference to the emeralds. "That ambivalence sounds odd coming from you. You said yourself you wanted this Prior job."

"Bah. Walstead's bringin' in other men, and 'e's got men workin' on it in Leeds. We are t' nannies now, watching over t' babies while others do t' real work."

Determined to stay on task, Anthony veered the conversation back to the jewels. "Ever heard of the King's Prize before this?"

Timmons stepped around the animal to brush its other side. "Never. You?"

Anthony shook his head. "No. Have the other men said anything to you about it?"

"Not much more'n Walstead told ye."

The cool indifference in Timmons's tone was concerning. "What do you think of Ames and Broadstreet?"

"Worked t' Swendel Bay transport job with Broadstreet. Why?"

"Curious. Is he a good sort?"

Timmons shrugged. "As good as any of the rest of us, I suppose. Keeps to 'imself. Nerves of steel."

"And Ames?"

"Never met 'im. Must be on Walstead's bad side if 'e stuck 'im out 'ere with us."

After leaving Timmons, the tense conversation stayed with Anthony. Nothing about it sat well with him, but even so, he was fairly certain Timmons did not know the whereabouts of the King's Prize. But at the moment, he had another pressing matter to consider: two other watchmen were on the property—neither of whom Anthony knew.

That needed to change.

Anthony found Ames as he was patrolling the back garden and jogged to catch up with him in the day's fading light. After Anthony called his name, the shorter, stockier man turned.

"Haven't had a chance to introduce myself," Anthony said as he approached the other watchman. "Walstead said this is your first assignment for him."

"That's right," Ames responded, his voice low and raspy. "Never expected to be stuck out in the country, though."

"This is an unusual assignment. I'll give you that." Anthony fell into step with him as he walked toward the back garden.

"How'd you go about getting on with Walstead? Last I heard he wasn't taking on new men."

"I was a thief-taker in London, with Thomas Smith. He recommended me to Walstead."

Anthony knew the name. "Why'd you leave London for Leeds?"

"I was part of an undercover assignment, and my identity was revealed. Doesn't scare me none, but it put the men I work with in danger. So I left London, and Walstead took me on. How about you? How long you been with Walstead?"

"Almost three years." Anthony shifted his efforts to finding out what Ames knew about this case. "Walstead said that the hunt is on for these emeralds."

Ames snorted. "Awful lot of fuss for some jewels that may or may not even be in the country. But the mill workers feel they're owed something, and you know what lengths folks'll go to when they feel like their backs are against the wall."

"Are there any leads to their location?"

Ames shook his head. "Some say Roland Prior hid them in Wolden House. Some say they've already been sold. Some say he gave them to his wife; others say he gave them to his mistress. There's no telling with a man like Roland Prior. But Mr. Walstead and Mr. Prior have a team of men searching for them 'round the clock."

Suspicion that Ames knew more than he was letting on flared. After all, Charlotte said she thought someone had been in her chamber. He tried to gauge the man's intent. "And you? Do you suspect Mrs. Prior has them here?"

Ames shrugged a bulky shoulder. "Suppose anything's possible."

Anthony did not want to say anything else on the matter, not until he'd had a chance to talk with Broadstreet and gauge what he knew about the situation. Regardless of what he would learn, however, Anthony was on alert. Never had he been on a case when he did not trust the watchmen he worked with, and that lack of trust was dangerous—for everyone involved.

Chapter 34

THE SOUND OF the wind gusting against her east window and the wooden rafters creaking overhead pulled Charlotte from her erratic sleep the next morning. A gentle roll of autumn thunder echoed in the distance, and a steady rain pattered the panes.

As soon as her senses were fully about her, she reached under her pillow and then, after confirming the King's Prize was still there, she let her head fall back against the pillow in relief.

She had known all along that it would be difficult to make a new life here in Hollythorne House, but the tides had turned in unexpected ways. Her thoughts drifted to Anthony, as they had so frequently as of late. In an environment where it seemed no one could be trusted, his sincerity and familiarity shone as a beacon.

She'd expected him to be understanding, to be helpful. But she had not expected to be drawn into his arms, nor the flame to be reignited in her in such a way. She had not even realized how much she longed for his touch, how much she missed the strength of his arms, until he offered it. Now it captivated her and opened her thoughts up to what the future could look like.

But as lovely as the thought was, she must continue to

diligently guard her heart—as diligently as she strove for freedom. After all, Anthony had promised to help her and not to leave her to face this alone. But he made no promises beyond that—just like he made no promises four years prior.

She propped herself up on her elbows and blinked in the darkness, allowing a few moments for her eyes to fully adjust, and she realized something was missing.

Normally, Rebecca would have a fire roaring by the time Charlotte awoke, but the silver strip of dawn outside her window confirmed the usual hour for the activity had passed, and all that was left from the previous night's flame was a faint orange glow.

She shivered in the morning stillness, and she moved to the fire and picked up the poker, intending to stoke it to see if she could revive any flame. As she reached for the iron utensil, it slipped from her fingers and clattered to the floor.

She whipped her head up, fully expecting the sound to wake Henry.

But it did not.

She frowned.

The baby was not a sound sleeper. Normally such a sound would send him wailing.

She returned the poker to the stand and approached the cradle, the floor creaking beneath her with each step.

The sight found therein froze her blood.

It was empty.

Frantic, she plucked the blanket away.

Nothing.

She fell to her knees to peer under her bed.

She called his name.

But Henry was nowhere to be found.

Rational excuses bombarded her. Perhaps Sutcliffe took him to the kitchen to let her sleep longer. Perhaps Rebecca woke early and decided to feed him.

And then as she yanked yet another blanket free from the cradle, a piece of paper fluttered toward the floor.

She snatched the missive before it even hit the ground.

It was as if she no longer had control of her own movements. Like a puppet, fear controlled her every movement, causing her fingers to tremble and her breath to shudder.

No part of her body would work fast enough as she popped the wax seal and squinted to see in the dark.

Bring the jewels to the cottage at the foot of Thoms Tor tonight at dusk. Come alone. Or else.

That was all.

Her mind mapped the facts: the note was demanding an exchange.

An exchange for her baby.

———————

The sound of his name, cried by a distant feminine voice, yanked Anthony from a light slumber.

Then another call of his name, followed by the pounding of approaching footsteps outside his door, catapulted him from the bed. Out of instinct he reached for his weapon but stopped mid-action when the bedchamber door flew open.

Charlotte, clad is a dressing gown, hair wild and loose, complexion ghostly pale, eyes wide, cried, "Henry's gone!"

Anthony winced. "What?"

She raced in, on open letter extended in her trembling hand.

He took it. Read it.

"We must go there. Now," she demanded, her every movement hectic and frantic. She reached for his coat, which was slung over the chair, and thrust it toward him.

"Wait, slow down." He shifted his feet and reread the letter, blinking to make sure he was fully comprehending the words before him. "Where did this come from?"

"It was in Henry's cradle, and he's gone. We must go now. Every moment, every minute, is—"

"You must stay calm."

"Stay calm! How can you say such a thing? He could be hurt! He could be scared, he could be—"

He stepped closer and put his hands on her shoulders, guiding her attention back to him. "We'll find him, but we must keep our wits about us."

She jerked his hand away, and her tone sharpened. "We're wasting time. Quickly, I—"

"*Charlotte.*" This time, his more forceful inflection silenced her.

She blinked, and a tear dropped from her dark lashes. And then another trailed down her pallid cheek. "I can't lose him, Anthony. Please. I can't."

The sense of failure rushed him as his mind raced to connect the few facts he knew.

How could this have happened?

A guard had been by the bedchamber door all night. Another guard walked the perimeter. He himself had been awake until just before dawn, patrolling the road in front of the house. A mental list of every precaution they'd taken formed—all of which should have prevented this.

But here, just inches before him, Charlotte stood trembling. Her chin quivered. Her hands shook.

The pleading and fear in her eyes lit a fire in his chest. He wanted—needed—to fix everything in that moment. He wanted to stop her tears. He wanted to run to get Henry. He would find whoever was responsible for this madness to bring them to justice.

Then another tear slid down her face. Panic radiated from her, hot and fiery, and he could think of nothing other than alleviating her pain.

So he folded her into his embrace.

At first she pushed against his chest in adamant resistance.

He held her more closely.

Anxiety tightened her every muscle, making her stiff and rigid.

But he did not let go. He whispered, steady and low, "I swear to you, we will get him. But you must stay calm. *We* must be smart and rational."

A sob shook her body, and then the tension in her released, and she melted against him. He tightened his arms around her as she wept against his chest, as if by doing so he could shield her from the terror he knew seized her.

When she eventually pushed away from him, she wiped her eyes impatiently with the backs of her forefingers, shook her head, and drew a deep breath, as if to dislodge fear and replace it with determination. "What now?"

"Who else knows of this note?"

"No one. I came straight to find you."

He snatched his coat that she'd attempted to give him a few moments earlier, pushed his arm through the sleeve, and reached for his boots. "Gather the house servants, and I'll find the watchmen. Then we'll meet in the kitchen and figure out a plan."

Chapter 35

AS CHARLOTTE RACED from Anthony's chamber to the room where Sutcliffe slept, his call for calmness echoed. He was right, of course. Now more than ever she needed to keep her wits about her and pay close attention. A clue could be found anywhere, and there was no margin for error.

Even as she instructed her mind to be still, her heart was screaming, and within her, anger raged.

Anger at the criminal who abducted her baby.

Anger at Roland for his selfish recklessness and his disregard for the safety and well-being of those who depended on him.

Anger at herself. What sort of mother would sleep through someone kidnapping her child?

Anger at the watchmen. How did yet another person come onto the property and invade her very chamber, no less?

Every decision she had made since Roland's death had been for Henry's safety and security, including her decision to allow Mr. Walstead's men to escort them to Hollythorne House. Clearly, she had made a grievous mistake.

She reached Sutcliffe's small attic chamber and flung open

the door. She hurried to the bed and shook her maid's shoulders. "Sutcliffe! Sutcliffe, wake up. Wake up!"

Sutcliffe rolled over, her gray eyes sleepy and her golden hair wild beneath a linen sleeping cap. "What is it?"

"Someone has taken Henry. He's gone! You must get up."

Sutcliffe bolted upright in bed. "What?"

"Someone abducted him while I was sleeping." She pulled the blankets away so Sutcliffe could move quickly.

"Are you sure it wasn't Rebecca? You know how she takes him down to the kitchen when he can't sleep."

"No, there was a letter. Remember those emeralds we found in my case? That is what whoever took Henry wants. Mr. Walstead said they were valuable. Something called the King's Prize."

Charlotte's frustration grew as Sutcliffe's pace did not increase. Charlotte reached for Sutcliffe's dressing gown, hanging on a hook next to the chamber's only window. "Why are you moving so slowly?"

Sutcliffe shook her head and pulled off her sleeping cap, her face twisted in odd confusion, as if attempting to comprehend what she was hearing, and reached to accept the wool dressing gown. "I didn't think the emeralds were significant."

Ice trickled through Charlotte's veins. Sutcliffe was notoriously bad at lying, and her current expression and uncharacteristically timid movements spoke volumes. "Did you tell anyone about the emeralds? About where we hid them?"

Sutcliffe pushed her hair from her face and hesitated.

"Did you?" Charlotte demanded, her patience growing thin.

"Only Mr. Timmons. But I did not tell him where they were! I only said we found some emeralds, that's all."

Charlotte felt as if she would be sick.

"But it was not him, surely!" The maid scurried from the bed, suddenly animated. "He would never do such a thing. He only asked me about the jewelry I was selling in Leeds, and the emeralds came up in conversation. Honestly, I did not know they were important!"

Indignation, fueled by shock, flared red hot. "How dare you discuss my personal concerns with anyone! And you think after a couple of weeks that you know Mr. Timmons's character so well to believe him completely incapable of a devious act?"

Tears pooled in Sutcliffe's eyes. "I-I . . ."

Charlotte refused to give in to tears again and she would not abide it in anyone else, not when there was much to do. "Hurry and dress. Mr. Welbourne wants us to assemble in the kitchen so we can decide our next course of action."

Charlotte left Sutcliffe in her chamber and made her way down to the kitchen. She felt as if the floor were going to shift beneath her, or as if she would awaken at any moment to find this experience naught but a nightmare. And yet she'd witnessed so many difficult situations she never could have possibly dreamed she would encounter—each one more incredulous and terrifying than the last.

This had to end—life would surely have to right itself soon. She *would* get Henry back. They *would* have a good life. And she *would* protect him.

Anthony raced out into the dawn and scrambled to put the pieces together. Broadstreet should have been at the main staircase.

He was not.

Timmons and Ames should be on the grounds. But neither could be seen from the mist-laden courtyard.

Anthony blinked away the rain as he jogged toward the front stables, hoping the presence of the horses would give him a clue as to who was where.

Anthony rarely surrendered to panic, but something about this was decidedly askew. This should not have happened. Enough watchmen were on duty that all should have been secure. Nausea gripped his stomach as another thought assailed him: one of the watchmen must be involved.

He pulled open the stable door, and the horses in the stalls turned their heads at the early intrusion, but Timmons's, Ames's, and Broadstreet's horses were gone. He groaned in disbelief and turned to leave when a muffled sound mewled and stopped him.

He grabbed the pitchfork by the door and inched toward the muted noise resonating from one of the back stalls.

Anthony stood completely still and listened. "Who's there?"

The sound, which now was clearly a stifled voice, echoed again.

The straw beneath his feet crunched as he stepped farther in and looked into the stall in question. There was Ames. A thick rope secured his feet and hands. A rag was tied around his mouth.

Anthony dropped the pitchfork and rushed to remove the rag from his face. "You hurt?"

Ames shook the rag away and drew a deep breath. "Just my pride."

"What happened?" Anthony's fingers felt thick and clumsy against the adeptly secured rope as he endeavored to release it.

"Not sure." Ames glanced over his thick shoulder to watch Anthony untie it. "I was patrolling this courtyard and I heard footsteps. Before I knew it something hit me across the face and then again on the back of the head. Next thing I know, I'm here, tied up. My pistol's gone, I think, and I don't see my horse."

Anthony loosened the rope, and Ames struggled to his feet. Sure enough, a deep-purple bruise circled his left eye and cheek.

"The baby's been kidnapped," Anthony said in a rush once Ames's hands were free. "He's gone, and a note has been left."

"What? I thought Broadstreet was standing guard at the stairs."

"Well, he's not, and I can't find him anywhere," Anthony snipped as he handed his colleague the note.

Ames's mouth set in a firm frown as he read the letter. "Did anyone see anything?"

Anthony shook his head. "No. I've asked Mrs. Prior to round up the servants. We're to meet them in the kitchen."

Ames brushed more hay from his sleeve. "Where's Timmons?"

Anthony found it difficult to answer.

"Timmons *is* here, is he not?" repeated Ames.

The words were gritty as they passed Anthony's lips. "I've not seen him all morning."

Ames spewed a slew of curses, echoing Anthony's sentiments.

But not all his sentiments.

For not only was he shocked, but he was also hurt.

Timmons had been his closest friend except for Charlotte. Anthony had known Timmons was having a difficult time with recent events, but now the exact picture of Timmons's frustration became clear, and it seemed like he had gone down a far darker path than Anthony would have ever expected.

"It's the King's Prize they're after. Right?"

Anthony drew a sharp breath. He still did not know Ames well, but at the moment, he had to trust someone, and based on the fact that Ames had been bound and gagged, he clearly was not involved in the kidnapping. "I'd say so."

"And have you found out for certain? Does Mrs. Prior have them?"

It was a reasonable question. Anthony was willing to work with him, but at the moment he was not willing to divulge Charlotte's secret. Not yet.

Anthony shrugged. "Let's go talk to them and see what we can discover."

The two men fell into step as they wordlessly crossed the back courtyard and headed toward the kitchen. Anthony's heart wanted to think that perhaps Timmons had ridden off in search of the child and would save the day. But his gut—the instincts he had conditioned himself to trust—told him something completely different.

Chapter 36

CHARLOTTE, WITH HER shawl pulled taut around her shoulders and torso, paced the kitchen as the early morning light found its way in the east-facing windows. She'd gathered Sutcliffe and Mr. and Mrs. Hargrave, and now they waited with her. But one servant was noticeably absent: Rebecca.

Charlotte's lips trembled. Her hands shook. And fire shot through her veins.

A state of shock had taken hold—one far more severe than when she had discovered Roland dead.

Sutcliffe was seated next to the fire, unmoving, unblinking. Her fair hair hung loose about her shoulders and her dressing gown hung askant on her frame. She was silent; she only stared into the hearth's leaping flames. The housekeeper and manservant bustled about, making tea and moving chairs around, as if by keeping their hands busy and going about their normal tasks they could ease the discomfort of all those gathered.

Impatient for Anthony and the rest of the watchmen to arrive, Charlotte stepped to the window and looked out at the courtyard. The weather was shifting. Gone was the rain that had awoken her with its gentle sounds, and now a thick Yorkshire mist had taken hold. Her stomach clenched tighter. Weather like this would make any sort of travel or search even more difficult.

Anthony and Mr. Ames emerged from the fog, their stony faces and stiff gaits exuding frustration. As they drew close, bruising became apparent on Mr. Ames's face, and one side of his coat and trousers was covered in dry mud, as if he'd taken a tumble.

Sutcliffe joined her at the window. Both were silent, for no one needed to speak the obvious. Three people were glaringly absent. Those three people each had been entrusted with Henry's safekeeping and had access to him.

It was no wonder she did not hear Henry in the middle of the night. He would not have cried if Rebecca lifted him from his slumber. He knew her. Trusted her. And that fact sickened Charlotte all the more.

Anthony and Mr. Ames entered the kitchen and removed their greatcoats. For several moments no one spoke, as if they were frozen in fear over what had transpired. The reality had settled over all of them like a cloak, dark and suffocating.

When Anthony did speak, his voice sounded gritty. Annoyed. Impatient. "The baby is gone. So are Rebecca, Timmons, and Broadstreet. When was the last time anyone heard or saw them?"

Anthony folded his arms over his chest and assessed the gathered crew.

Every muscle of Charlotte's jaw appeared tense.

Sutcliffe's face flushed blotchy and crimson, and her eyelids were puffy from crying.

The housekeeper and manservant slowed their tasks, eyes wide, quietly observing.

Someone *knew* something. Someone *heard* something. He fixed his gaze on Tom Hargrave. "When was the last time you saw any of them?"

The manservant shrugged a scrawny shoulder. "Last I saw 'em was last night when we was beddin' down the 'orses for the night. Mr. Timmons and Mr. Ames took their 'orses out. Isn't that right, Mr. Ames?"

Next to him, Ames nodded. "That's right."

"I ne'er 'elp with the midnight change of 'orses," continued Tom. "I was asleep after that."

Anthony shifted his attention to Mrs. Hargrave, who was anxiously knitting the edge of her apron with her work-worn fingers. She blurted out, "Same as Tom. Saw 'em for their meal last night, and that was t' last I saw of 'em. I was asleep all night. Didn't 'ear a thing."

Anthony weighed their statements. His gut told him they were telling the truth. "Ames, take these two and go through the house and see if you can find any clues."

No one argued, and soon he was left alone in the kitchen with Charlotte and a flushed Miss Sutcliffe. The light from the freshly built fire reflected the lady's maid's tearstained face, and she averted her eyes from him. He knew about her relationship with Timmons, and based on her reaction to what was happening, he could only assume that he'd not been the only person with whom Timmons was not truthful.

"Miss Sutcliffe, it is very important that you are honest. Henry's safety is at stake. Do you understand?"

She nodded, glanced warily toward Charlotte, and pushed the handkerchief against her nose with a sniff.

"You were aware of the emeralds in Mrs. Prior's case?"

"Yes," she whimpered, "I saw them."

"Are you aware of the significance of them?"

"I was not until this morning."

"Did you tell anyone about them?"

She sniffed again. "Just Mr. Timmons. We spoke about them last night. Honestly, if I had any idea of their significance, I never would have said a word."

Anthony could feel Charlotte's eyes on him—and her frustration. He dare not meet her gaze. He focused on Miss Sutcliffe. "How did it come up in conversation?"

Miss Sutcliffe gripped her finger in her lap, and her knuckles turned white. "Mr. Timmons asked me when I'd be returning to Leeds to sell more jewels. He said he enjoyed our errand to Leeds and wondered whether we could repeat our journey. One topic in the conversation led to the other, and he asked why I was selling them. He told me he knew of a jeweler in London he could introduce me to and inquired after what sort of jewelry Mrs. Prior would like to part with. It seems so odd to say it aloud now, but it really did just come up naturally during conversation."

Anthony was not surprised. Timmons knew how to get information out of a criminal, let alone an unsuspecting lady's maid. He flicked his gaze to Charlotte to gauge her reaction. Color replaced the pallor on her cheeks, and her teeth were clamped tight over her lower lip. She said nothing but jumped from the settee and whirled to the window.

Miss Sutcliffe followed Charlotte's retreating form. "I am sorry, Mrs. Prior. I knew better than to discuss your personal matters with anyone. I don't want Jonathan to get in trouble. He's a good man. I really believe that. He would never—"

Charlotte spun around. "He was using you, Sutcliffe. Do you not see that? We've all been made to look the fools, and now Henry is the one who will suffer."

Miss Sutcliffe burst into fresh tears, and fearing the emotions could get out of hand, Anthony interrupted her. "Did he tell you anything else? Any clues to his future plans? Anything of the sort?"

She inhaled sharply and shook her head. "He only said that as soon as he was done with this assignment, we would leave and begin a life together. But you are right, Mrs. Prior. He was using me. I see that now."

Anthony softened his tone toward Miss Sutcliffe. "If it is true that Mr. Timmons lied to get information from you, then it is he who is to blame. Not you. You may go now."

Neither Anthony nor Charlotte moved until the kitchen door latched shut behind Miss Sutcliffe. Charlotte let her breath out in a huff. "Unbelievable."

"Let's not place blame on the wrong person." Anthony joined her at the window. "Timmons knows how to solicit information."

She folded her arms over her waist and stared into the morning stillness. "I thought you said Mr. Timmons was trustworthy."

He couldn't miss the accusation in Charlotte's words. "I did say that. And I meant it. I'm as taken aback by this turn of events as Miss Sutcliffe."

Nothing about what had transpired made sense. Anthony had learned about the King's Prize only the day before, and yet Timmons had been playing a part with Miss Sutcliffe almost since their arrival. Perhaps his initial interest in the maid had been sincere. Or perhaps he had started this scheme much earlier. But why? And how did he know about the emeralds when Anthony had never heard of them?

Charlotte tightened the shawl around her shoulders. "We must go to the cottage by Thoms Tor. I see no reason to delay, do you? I have the jewels, and now, because of Timmons, anyone may know that we have them. We will just go—"

Alarm assailed him. "We cannot just go there, Charlotte, King's Prize in hand. 'Tis far too dangerous. We must inform Mr. Walstead. He'll provide the reinforcements and the legal permission for such a mission. There's no telling how many others are involved in this. It is far too dangerous at this point."

She scoffed. "What does my safety mean to me? I am *nothing* without Henry."

She was speaking from her pain, but he also knew he was challenging her stubborn streak. He'd not be the first to look away. "Charlotte, I—"

"Besides, how could I possibly trust Mr. Walstead or his watchmen now? When one woos my maid, kidnaps my son, and beats his partner? And you? Can you even be trusted?" she hurled as the pitch of her tone rose. "I'm going to the magistrate. I will find him first, and he can accompany me . . ."

He reached out to touch her, and she reeled back. "Do not touch me."

He pulled back, lifted his hands as if declaring innocence, and kept his voice low. "I'm on your side. Yes, we should go to the local magistrate. But I should also send word to Walstead immediately. He will have men out here in a few hours. This operation will have the numbers and manpower to—"

"Absolutely not. The letter says to come alone, and I refuse to take any chances."

"But, Charlotte, consider this: If Timmons or Broadstreet wrote that letter, or even if they were complicit in any capacity, they'll be prepared for a team of watchmen to come to the rescue. If you go alone, it could put you in even more danger. We must think with our heads, not our hearts."

"My heart?" She winced as if he'd struck her. "You don't know my heart. What do you know of who I am or who I have become? I've told you before, I'm not the same person you remember. Do not speak as if you know me or as if you understand me."

If the words were spoken in any other context, they might have stung. But she was scared and going on the offensive. He recognized the wildness in her eyes—she was frightened, with nothing to lose. How could he protect her if she was unwilling to protect herself? If she was willing to be impulsive and impatient?

"Charlotte, I'm fighting with you for Henry. I want him back here too. I swear to you I will get Henry back in your arms."

Chapter 37

AFTER LEAVING ANTHONY in the kitchen, Charlotte hurried up the parlor stairs to her chamber.

How could he not see what needed to be done? Why was he being so passive?

That frustration, combined with the pain from Sutcliffe's betrayal, cut her deeply. Sutcliffe's remorse did seem genuine, but it would not bring Henry home.

Once in her chamber Charlotte quickly changed to a heavy wool petticoat and gown of charcoal wool. She secured her hair at the nape of her neck and grabbed her heaviest cloak.

She paused at the sight of the empty cradle and, for but a moment, permitted tears to fill her eyes. How had her life come to this? At each turn she believed that nothing worse could happen— that she had experienced all the pain one person could withstand.

She retrieved the King's Prize from the pocket of her apron and dumped them on the bed.

Seven stones of varying refinement. Size. Shades. Shape. Something about these gems made them so valuable that men were willing to steal, lie, and perhaps even kill for. Like it or not, she'd been unwittingly ensnared in this corrupt plot, and yet she could not overlook her own missteps. She had trusted the wrong people. Made the wrong decisions. And while she would be able to forgive the others for their shortcomings, she could not forgive herself.

She gazed at the empty bed where Henry had been sleeping. She would not fail him. Anthony might be content to wait. She was not.

She quickly donned her sturdiest pair of boots, then tied the pouch of emeralds to a pocket in a slit in her gown.

She would not wait for Anthony. She would not wait for anyone.

Anthony's fingers flew as he penned a letter to Mr. Walstead, refusing to give voice to the doubts running rampant in his mind.

How did this happen right underneath him? He had to have missed a sign somehow. Somewhere. He'd failed Charlotte, plain and simple, and for that he would never forgive himself. He would also never forgive Timmons for the betrayal.

But he could not linger on the emotion incited by either fact. After all, he'd been trained to deal with such illicit events. He'd carefully assessed the facts at hand, and his intended plan of action was prudent. Writing this letter was one of the first steps, and with every word he wrote he checked it, making sure he was acting professionally and not as a man in love. He was, after all, still tasked with keeping them safe.

Mr. Walstead,

The Prior baby was abducted during the night, and a ransom note has been discovered. Timmons, Broadstreet, and Rebecca have abandoned their posts, and I suspect their involvement. They are demanding the King's Prize in exchange for the boy. We have discovered the emeralds, but we need more men before approaching the exchange site. Send at least five men and horses. I will contact the local magistrate. This situation is dire. We must act without delay.

He finished the letter, sealed it, and left his chamber to find Ames in the front courtyard. The watchman was ready with his horse and was clad in his high-collared coat, with tall top boots and a leather satchel hanging from the saddle.

"I've just finished the perimeter check," Ames shared, his tone somber. "Fresh hoofprints, from three horses, lead out the garden gate to the moor, due west."

Anthony's gaze lifted toward the indicated direction. *Thoms Tor.*

"Is the letter ready?" Ames pulled Anthony's attention back.

Anthony extended it to him, and Ames accepted the missive in his gloved hand and tucked it in his coat.

"I'm going to the village to find the magistrate," explained Anthony. "It will take you several hours, no doubt, before you return, but we will meet here and proceed together. I'll ride out to the site to stake it out and see what we're up against."

After seeing Ames off to Leeds, Anthony needed to get to the village. He had no idea who the magistrate even was, but he did know that many local magistrates refused to involve themselves in affairs outside of their own jurisdictions, especially ones of this magnitude. Some magistrates would be eager to put their names on a case like this, and others endeavored to keep city business as far from their villages as possible. But one thing was certain: If Mr. Walstead and his men did not arrive in a timely manner, the local magistrate would be imperative.

He gathered his caped greatcoat and hat, but he had to speak with Charlotte before leaving. She'd been angry, and rightfully so, but he didn't want to depart without checking on her one last time. He climbed the narrow parlor staircase and ducked under a low beam toward her chamber and, once there, knocked on the closed door.

No response.

He knocked again. "Mrs. Prior?"

When no response came the second time, he turned the door handle and pushed it open.

An empty chamber met him.

She was nowhere in sight.

In that moment he knew—she'd gone on her own.

She could be halfway to Thoms Tor by now.

Scenarios rushed him. Did she have a weapon to protect herself? If she did, did she know how to use it? He needed to stop her before another tragedy ensued.

Pulse racing, he spun from the room and sprinted from the house. She'd likely gone on foot, so he ran to the stables for his horse. His task was simple. He'd simply have to get there first.

———

Charlotte's father had always warned her that her temper and impulsiveness would get her in trouble.

She'd spent the bulk of her adolescence fighting her impetuous tendencies, and she'd thought that her marriage, and the strict rules and restrictions Roland had imposed, nullified such inclinations.

But now, as she hurried along the overgrown path that cut through Blight Moor, she realized that was not the case.

For she *was* impulsive. And she did have a temper. They were as much a part of her character as anything else.

Her gaze fell to the moorland grasses at her feet, and a memory flared bright.

When she was eight years of age, she'd found an injured tawny owl on the moor. She'd brought it back to Hollythorne House and made it a box in the stable, fully intent on nursing it back to health. When her father learned of her actions, he'd insisted that she return it to where she found it, claiming it would die away from its natural surroundings, and explained that nature abided by different laws. Yet she did not heed his warning. Ultimately, the bird perished. She'd cried and bitterly regretted her actions, but regardless of her remorsefulness, the bird would never live again.

Her intentions had been prudent, but they'd not been appropriate.

She had never been good at accepting that some things were simply beyond her control. Roland's severity almost squelched that part of her, but with her newfound freedom, it came roaring back, breathing life into those aspects of her character.

Anthony's methodical mannerisms reminded her of her

father's. Steady. Strong. Both men possessed a healthy respect for the laws of nature and humankind. They understood the parameters and worked within them—something she'd never been able to master.

She lifted her skirt to step over a stone.

Was she making the same mistake now?

What could she really do, on her own, to rectify the situation? Just knock on the door and offer the emeralds? Would they give her Henry and let her be on her way? Anthony had tried to explain the order of things. He'd evidently mastered the art of patience, whereas she never had.

Yet the thought of simply waiting for something else to happen sickened her. What if they waited too long? What if they were too late? How could they possibly be idle, waiting for other people to come and help them?

A sharp gust swept in, bringing with it a fresh bout of rain. She'd be soaked through soon if she continued.

But what if her actions made matters worse? What if she knocked on the door and a man took her captive as well? She hated the fact that her impulsive thoughts could endanger Henry further.

She took one step. And then another.

From where she now stood she could see the stony top of Thoms Tor in the distance, and the cottage would be just beyond it, in a small clearing that dipped down to a valley. She was not as familiar with this stretch of Blight Moor. It was much closer to the village of Lamby on the far side, much closer to where Anthony grew up.

This was his area of familiarity. Not hers. His area of expertise. Not hers.

As she took another step, she realized—it would not be wise to continue on her own.

It did not matter how much she wanted it.

It didn't matter what she was willing to risk or how hard she was willing to work.

Just like with the bird, she did not have the knowledge and expertise necessary.

Before, the scenario had ended in tragedy. And now the stakes were too high.

She stopped in her tracks and pressed her hands against her forehead as thoughts bombarded her.

Everything within her screamed to forge ahead.

Yet she and her small blade would be no match for a large man with a pistol. And where would that leave Henry?

She squeezed her eyes shut and turned into the wind, allowing the earth-scented air to wash over her face. Her neck. Her hands.

Anthony was right.

This was an instance where one needed to think with one's head and not one's heart.

Chapter 38

ANTHONY ADJUSTED HIS pistol at his waist, tucked an extra pistol in his satchel, hid his blade in the calf of his Wellington boot, and pulled his wide-brimmed hat low over his eyes.

Charlotte could not have gone very far on foot, and he knew exactly where she was headed. He would overtake her, surely.

He guided the horse from the courtyard and out the gate in the direction of Thoms Tor, where he allowed his horse to break free into a canter. Bits of rain pelted his face as he and his horse flew over the grassland and faded heather. A glance up at the sky confirmed that the rain was not likely to end anytime soon. He urged his horse to move faster, all the while scanning the landscape, looking for any sign of her.

He found her quickly, not far outside of Hollythorne's property. He pulled his horse to a halt and sighed in relief. She was not walking as he'd expected but standing completely still with her back to him, looking out over the broad Blight Moor, with the wind tugging at her cloak and streaming her hair about her. Relief that he'd not found her in a perilous situation prevailed, and he dismounted and led his horse to her.

Neither spoke when he stopped next to her. When she finally turned to him, her face was raised and her eyes direct. "You were right, Anthony. I should have listened, I . . ." Her words fell silent.

But he needed no apology or affirmation. Relief flooded him, and he pulled her close. And this time she did not resist. She melded against his chest, and he tightened his embrace. The nearness and transporting sensation of her in his arms sent fire through him.

He *would* protect her. He *would* fix this. For she was what he had been fighting for all these years—the dream behind every hope.

She wrapped her arms around his neck to draw nearer, and she looked up at him—the entrancing hazel of her eyes the same as he remembered. "I'm such a fool. It is that I—"

"No, no. You are not a fool." He brushed her hair away from her brow, allowing his hand to linger as the memories of their previous times together rushed him. "You love your son and want to protect him. And we will."

"I just keep thinking about what could be happening. He could be hurt, Anthony. He could be scared. Hungry. I can't bear it."

He cupped her face with his hand and wiped a tear from her smooth cheek with his thumb and redirected her focus to him. "Timmons or Broadstreet or whoever else has taken him wants the jewels, so Henry is the only power they have. They will not hurt him. For if they do, they'll lose any bargaining tool they have. Their goal is to obtain the jewels, not to hurt a child. It is hard to think in those terms, but you must. It will help you to think practically."

"'Think practically,'" she repeated. "I've never been very good at that, have I?"

"My dearest Charlotte, you are impulsive and wild, emotional, and passionate. And that is why I have loved you from the first day I laid eyes on you on this very moor. And it is why I love you still."

Something intangible shifted in the air; something ignited between them, like lightning striking during a summer storm. In the midst of a tragedy, the irresistible force of hope and desire, devotion and security, drew them closer together. They were not strangers. It was clear now—not even time could fracture the bond that had been forged between them years ago.

She rested her bare hands against the rough fabric covering his chest and fixed her gaze on him in a visceral manner that reopened the floodgates to the past and left no opening for mis-interpretation. "You and I belong here, don't we? We have done our best to leave Blight Moor, and the moor is reclaiming us. And Henry too."

He slid his arms around her waist, pressing close. "I'm afraid we'll never escape it."

"I never want to." She shook her head as she fussed with the button of his coat. "I want Henry to grow up here. To live this life. To be free."

"And he will. He'll grow to love it as we do. But before we go there is one more thing we need to do." He framed her face with his hands, lowered his head, and kissed her lips with all the fervor that four years' separation could muster. She melted to him, evoc-atively. Invitingly. Encouragingly.

This was home. *Charlotte* was home.

The ardor in her return kiss matched his in intensity, and she tightened her arms around his neck once more and trailed her fingers through his hair. He became lost in her intoxicating scent. Her allure. Her beauty.

At length he reluctantly released her, and she touched her fingertips to his face. "I love you, too, Anthony Welbourne. I always have, and I fear I always will."

———————

Charlotte loved him.

The very thought infused Anthony with a renewed sense of determination.

For now, his future was laid out before him in great clarity.

No, she'd made him no promises, but he knew that unmistakable expression in her eyes. He could feel it in the passion of her kiss—in the gentleness of her touch. Circumstances had separated them once before. He would do whatever was necessary to make sure that would never happen again.

But first, a very serious obstacle stood before them.

Charlotte and Anthony stood together in a copse of trees at the moor's edge, looking down in the mist-soaked valley at the thatched cottage at the foot of Thoms Tor. The wind whipped through the bare ash and oak trees and over the dormant heather and scattered leaves, as if spurring them forward. For now, the rain had ceased, and a heavy fog blanketed all. They decided that since they were in such proximity to the small, crumbling stone cottage, Anthony would investigate the site so he'd have information to share with Walstead when he and the men returned with Ames from Leeds.

"There it is." Anthony tied his horse to the tree. "Do you recognize it?"

"I've heard about it, of course"—she lifted her hand to brush her hair out of her eyes—"but I have never been here. It looks empty."

He cast another glance at the stone structure and took his pistol from his waistband. "Stay here with the horse." He paused and squeezed her hand.

"Be careful," she whispered, her brows drawn together.

Anthony pressed a kiss to her lips and left the small cluster of trees, careful to crouch as he moved to be hidden by the moorland grasses, all the while scanning the area.

For as long as he could remember, this cottage had stood empty. According to local folklore, a man name James Thom had once lived in this house. Legend had it he murdered his wife in a jealous rage when he found that she had taken a lover. Now the murdered wife haunted the grounds, and no food would grow on the premises, and no flame would stay lit within the house, keeping it in perpetual darkness. As a result, the house had remained uninhabited for nearly a century, and no one ever stepped foot on the overgrown property.

It was merely a story, and Anthony did not believe in ghosts and curses, but the tale made this location perfect for a hideaway after a heist of this sort. It was out of the way. Unobserved. Avoided.

He crept down through the tall grass and stones a fair distance from the cottage. Charlotte was right—at first glance it did appear empty. No smoke puffed from the chimney, and no light shone from the windows. But as he rounded the cottage, he noticed a small stone shed, and out of it a horse's black tail swooshed. His heart squeezed.

Someone was here.

He glanced back in the direction of where he'd left Charlotte. Feeling confident she was safe and out of sight, he made his way to the shed and approached it from behind. He peered through the wooden planks to see two horses—Timmons's and Ames's.

The sight propelled fresh fire through him, for it confirmed his suspicion.

Despite everything, Timmons's betrayal stung.

Anthony *had* trusted him. He searched his memory for signs that Timmons was involved in something nefarious but could find none.

Perhaps he did not want to find one.

Verifying no one else was present in the area outside the house, Anthony readied his pistol. The back of the stone cottage had but one window. He approached it at an angle to ensure he'd not be detected, and he crouched beneath it for several moments. Despite the cold and rain, beads of perspiration dripped down his temples. He pulled his hat low and took several deep breaths. He had completed assignments like this dozens of times, but the fact that Charlotte's son was possibly inside added a challenging level of complexity.

He inched his way up until he could see through the deep window.

The cottage was a single, narrow room. No fire danced in the fireplace at the room's end. A single bed stood in the dark corner, and a table with two chairs was positioned in the middle. There were two entrances to the cottage—one on the south end and one on the north. He spied Timmons, sitting at the table, cleaning a pistol. He pivoted to see Rebecca sitting near the bed, and it appeared that Henry was sleeping on the bed.

Shock held him captive. He expected more of an armed presence. He had told Charlotte that it was imperative they wait for reinforcements of some sort. But based on what he saw, that would not be necessary.

He'd assumed Broadstreet was involved in this. But he wasn't here.

And an idea formed.

Chapter 39

SECONDS TICKED INTO minutes as Charlotte waited anxiously with the horse for Anthony to return. Her nervous impatience impacted her sense of time, and she had no idea if a quarter of an hour or an hour had passed. She focused her attention on the decrepit structure with steadfast intensity. The fact that her baby might be in there, cold and scared, sent a bolt of fire through her. It took everything she had not to take the emeralds, burst through the door, and demand her baby back.

But she had promised Anthony she would wait for his return, and had she not just learned her lesson? It was not wise to do this alone. What was more, she did not want to do it alone. She trusted Anthony—genuinely trusted him.

When he did finally emerge through the grass and trees, she secured the horse to the tree and rushed to him. "What did you find?"

He drew a deep breath and stepped past her to the horse. "Two horses tied in the back. I was able to creep up to the cottage and peer in one of the back windows."

"And Henry?"

Anthony nodded and pulled another pistol from the satchel. "He's there."

Relief, powerful and enthusiastic, overcame her.

"'Tis only one large room in the cottage, which is helpful for us," he continued. "Timmons and Rebecca are in there. That's it."

She frowned. "No one else?"

"Not that I saw. And I watched for quite a while. Rebecca's sitting near Henry, who appeared to be sleeping, and Timmons was sitting at a table, cleaning his pistol, so at least for the moment it is in pieces and not useable."

Indignation flared at the report that Rebecca was near her son, and fresh determination surged within her. "What do you want to do?"

He held up the pistol and fixed his gaze on her. "Do you know how to use one of these?"

"No. I've never even held one."

"If we are going to do this now, while there are only the two of them, you will need this."

She licked her lips and nodded eagerly. "Of course. I will do whatever is necessary."

He handed it to her.

It was far heavier and colder than she'd imagined.

"We'll leave the horse here and go around to the back of the house. The door will likely be locked, but I saw the latch on another door through the window, and I'm certain I can kick it in. We must take them by surprise; 'twill give us the upper hand. When we get inside, point your pistol at Rebecca, and I'll handle

Timmons. But don't shoot. I will instruct Rebecca to step away from Henry, at which time you will give me your pistol and put Henry on the floor behind you. There is a rope in my satchel. You will then tie her to a chair, and I will cover you. Then you will tie Timmons. Do you think you can do it?"

Doubts swirled. Never had she held a pistol. Never had she tied anyone with a rope. "I-I think so."

"Charlotte, you must *know* you can do it. Otherwise you will fumble. Do you understand?"

She nodded, garnering every bit of confidence she could muster. "Yes, I can do it."

"Once they are both bound and secure, we will return here when Walstead arrives with the others. Keep in mind that Henry will likely scream during the bustle. Do not let that distract you."

He gave her directions on how to use the weapon, and she did her best to retain them. Point the pistol. Tie the rope. Get Henry. He made it all sound so simple and matter-of-fact. He might be used to doing this sort of thing, but it struck fear deep in her core. For one wrong move, one mistake, could spell disaster for them all.

"Give me the King's Prize," he said abruptly, interrupting her thoughts. "I'd rather it be on my person than yours in case anything goes awry."

Alarm pricked at the statement. "What do you think could go wrong?"

He jerked his head, and she retrieved the pouch from her pocket. "Let's just hope nothing does."

A confident energy simmered about Anthony now, one she'd never encountered before. She'd always known him to be strong and determined, but his presence of mind and coolness in such a treacherous event astounded her.

He retrieved the rope from the satchel and hoisted it over his shoulder. "I'll carry this in and give it to you once we are there. It's heavy, so prepare yourself for that fact so you aren't taken off guard when you go to use it. Ready?"

Perspiration began to gather on her brow, despite the cold breeze. The sequence of events from the time she'd left Wolden House reenacted in her mind. She nodded with determination, more to bolster her confidence than his.

"If anything goes wrong, anything at all, you do exactly as I say. And if anything happens to me, you get Henry and you run. Hear me?"

At the warning she sobered.

He reached for her hand, and his expression softened. "We are going to get Henry. And then we will start on a new life together, right?"

She smiled, despite the nervous tremor coursing through her.

He leaned toward her, kissed her once more, and squeezed her hand. "Time to go."

Chapter 40

ANTHONY FACED THE door. Charlotte was right behind him. All was silent and unsettlingly still.

His heart drummed wildly—a rapid staccato within his chest. Just as it used to before a battle.

He knew what was before him—the possibility that something would go amiss, the possibility that he might be injured or even die.

But this time the stakes were even greater. For Charlotte was right behind him. And Henry was inside. Both were relying on him to make the right decisions.

He ignored the voice within him telling him he should have made Charlotte return home, that they should have waited for reinforcements. But by dusk, more people could arrive here. As it was now, they were evenly matched.

He glanced over his shoulder at Charlotte. She'd left her cape with the horse for ease of movement, and he'd left his coat behind. The wind was ripping at her gown and at her hair, and yet she did not look afraid. Instead, she nodded encouragingly.

He refocused his attention on the door.

One swift kick should do it.

Three. Two. One.

With every ounce of strength Anthony possessed, he kicked the heel of his boot toward the door's wooden center. Wood splintering shattered the morning stillness and Anthony rushed, taking an immediate assessment.

One room.

Timmons still at the table.

Rebecca in the corner.

Henry crying.

Anthony aimed his pistol straight at Timmons.

Charlotte raised hers toward Rebecca.

"Do as we say, or we will shoot." Anthony stomped toward Timmons. "On your feet and against the wall."

Timmons's face blanched, and hardness glazed his light-chestnut eyes. He stumbled back, nearly tipping the chair in surprise. His weapon still lay in pieces on the table.

Anthony refused to break his glare on Timmons. "Stand up, Timmons, and against the wall. Now! Rebecca, step away from Henry."

Rebecca broke into hysterical sobs and inched away from the bed. Timmons, too, did as he was bid, slowly. The noise and movement added to the confusion, but Anthony held firm. From the corner of his eye, he saw Charlotte doing the same.

Anthony did not recognize the man standing against the wall. The Timmons he knew—the man who had nursed him to health and who had helped him find employment—never would have deceived anyone. But now, he'd kidnapped a baby.

"Why are you doing this?" Anthony thundered, his anger briefly taking control. "What could you be thinking?"

Timmons scoffed and shook his head. "Ye couldn't just leave it alone, could ye?"

"This isn't you, Timmons. *You* don't do things like this."

Timmons sneered in the cottage's dark shadows, like an animal caught in a trap. "Ye don't know what I'm capable of. Ye may 'ave come out of things unscathed. But me—this was my opportunity t' right the wrongs I've dealt with. I'll naught let ye ruin this."

"Tell me what is going on. I'll find out eventually. You know I will."

"I'll tell ye nothin'." Timmons seethed. "So go ahead and do your little investigatin'. Play t' role of thief-taker and learn what ye can. But in t' end, ye may be able to stop me, but ye won't be able t' stop 'im."

Anthony jerked. "Stop whom?"

"Ye know. And who are ye to question me and my decisions? For ye are no better than I. And if it weren't for me, ye would 'ave died on that ship. And this is 'ow ye repay me? Ye need t' leave and t' stay out of me way."

Timmons was rambling. His light-brown eyes were bloodshot and wild. His skin was growing splotchy. He was starting to crumble under the weight of whatever caper had brought him to this point.

"Abducting a child is not the way to redemption." Anthony was powerless to control the harshness in his tone. "I don't care what you say, you'd never be able to live with yourself if something happened to this baby."

The color drained from Timmons's face, and even in the shadowed light, perspiration beaded on his face. "I'll never be able t' live with myself regardless o' what I do. But one word from 'im could restore any of us back t' a respectable place."

Anthony winced at the nonsensical words. "What are you talking about?"

Timmons flicked his gaze to Charlotte tying up Rebecca. "Friend or no friend, I let ye stand in my way too long."

Anthony glanced at Charlotte as she pulled the rope to tighten it, and in that split second Timmons reached in his coat.

Anthony did not think. He acted.

He launched toward Timmons at the very same moment that Timmons seized another pistol from his coat.

Rebecca screamed.

Henry wailed.

Anthony smacked Timmons's hand, which sent the pistol clattering to the stone floor. "Get it, Charlotte!"

Anthony slammed his fist into Timmons's jaw. Timmons hit back with a fist to Anthony's gut, hurling the air from him, but he grabbed Timmons by the arm, twisted it behind him, and then shoved him against the wall. Anthony thrust his pistol at Timmons's back. "The other rope!"

In seconds Charlotte was at his side, with both the rope and her own loaded pistol. He gave Charlotte his pistol and repositioned Timmons's arms and tied them. He patted him to search for other weapons.

Timmons resisted, thrashing the best he could, and Anthony forced him into the chair and tied him securely.

"He's going t' kill ye for this, you know," jeered Timmons. "He'll kill ye and 'er. You should 'ave left it alone."

Was he referring to Broadstreet? Perhaps Silas Prior? "You know me, Timmons," muttered Anthony, testing the rope. "I would never leave this alone."

Anthony glanced behind him.

Charlotte still held the pistol steady, her eyes wide. Henry was still screaming on the floor. Rebecca was sobbing against the wall.

Anthony cut another length of rope and double-checked Charlotte's knots and bound Rebecca's legs, and then he secured her to the heavy leg of the table so the two could not get to each other after Anthony and Charlotte left. Anthony cinched the knot even tighter and then used the blade in his boot to cut off another length of rope to tie Timmons's legs.

Anthony stood, stepped back, took the pistols, and motioned for Charlotte to pick up Henry.

He looked back to the man who had been like a brother to him these past years. So much he wanted to say. So many questions he wanted to ask. But he resisted. "I'll be back with the magistrate."

Timmons chuckled. "There's nothin' ye can do t' me, *Captain*, and ye know it."

Anthony did not look away. "Go, Charlotte."

Anthony heard her feet retreat, and the sound of Henry's crying faded. He then backed out of the cottage, not turning his back until he cleared the door.

Once free of the cabin and once again mounted on the horse, the three of them raced over the moors. The landscape flashed by them in shades of brown and gray. He should be happy, for

Charlotte was riding in front of him, Henry in her arms. Timmons and Rebecca were tied in the cottage. But Anthony was far from at peace.

Timmons might have been telling him the truth. Maybe he was lying.

But regardless, he had been betrayed and lied to by a friend. And it did not sit well with him.

The only thing he could do was what he knew to be right.

Chapter 41

THE HORSE CARRYING Charlotte, Henry, and Anthony thundered over the uneven moorland terrain. Each second put more distance between them and Thoms Cottage. Charlotte blinked away the moisture and tightened her grip on Henry, and she pressed her back against Anthony's chest, welcoming the sense of protection it offered and drawing from his strength.

They'd done it.

They had gotten Henry back from the kidnappers.

But she felt far from relieved, and she sensed Anthony was not at peace either.

Even as Anthony's arms encircled both her and Henry as he held the horse's reins, she could feel the tension in them. She wanted to soothe him and reassure him after the blow of betrayal he'd received from a friend. But the whistling wind blasting them as they rode made talking nearly impossible, and besides, what could be said?

They cantered into the stable courtyard. The cobbles were dark and slick with rain, and as the horse came to a stop, Sutcliffe ran out. "Oh, you're safe! And Henry! I'm so glad!"

Charlotte handed Henry down to Sutcliffe.

"Please tell me you are not hurt." Sutcliffe forged ahead, but when Charlotte didn't answer, Sutcliffe frowned. "What is it?"

Anthony helped Charlotte dismount and she faced Sutcliffe. As soon as her feet were on the ground, she embraced her friend. She wanted to apologize for her harsh words. She *didn't* want to tell her how awful the man she fancied truly was. And yet she did not have the opportunity, for Anthony dismounted right behind her.

"Any sign of Ames or the other watchmen?" Anthony asked.

Sutcliffe shook her head as she adjusted Henry in her arms. "No. But what of Mr. Timmons? And Mr. Broadstreet? And Rebecca?"

"There's time for all that later," he said. "Go upstairs and pack a few things. I'm headed to the village to track down the magistrate, and I'm taking you three to the inn in the village until all is sorted."

"Where's Mrs. Hargrave? And Tom?" asked Charlotte.

Sutcliffe blinked and gripped Charlotte's hand. "They're gone! They left soon after Mr. Welbourne, and without another word. Oh, please do tell me what is happening."

Charlotte's stomach clenched.

Suddenly this very house, which had seemed so isolated for so long, now seemed to be danger itself. She looked back to Anthony. "You're right. We shouldn't stay here."

"Quickly, get your things. Put on dry clothes. I'll tend the horse and then be right in."

She was standing near him, and he gripped her hand with his.

She squeezed back. Tighter. She did not want to let go. He was the last stronghold—the last place she could garner strength.

Anthony headed toward the stables, and Charlotte and Sutcliffe hurried into the empty kitchen. The familiar warmth rushed her and soothed her trembling limbs, but a new, much more sinister atmosphere had gripped the household. She wanted nothing more than to hold her son tightly to her and never let go, but there would be time for that when they were certain they were out of danger. Now she needed to stay focused.

"Henry's freezing," Charlotte ripped her cape from her shoulders, "and no doubt starving. Please get him out of those wet things and feed him. I am going to change and get him a dry gown. Alright?"

Gooseflesh prickled her skin, and the pins holding her hair had long since given way, and her hair hung wet about her shoulders. Her mind raced ahead to the next steps. The inn in the village, and then Anthony would probably return here to meet with the watchmen, if they were indeed to come. Henry would need fresh gowns, his blanket, and—

She stepped from the kitchen through the corridor but as she crossed the great hall, a singsong yet gritty, masculine tone stopped her in her tracks.

"You lied to me, Mrs. Prior. Didn't you?"

She froze and turned her head in the direction of the familiar voice.

William Walstead exited through the parlor door and stopped just outside the threshold.

She should be happy to see him. Surely he was here to assist.

But a frown creased his brow. His russet eyes were dark and hard. And the sinister grin on his clean-shaven face was probably the most frightening thing she had ever beheld.

She resisted the urge to inch backward.

No, he was not here to assist.

She held up her trembling chin, determined to hide the fear—and the confusion—welling within her. "I could say the same thing to you."

He smirked and stepped forward, his polished boots snapping against the stone floor. "I asked whether you knew about the King's Prize. You told me you didn't know to what I was referring. Furthermore, when I asked whether you knew where the emeralds were, you looked me dead in the eye and lied. I find that exceedingly offensive."

She could only stare as her mind attempted to make sense of his presence.

"Your husband owed me money," he continued. "A great deal."

Her voice felt airy and weak, despite her best effort to bolster it. "I've told you before that I know nothing of his business deals."

Walstead chuckled. "Roland Prior was a devious man. A very devious man. But I suppose I should give credit where credit is due. He bested me. Tricked me. But now he is dead, and someone must pay his debts."

She stammered, grasping at any delay tactic she could summon. "H-how had he bested you?"

Walstead dragged his finger over the windowsill and then looked at his fingertip to examine the dust. "He said he would pay those poor fools who work for him at the mill to go to Plymouth to get his rather large shipment when it arrived from Spain. But he never had any intention of paying them, so he hired me and a few of my best men to steal his goods and return them to him in secret. Since the goods were stolen, he did not have to pay the mill workers for transporting the goods since they did not complete the job and deliver the cargo. Clever, eh? But you see, he then put me off and refused to pay me for not only that job but several others we completed for him around the same time." He clicked his tongue. "And *that* is never a good idea."

"If that is the case, then take it up with the solicitor," she challenged with a tone much more confident than she felt.

"That's where you're wrong, my dear Mrs. Prior. Remember how I told you he'd made unscrupulous investments? His estate is bankrupt. I doubt even Silas Prior will be able to save it. But your husband did have one thing in his possession that was very precious indeed—the King's Prize. And I know because I witnessed it being confiscated from the mill workers. Mill workers, you see, are no match for my men. But oh, what a tangled web. But Roland surprised me—I never would have guessed he hid it in his mousy wife's belongings. Very clever. Very clever indeed."

"You are despicable," she sneered.

"I've long suspected that you played a part in all this, and you, my dear Mrs. Prior, have been a thorn in my side. What am I to do with you?"

She stared at him. He exuded frightening confidence—and it struck her to her core.

"You will give me the emeralds now." He stepped closer. "And if you comply, I might just let your son live."

He retrieved a pistol from his coat and pointed it at Charlotte. He cocked it.

The air vacated Charlotte's lungs. The sight of the pistol incited a fear that flew in the face of the hope the day had otherwise brought.

She sputtered, searching for protest, when another voice behind her spoke. Smoothly. Confidently. "She doesn't have the emeralds. I do. So if you want them, you will have to speak with me."

Chapter 42

ANTHONY MATCHED WALSTEAD'S hard glare with his own.

Never did he think he would be on this side of Walstead—opposing him instead of working with him. But he'd left Anthony with no choice. Anthony was acutely aware of his pistol in his waistband. But he would not make a move for it until he was certain he had the upper hand.

For Walstead was pointing his weapon at Charlotte.

"I said she doesn't have the emeralds," Anthony repeated.

"Ah, there we are!" Walstead threw his hand up in mock celebration. "Welbourne. I have to say, you surprised me as well. I never would have pegged you for such a romantic soul. Who would have thought that a stoic man such as yourself would have a softness for a woman? I'm not often surprised. Nor am I often deceived. But you did both. As I was just telling Mrs. Prior, I abhor deception."

Anthony was determined to keep Walstead's focus on him and not Charlotte. "Release her."

Walstead laughed. "So gallant! But don't forget who I am. I

know how skilled you are at this sort of negotiation. But we both also know something else—I am better."

Sudden movement in the courtyard sounded, and a horseman and a carriage rumbled up. Anthony's stomach tightened. Ames's profile flashed next to the driver, along with other men he did not recognize.

He thought that Ames went to get Walstead—but why was Walstead already here?

In an instant Walstead's expression hardened. He stepped to the window and looked out. His brows drew together, and he cursed under his breath. He extended his palm. "Toss them here. Now!"

Sensing an opportunity during Walstead's break in concentration, not to mention the fault in Walstead's request, Anthony reached into his coat as bid. But he did not retrieve the emeralds. Instead, he snatched his pistol from his waist.

Walstead reacted and lunged forward, grabbed Charlotte, and pulled her tight against his chest, blocking any shot Anthony might have. And then Walstead pointed his pistol straight at Anthony.

———————

Charlotte stood frozen, her gaze locked on Mr. Walstead's pistol, her wet boots fixed to the flagstone floor.

His fingers dug, sharp and hard, into her arm through her soaked wool pelisse.

Every heartbeat pulsed through her ears.

Every breath wheezed with desperation.

She slid her gaze to the commotion in the courtyard that had caught Mr. Walstead's attention: Mr. Ames and other men. Perhaps watchmen. And if these were watchmen, she had no way of knowing whether they would assist Anthony and her or would support Mr. Walstead.

He spewed out another slew of curses, the first sign of a break in his haughty composure, and Charlotte's heart leapt. He pulled her back to him even tighter, his scent of horses and brandy overwhelming her.

And she did not have time to contemplate it further, for Mr. Ames burst in the front door, pistol drawn.

One shot fired.

Then another.

The cracks echoed from the archaic stones and wooden beams.

Charlotte cried out with the shock of it, then stumbled forward as Mr. Walstead's tight grip on her suddenly released. She fought for balance, and Mr. Walstead dropped to the ground behind her.

She gasped for air.

But there had been two shots, and she had not been hit.

She lifted her gaze.

Anthony was on his feet, but he was stumbling backward. Blood seeped through the white fabric of his neckcloth and his gray coat. He fell to the ground.

Horror froze her to her spot. Suddenly men seemed to be everywhere—shouting, running. She regained control of her limbs and rushed toward Anthony and dropped by his side. "Anthony!"

She touched his face, forcing him to look at her. His vibrant eyes were wide. But he said nothing. He gasped for air and looked down to his chest.

Her panicked words tumbled forth. "It's going to be alright, Anthony. Breathe, my love, breathe."

Mr. Ames pushed her away and she fell back. He ripped off his own coat and tore a sleeve free.

Anthony exhaled and leaned his head back against the stone floor. Every second seemed an eternity as Mr. Ames assessed the wound. She felt sick at the gory sights around her, and the acrid scent of gunfire and death turned her stomach. She reached for Anthony's hand and held it as if both their lives depended on it.

She could not look at the wound as Mr. Ames cut away the fabric of Anthony's coat or at the man who came to assist him. Instead, she leaned close to his face and spoke firmly. "Don't close your eyes, Anthony, don't you dare."

Mr. Ames nudged her, jolting her from her shock. "Go find wine, whiskey. Ale. Anything. Now."

She flew to the kitchen and retrieved a bottle, barely noticing one of the other men standing over Mr. Walstead's body. She returned and knelt by Anthony.

"Get as much in him as you can," instructed Mr. Ames. "He'll be glad you did."

She adjusted Anthony's head just enough to get the bottle to his lips. He coughed and sputtered as she assisted him.

After several moments, Mr. Ames looked up. "The bullet went through his shoulder, close shot like that."

She turned back to Anthony, whose eyes were beginning to

flutter closed. He seemed weak, and yet he reached his other hand to her just enough to touch the fabric of her gown.

As Mr. Ames continued his work, she leaned down and kissed Anthony's forehead. "I love you, Anthony Welbourne. Please do not leave me."

Chapter 43

AS CHARLOTTE SAT next to Anthony's bed in the upstairs chamber, she lost track of time. The sky outside the window was black. Not even a small star dared to make an appearance. The day's events played before her in vivid detail—the elation of saving Henry. The fear of encountering Mr. Walstead. The horror of Anthony getting shot.

Her eyes burned with exhaustion, but she would not sleep.

She *could* not sleep. Not until there was evidence that he was alright.

Anthony, on the other hand, had not woken since the incident. Perhaps it was the spirits poured into him, the laudanum that the surgeon had given him, the shock of the bullet to his body, or the loss of blood.

Whatever the reason, she would not leave his side. Not until she saw the blue of his eyes. Not until she told him again that she loved him.

At present Henry was asleep in the bedchamber with Sutcliffe. Mr. Ames, the magistrate, Mr. Greenwood, and the other men

Mr. Ames had assembled had since removed Mr. Walstead's body and departed to collect Timmons and Rebecca.

All was finally growing quiet, growing still, and yet anxiety wound through her, squeezing and choking. Thoughts about what might have happened plagued her, and every time she closed her eyes, the sights from earlier in the day were as detailed as they had ever been.

She brushed a wayward sable curl from Anthony's brow. He was clean now. His bloody clothes had been cut away, and linen bandages wrapped over his shoulder and around his chest, leaving his other shoulder and arm exposed. The scent of the tincture the surgeon brought filled the chamber. Anthony seemed to sleep peacefully enough, but he looked broken, and yet she knew he possessed a strength most could only strive to emulate.

With his chest bare she could see the full extent of his war injury—of how something had crossed down the side of his face and caught again on his shoulder and appeared to deepen as it reached his arm, just as he had said. Uneven scars from hasty stitches were purple and pink on otherwise fair skin. Now his opposite shoulder and arm were bandaged—not because he was fighting for king and country but because of her.

For her.

His chest rose and fell in deep, rhythmic breaths, and she leaned forward and kissed his forehead.

She did not know what would happen next. But she had fought for Henry. And now she would fight for Anthony. It was glaringly clear now. Hollythorne House was their home, but now it would not be complete without Anthony. She loved him. Every memory, every heartache, every smile was written on her soul. On her heart. Circumstances of every kind threatened to unbind them, and yet they had found their way back to each other.

She reached out and took his large hand in hers. It seemed so much larger than she remembered. Much rougher. Calloused and scarred. It was so different from Roland Prior's. And she never wanted to let go of it.

———

Noises.

Movement.

Searing pain.

Anthony was pretty sure he was dreaming—trapped in that unconscious space of alertness and decision, daydream and lucidity. He'd been here before, in the days following the Battle of New Orleans while in the field hospital and on the hospital ship. His eyes were closed. He attempted to adjust his hand, but his fingers were swollen. He seemed to vaguely recall a bout of fisticuffs.

Pain scorched through his shoulder and down his arm. His head was heavy and thick, as if emerging from a drunken fog. He pried an eye open and was met with a brightness from a candle that felt like a fiery poker stabbing his eye. He promptly closed it again. As he became more aware of his limbs, it all rushed back.

Charlotte and Henry were safe.

He'd been shot.

Walstead was dead, he thought.

Timmons had betrayed him.

Anthony drew a breath, then stopped. The simple action incited pain in his ribs and lungs. He was certain he lost consciousness at some point when the surgeon was here. It was the last thing he remembered.

He did not open his eyes, yet he slowly touched the linen bandage across his chest.

"Are you awake?"

The feminine, eager whisper enticed him from his foggy slumber.

He did not want to open his eyes, fearing the soft voice was but a figment of his imagination.

He heard sounds of movement as someone approached the bed. The scent of lavender met him.

He eased open an eye, squinting to adjust his sight to the bright candle glowing on the bedside table.

Pain dominated, and yet she drew every bit of his attention. He attempted to change his position, to push himself up slightly on the bed. But his head spun, and blackness eclipsed his vision. His arm gave out beneath him.

She was at his side instantly, both hands, cool and soothing, on his good arm. "Shh. Be still."

He heard her draw a chair close to the bed and settle near to him. A gentle, soft hand covered his. She leaned near, and soft chestnut hair fell over her shoulder and brushed against his bare arm.

He might be intoxicated.

Surely someone had administered something for pain, and the effects of it lingered.

Charlotte took the hand of his good arm in her own and pressed her lips against it. The movement slow. Deliberate. "We must find a way to keep you out of danger, Anthony Welbourne."

"Don't worry." His words were gruff and harsh against his parched throat. He attempted to clear it before speaking an absolute lie. "'Tis nothing."

"Well, it may be nothing to you, but it nearly broke my heart." She shifted, as if preparing to stand. "You must be thirsty. Let me—"

He grabbed her hand and stopped her with a force that surprised even him. "Don't leave. Please."

She slowly sat back down, silent.

He opened his eyes farther. The candlelight flickered on the precious angles of her face. How well he could read each twitch. She was trying to smile, but an element of fear lingered in the depths of her changing expression. Her chin trembled, and as if aware of it she bit her lower lip.

He squeezed her hand. "I want to make sure that you are really here."

She said nothing but covered his hand with her other one. "The surgeon says you'll recover. The bullet went through. Do you remember any of it?"

The image of Walstead's pistol pointed in his direction would forever be imprinted on his mind. But there had been a second shot. He recalled seeing Walstead on the floor. "Is Walstead dead?"

"Yes."

Details began to return. "And Timmons?"

She rubbed her fingertips over the back of his hand. "Ames

took it upon himself to fetch the magistrate, and they took a group of men to the cottage right afterward. Apparently he saw Walstead already in the village after he left Hollythorne House with the letter and grew suspicious. I've heard no update."

Anthony's stomach tightened as he remembered the sight of his friend tied and bound in the cottage. He didn't want it to be that way.

Conflicting emotions warred in his chest. He'd loved Timmons as a brother. Respected Walstead like a teacher. They were both exposed now. And neither was who he'd thought they were.

The soft caressing of her fingers on his hand brought him back to her. "Where's Henry?"

"With Sutcliffe. He is sleeping. He's had quite a day."

"I shouldn't keep you from him." Anthony released her hand. "You have waited a long time for him."

"Henry and I have many years together ahead of us. It is you I am worried about now."

He studied her again for several moments—the beauty of her dark lashes. The curve of her slightly parted lips. Fierce protectiveness clawed through him. He was ready to jump up and fight for her again. He would never stop doing so.

She seemed oddly hesitant in this moment of privacy, but he was emboldened—by years of loneliness, by years of yearning for her, by the closeness of death and the brevity of time. His head pounded, his shoulder throbbed, and he did not trust his voice to speak, yet he'd never felt more at peace or more certain about what needed to be said.

"I've cheated death twice. For some reason, I'm still alive. I want to wake up to you every day, not just this one. You have years ahead of you with Henry, and I'm happy for it. But I would gladly give you every day I have left, if you would have them. For another chance at life would mean nothing without you in it."

Her eyes, rid-rimmed and dark, met his.

She drew a shaky, thin breath, and a tear fell down her cheek. She lifted his hand and pressed her lips to it. "I've been so frightened. And how I've missed you. Every day I've missed you and thought I would never see you again. But I-I-I'm so different now. I'm so broken. How can—?"

"Charlotte."

She fell silent at his word.

"You may feel broken now, but you—every part of you—is beautiful to me. You and Henry."

She wiped her cheek with the back of her hand. "It's just with everything that has happened, I don't know where I belong or even where to begin."

"With me, Charlotte." He reached for her hand and looked her directly in the eye. "You belong with me. And I belong with you."

She scooted close and leaned into him, gently at first and then burying her face into his neck. He wrapped his good arm around her, cursing the fact that his other arm was not free to embrace her properly.

This.

This moment.

This was what he had fought for, strived for, dreamed of, even when he didn't know what was before him.

She eventually pulled away from him, and he wiped her face

with his thumb and tucked her long hair over her shoulder. He leaned forward as much as he could, and she met him halfway. He framed her face with his hand and kissed her, allowing the softness of her touch to numb any pain and to shed optimism on their future.

"Marry me," he breathed, unable to hold the request back. "I will protect you and Henry. I will love you—both of you—until the day I die. These last few years have been an endless nightmare without you. Thank God I've woken up."

Her face was mere inches from his, and her eyes met his with such honesty, such intensity, it seemed as if they had never been apart. She leaned forward, and her loose hair fell against his skin. A grin toyed with her lips, and a bit of brightness flashed in her topaz eyes. "Not even war or smugglers can keep us apart, can they?"

She trailed her finger through his hair and pressed a kiss to his lips before whispering, "Of course, I will marry you. It was only ever you."

Chapter 44

CHARLOTTE SMILED DOWN at Henry as he yawned in her arms. His white eyelashes fluttered against his pink cheeks, and his chest rose and fell with comfortable sleep.

She could not resist smoothing her hand over his white-blond curls and covering his little hand with hers.

Memories of his abduction and the horrifying events that accompanied it would always haunt her, but in this singular moment he was safe, and with any mercy he'd never remember a bit of it. She wished she could be so fortunate, but the events of the past month were seared into her brain with such intensity that they would always be a part of her.

She recalled the sight of Mr. Walstead's lifeless body on the stone floor. Of Roland's lifeless body on the Persian rug. Of Anthony injured. Of Henry screaming in fear at Thoms Cottage.

She squeezed her eyes closed to black out the thoughts.

It was over.

Now, they only had to figure out what to do with the King's Prize. Technically, the collection of emeralds was owned by Roland, and as such was a part of his estate. Even so, she would not rest fully until they were out from beneath Hollythorne House's roof.

The door opened, as did Charlotte's eyes, and Sutcliffe stood in the doorway to her bedchamber with a stack of linens in her arms.

"I did not hear you." Charlotte motioned to the lady's maid. "Come in."

Sutcliffe did as she was bid, but her every movement was void of her usual enthusiasm. A shadow crossed her round face, and she stopped in the middle of the chamber. "May I beg a word with you?"

Charlotte turned to place Henry in his bed. "Of course."

Sutcliffe set the linens on the bed before she faced Charlotte. "I owe you an apology, Mrs. Prior. A formal one. I want to tell you with the highest sincerity that I never meant to tell Mr. Timmons about the emeralds. I honestly was not aware of the significance, and I never would have intentionally betrayed your trust."

"Oh, my dear. You have nothing for which to apologize. Mr. Timmons deceived you. Cruelly."

Sutcliffe shook her head, her fair brows drawing together. "I still don't know how I could have been so foolish. I fear I will feel shame for it until the day I die."

Charlotte reached out to take the woman's hand in her own. "You are not foolish. Do not allow yourself to believe it for a minute. You have a good, trusting heart. 'Tis only a pity that such goodness was not matched."

Sutcliffe nodded. "You are kind to say so."

"One day a man will come who deserves the loyalty and trust you have to give him, but Mr. Timmons proved to you, quite clearly, that he is not that man." Charlotte drew a sharp breath. "And while we are speaking of forgiveness, it is I who should be apologizing. In the midst of my own anger, I spoke very harshly to you the morning we discovered Henry missing. At the time I was so blinded by fear that I could not see the anguish others were enduring. As your friend, I beg your forgiveness."

"All is forgiven." Sutcliffe smiled tentatively, slowly pulling her hand from Charlotte's. "But there is something else that must be spoken."

Charlotte tensed.

It was quite unlike Sutcliffe to be timid and hesitant.

Sutcliffe pressed her lips together and then drew a deep breath. "I appreciate every opportunity you have extended to me, but I must find another position. Given what has transpired I cannot remain in your employ."

The words echoed. And hurt.

But they were not a surprise.

After what they'd all just experienced and the embarrassment Sutcliffe likely felt about her relationship with Mr. Timmons, Charlotte did understand.

She wanted to plead with her lady's maid, her *friend*, to change her mind, but she knew Sutcliffe. She would not have made such a decision lightly, and now that her decision was made, it would be useless to attempt to sway her otherwise. "Where will you go? Back to Leeds?"

"Heavens, no." Sutcliffe wrinkled her nose. "I shall never, ever, return to Leeds. No, I will go to my cousin Charles in London. I'm certain they will welcome me. He and his wife have four children and no doubt could use my help."

Charlotte tilted her head to the side. "Selfishly, I wish you would stay. I will miss you tremendously. But I understand."

Sutcliffe tucked a lock of golden hair sheepishly behind her ear. "Have you heard if they have apprehended Mr. Timmons yet and what will happen to them all?"

"Yes." Charlotte hated to be the person to share this news with Sutcliffe. "Mr. Timmons is in the village gaol. Mr. Ames told me there is a transport arriving in the next day or so to return him to Leeds. Rebecca was taken to a gaol in the village over and will also be sent away. Mr. Broadstreet was apprehended in Leeds. Apparently it was he who notified Mr. Walstead that they had kidnapped Henry and prompted his visit. They will go to trial for their parts in all of this."

Sutcliffe nodded slowly as she took in the news. "As they should."

Charlotte reached out and gripped Sutcliffe's hand in a show of solidarity. "I know you are hurting now. You do not need to say it for me to know it's true. I know you will come from this stronger. Wiser."

"I hope you're right. And I wish you happiness as well. I confess, I was not even aware that you and Mr. Welbourne were acquainted to such an extent. I suppose I was so locked in my own happenings that I failed to notice."

A memory fluttered in her mind of her conversation with Anthony—of their promises to each other. "I've known Mr. Welbourne for years. And, in truth, I've loved him for years, but I thought I would never see him again. I am only sorry it took such dramatic events to reunite us."

"Dramatic, indeed." Sutcliffe chuckled softly before sobering. "I, for one, hope never to keep another secret again."

"As do I. But life is beginning anew for both of us. And I hope we both seize the opportunities that have been given us."

———————

Anthony ran his fingers through his dark hair, loosening the tangles and smoothing it into place. Then he ran his hand down his face. His stubble had grown into a beard that would undoubtedly be considered unfashionable by most.

He'd been abed two days, per the surgeon's instructions. But he could stand to be in his attic chamber no more.

His shoulder throbbed, but he'd managed to wash his face and don his extra shirt. He'd shave another time when he had better use of his arm and hand, and he did not bother with a waistcoat. He turned to reach for his boots, and his eyes fell on his coat and the brilliant-blue armband.

Anger surged through him at the very sight of it.

Had he been oblivious? Tricked? The time he'd spent recovering had afforded him ample time to contemplate the situation. Surely there had been signs that he either missed completely or hadn't wanted to see. Now it all seemed so obvious. He had spent many years believing that he was destined for a life of solitude—of chasing criminals in dark alleys and guarding eerie warehouses. In truth, he'd been hesitant to leave that life, where he answered to no one and was responsible only for himself. But he'd been using his role as an excuse not to face his guilt for leaving his uncle alone with the mill. But oddly enough, it was that very life that led him back to the one person who could make his life whole.

And he was ready—ready to be a husband to Charlotte. A father to Henry. To allow himself to be happy and content. And he would restore the mill and do right by the past he'd so ardently tried to escape.

Upon leaving his chamber Anthony found Ames in the stables. Charlotte had engaged Ames to keep an eye on the grounds until Anthony was well enough to do so. For a threat did still exist—the King's Prize was in a strongbox within Hollythorne House, and as long as it was there, an element of danger would reside with them.

"Good to see you up and about," called Ames in a raspy voice as he led a horse away from the stables.

Anthony squinted in the afternoon sunshine. "All is well, I trust?"

Ames scoffed and tipped his hat lower. "Yes."

"Any updates?"

Ames paused to adjust the glove on his hand. "The magistrate was by early this morning. He's heard from Leeds, and the transport will be coming to collect both Timmons and Rebecca tomorrow."

His stomach lurched at the thought. It would take him some time to come to peace with this news of Timmons. But Timmons was a grown man who had made his own choices. He would have to face the consequences. "Did you have any inkling at all that Walstead was involved in this?"

Ames shook his head. "At first, no. But something was not right about that Broadstreet fellow, and Walstead was unusually involved in the assignment. Then, when I was riding back through the village on the way to Leeds with the letter, I encountered Walstead outside of the traveling inn, and in that moment I knew he was involved. So I abandoned the plan and went straight for the magistrate and drummed up all the help I could. Looking back, I suppose I should have been suspicious. But Walstead always was an intense man. One could hardly tell what was normal for him and what was not."

"Do you know how exactly Broadstreet fit into the scheme?"

Ames nodded. "Apparently both Timmons and Broadstreet were involved with the King's Prize from the very beginning. Prior hired the both of them to make sure that the emeralds never made it back to Leeds so Prior wouldn't have to pay his workmen. Something about work at a place called Swendel Bay."

Anthony stiffened at the familiar name. "Swendel Bay?"

"Aye."

Anthony thought back to their conversation after the dirty workmen had confronted him with a message for Walstead outside the pub. Timmons had clearly stated he was with the Raunten Bay assignment. It must have been the first of many deceptions.

Ames continued. "The relationship between Roland Prior and Walstead soured when Prior was falling behind on payments for services rendered by Walstead. When Prior died, he still owed Walstead a lot of money, since most of their transactions had been conducted with a gentleman's agreement and had no formal paperwork or documentation. Walstead knew Prior was likely still in possession of the King's Prize, so he started to search for it.

"Since Timmons knew of the King's Prize from the time they stole it from the mill workers, Walstead tasked him with the job of finding out if Mrs. Prior knew anything about it. Timmons wooed the lady's maid until he learned what he needed. Once they were certain who had the King's Prize, the three of them planned the kidnapping for a ransom situation. Timmons and Rebecca abducted the baby, and Broadstreet rode to Leeds to inform Walstead that the act was happening. That is why Walstead was already in the area at the time of the abduction."

The facts raced through Anthony's mind. They sickened him. Frustrated him. Embarrassed him—because he should have foreseen it. "Are you returning to Leeds when this is over?"

"No. From what I'm told, the details are coming to light, and it is causing quite a stir. Men in our profession have unique reputations as it is. This is going to make them worse." Ames shifted. "And you? From what I see you seem to have found your place here. I can't imagine you'll be leaving anytime soon."

Anthony chuckled and looked out to the moors—to the vast expanse that he had at one point been so eager to escape for something grander. But now, as he took in the wavy grass and rocky mounds, he felt as if he'd finally found freedom. He drew a deep breath of the earthy air, and a deep sense of gratitude settled over him. "You're right. This is now my home."

Chapter 45

A FEW DAYS later the gloomy clouds parted at last, and the gray morning had given way to a bright bit of sunshine as Anthony waited for Charlotte to emerge from Hollythorne House. A month ago, he never could have predicted how significantly his life would change—he'd been challenged and betrayed. But from a bewildering situation, such clarity and beauty had emerged, and he now stood on the precipice of a different life. And it infused him with optimism.

After days of being inside and resting his shoulder and arm, he was eager to be out of doors. When Charlotte joined him, they would ride out to the mill. He'd not had the opportunity to visit it until now, for his responsibility and attention had been here at Hollythorne House. But Ames had the grounds under control, and Anthony could feel comfortable leaving. What was more, he had no choice but to take up residence in the mill house, for it would be weeks before he and Charlotte could marry. Banns were required to be read and a great many things needed to be settled. He was her fiancé, and as such, he could not reside under the same roof as her, regardless of whether he was injured or not. He would not compromise her reputation with her tenants.

At length Charlotte joined him in the back courtyard, and his breath caught at the sight of her approaching. Her expression was bright in the morning glow, and her cheeks were vibrant with the chill of the air. She was every bit as captivating as he remembered from that summer four years ago—if not more so. He'd always known her to be confident and outspoken, but he'd witnessed a different side of her over the past month—the side that confronted injustice and would stop at nothing to protect those she loved. It was an attractive quality—one he respected perhaps more than any other.

She smiled brightly as she approached and called, "Are you ready?"

His breathing slowed as she drew nearer. Charlotte had been clad in severe black and dark hues of browns and grays almost every day since they arrived at Hollythorne House, but now she was in a riding habit of pale green wool, with ivory flowers and vines embroidered along the hem and on her sleeves. An ivory satin ribbon was woven in her hair and beneath her bonnet, and for the first time, a shade of pink was returning to her cheeks. Gone were the dark circles beneath her eyes, and her warm hazel gaze enticed him and invited him to share her secrets and her heart.

The sight—the powerful allure of her—made him almost forget to respond to her question.

He whispered, "You are beautiful."

An even prettier flush rose to her cheeks. "I-I thought it only appropriate that if we are to build a new life together, we should start over. I can't abide black. Not anymore."

"I wholeheartedly agree." He longed to reach out and take her hand, but he refrained. They would be married, but people were still milling about. In the last few days a new housekeeper had been hired, along with a groom and a stable master and two maids. Workmen were finishing repairs to the roof, and glaziers were busy tending broken windows. Discretion was still key, regardless of what they had recently endured.

He pivoted to hand her the horse's reins, and he winced when a sharp pain jolted through his shoulder.

Her brows furrowed in a sympathetic arch. "You're in pain, aren't you?"

He grinned reassuringly. "No."

"You're lying. I saw the wound myself. There is no way you are not still in pain."

He sobered. When she saw the wound she undoubtedly saw the other wounds too—the hastily repaired ones that, even though healed, were far more physically altering than a bullet wound. He was not embarrassed by the unseemly scars, but they were like a window into his past—into the dark things he had done, seen, and survived. As a result, he relived them every time he saw the grisly marks. He did not want her to think the same.

But she smiled at him—the sort of smile that would soothe every ache and push those tarnished memories far into the past where they belonged. Her gaze did not break away. Instead, she took the reins from his hand, allowing her gloved hand to brush his.

Together they rode into the fresh air and over the moor's uneven terrain, past Even Tor, past Thoms Tor, past the places that had been so significant. It had been years since he traversed this specific path, yet he knew the way like the back of his hand.

He knew they were getting close when they crossed the arched stone bridge above the River Lamby. At the gate, the white-stone mill cottage he grew up in and the damaged mill building were visible, and the hum of rushing water in the river met his ears.

He'd been in shock the last time he was here, for he'd just learned of his uncle's death. The sorrow over it, coupled with the guilt of not being here to save him, had been so overwhelming that he'd barely been able to look at what remained after the fire. He'd shut himself off that very day and given himself dozens of legitimate excuses not to return. But now everything was different.

Once at the gate to the millhouse, they dismounted and secured the horses. Anthony turned to Charlotte. "What do you think of it? Is it what you expected?"

Charlotte wrapped her arm around his and leaned against him. "It is as you described it."

He followed her gaze and tried to assess it with fresh eyes.

The mill itself, a square structure of stone and brick, had two large windows on each side, many of which were damaged or missing, and it was positioned on a small island in order to harness power from the River Lambey. The island was large enough for the building and several mature trees and could be reached by a smaller bridge. Spencer had been right. The roof and wheel were gone, but from where Anthony was standing, the stones of the mill walls appeared largely intact.

"Can it be saved?" Charlotte's question echoed the one that had simmered in the recesses of his mind since the day he learned of the fire.

He looked up to the charred remains of the mill. But despite the obvious damage, the inner and the outer walls were standing, and the millstone appeared intact. He was by no means an expert in construction, but he knew enough about this particular building and how it needed to function. What was more, his focus was shifting. Determination and motivation would go a long way to overcoming the obstacles.

"Yes. It can," he responded. "And it's time I saw to it. My uncle would be angry that I allowed it to remain in such a state for so long."

"I think he'd understand," she said with a coy smile. "What he would not understand is how a Grey and a Welbourne saw fit to even speak to one another, let alone become betrothed."

Anthony chuckled at her playful tone. "If he ever met you, ever spoke with you, he'd be in agreement with me."

Her cheeks flushed at the compliment.

How he loved seeing her like this—happy, carefree, flirtatious. Each day she was shedding the protective armor that had been her constant companion since their reunion.

She stepped farther into the mill, lifting her gaze to where the roof should have been. "It might be reparable, but do you not think it will be expensive? You may be marrying a landowner, but you've seen the ledger and the state of things. I will no longer receive money from Roland's will, and I—"

"I will stop you right there." He raised his hand. "We do not need Roland Prior's money. My pride will not allow it, and I dare-say yours would not either. Besides, I am not destitute, after all. I have money from the sale of my commission and my wages for the past several years. And speaking of the ledger, I do believe that if we can save the tenants money by using this mill and implement a few practical changes, the situation will eventually right itself. The estate's been neglected, that's all. We'll simply change it. We will cancel any contracts with Clarett, and given the circumstances, not to mention the unsteady state of Prior Mill, there is no way that agreement could possibly hold. Once I get Welbourne Mill operational once more, the customers will come."

She sobered and looked down to her hands. "And then there is Hollythorne House and the estate. When we marry, it will all legally belong to you."

He stiffened. Yes, the transfer of property was a fact that would come with marriage, and he had wondered how that would affect her. It was not something they'd yet discussed, and he knew how much pride she took in her ancestral home and her dreams for its future.

"Perhaps legally," he offered, "but Hollythorne House will always be yours. And Henry's. And any other children that may come. That I swear to you, because I know it belongs to you as much as you belong to it. You have fought too hard for it not to be so. I can only imagine what your father would think—a Welbourne, a lowly mill owner—taking up residence there."

She smiled. "I loved my father dearly, but he was pretentious, wasn't he? I don't think that even he would deny that."

"And you? Will you be able to bear marriage to a hardworking man who labors in a mill? It will hardly be the elegant city life you've been used to."

"The life I was used to was cruel and calculating. The man I am about to marry is opposite in every way. And I am so very grateful."

"Come on," he said, taking her hand and lacing his fingers through hers. "I've seen where you were raised. Let me show you where I grew up."

He led Charlotte to the two-story stone mill cottage, which, like Hollythorne House, was built of gray gritstone and blackened with age. But that was where the similarities ended. He lifted his gaze to the thatched roof and the overrun ivy clinging to the cottage's humble facade. He retrieved the key from his pocket and opened the door.

The scent of damp disuse met him, and despite the shining sun, all was dark. He'd prepared himself to be uncomfortable stepping in here once again, but that was not the sentiment that dominated him at all. Instead, a peace settled over him—a peace quite different from being in Charlotte's presence or even by being on Blight Moor.

It was the peace of coming home.

Hand in hand they wandered through the shadowed, low-ceilinged rooms, and he allowed himself to feel the memories that existed here—the moments that laid the foundations for the man he was now. The lessons learned. The disappointments endured. How he could recall running through these small chambers, past the stairs, through the kitchen, and out the back door to the open moorland. He stepped up the creaky stairs, remembering how effortless this climb used to be as a boy, but now he had to duck to prevent hitting his head on the ceiling. This entire visit was like stepping back in time, but with the benefit of time and experience to truly appreciate the beauty of what was around him.

When they returned to the cottage's kitchen, he stepped to the empty hearth and lifted his gaze to the rifle above it. Charlotte drew to a stop next to him and tucked her hand in the crook of his arm.

"That was my father's rifle," he said after several seconds.

"He would have been proud of you, Anthony."

Her words sank in. For he'd shared with her how important it had been for him to fulfill his father's request and be a soldier. Anthony only wished he would have known the price he'd have to pay to do so. "Do you think so?"

"Of course. Do you not?"

Anthony lifted the weapon from where it was hung above the mantel. The rifle's wooden barrel, smooth with age and use, felt cool against his fingertips. Yes, his father would have been proud. But Anthony realized, perhaps too late, that his uncle's steady influence on him was even stronger. And he wanted to make that man—the man who had given him so much—proud too.

At this, rare emotion tightened the back of his throat. The guilt he carried with him was multifaceted, and his uncle's words rang in his mind.

"You are young. Your life is ahead of you. You don't believe me now, but one day you'll want a home to rest in. Permanency. Do not discount steadiness and security. You don't have to go to war to fight to be

important. You don't think it, but the work we do here, now, is important to every farmer we work with."

Uncle Robert had been right. Anthony did long for home. He did long for permanency.

He returned the weapon to its place and wrapped his good arm around Charlotte. He pressed his lips to the top of her head and then drew her close, holding her in the cottage's silence. She, in return, wrapped her arms around his waist, and in the stillness he could hear the gentleness of her breath, feel the softness of her warmth, and sense true purpose and peace in her presence.

"I'm a very fortunate man." He let his hand fall to the small of her back. "For I know what it is like to have lost everything and then have it restored. I will never take it for granted."

Chapter 46

ANTHONY STEPPED INTO the constable's office, satchel in hand, allowing several moments for his eyes to adjust from the afternoon's brightness to the dingy dimness of the closed space. The transport would be by later to convey Timmons to Leeds, and this was Anthony's last opportunity to address the former watchman before his departure. He'd accompanied several perpetrators into a similar structure before, but never did he think he would be visiting his friend in one.

He stepped toward the iron bars, and Timmons stood from a stool as Anthony approached. It had only been a few days since he last saw Timmons, but Anthony was struck at his altered appearance. The lines around his eyes and mouth seemed deeper. The shade of his eyes seemed to have dulled, and the start of a beard hugged his jaw. It was the man's posture, however, that was the biggest window into his state of mind—he was hunched, just as he had been the morning they had met at the public house when he had not been granted the constable position.

For several moments neither man spoke.

Anthony had expected to be frustrated or perhaps even

indifferent when seeing his friend after what had transpired, but he was not prepared for the rage that flared within him at the sight. He drew a steadying breath. This conversation needed to happen—for both their sakes. "I debated on whether to come."

"Felt sorry for me, did ye?" Timmons smirked in a failed attempt at lighthearted banter.

Anthony stiffened. He did feel a measure of pity for the man who had been as close as a brother. This was not the future he wanted for his friend. But now, outrage for the danger he'd put Charlotte and Henry in flared afresh.

"I 'eard ye got shot." Timmons nodded to Anthony's shoulder.

"It's not the worst injury I've received. I'll recover." Anthony kept his tone flat as he handed the satchel through the bars of the gaol. "I brought you some apples. The magistrate said you'd not eaten."

"Very thoughtful," Timmons responded in a measured tone. "Are these t' give me enough sustenance so I can walk on me own t' the gallows?"

Annoyed at the dark jest, Anthony pushed the satchel farther. "Just take them."

After several seconds, Timmons grabbed the outstretched offering.

Anthony paced the small space before Timmons, allowing his thoughts to calm. He'd contemplated what he wanted to say and what questions he would ask. But now that he was here, they would not form. At length he said, "You and I have found ourselves in some precarious situations before, but this is one I never would have suspected."

Timmons fixed his eyes hard on Anthony. "And I never expected ye t' woo our client. Ye ruined everything, ye know—ye and your romantic conquests."

Anthony shrugged. "I've known Charlotte for years. Besides, my personal life should have no bearing on your actions."

"That may be so, but this would 'ave gone differently if you'd been 'onest and told me t' truth straightaway."

"You speak of being honest?" Anthony blurted incredulously. "When I think over the last several months, even years, I don't know what part of what you said was true and what was a lie."

The words echoed from the stone wall, capturing the attention of the constable, and Anthony checked his rising volume and tugged at his neckcloth, and he refocused his concentration. "How did you even get involved in this?"

The war battling within Timmons wrote itself on his face before he spoke. "Years ago, when I was involved in takin' the jewels after Swendel Bay, I knew it was wrong, but Walstead told me if we kept Roland Prior content, then I'd be able t' pick and choose me assignments."

"Swendel Bay," repeated Anthony. "You told me you were at Raunten Bay."

"'Twas a lie." Timmons shrugged matter-of-factly.

Anthony scoffed and shook his head.

"I lied t' protect ye," Timmons blurted.

"I wouldn't have wanted or needed your protection."

"As soon as I 'eard about Roland Prior's death, I knew there might be trouble. T' less ye knew about me involvement, t' better. Besides, I didn't want ye t' get suspicious." Timmons cleared his throat. "Anyway, after Prior died, Walstead told me t' watch 'is wife t' find out what she knew about t' jewels. Said it would get us paid for t' job we did. It seemed simple, so I played up t' the maid and found out what I could. And then ye complicate it by bein' in love with t' woman I was t' watch. I didn't know 'ow t' get out of it."

"Then why did you not say something? I would have helped if I'd known."

"By t' time I realized t' extent Walstead would go t' get the King's Prize, I was too far in. Ye know Walstead. 'E demanded complete loyalty. T' job was not supposed t' include ye, but when 'e mentioned Blight Moor, I knew ye were from there and that we all stood to make a great deal of money. So I suggested you join. It was t' perfect setup."

"If you are expecting me to thank you for including me in this venture, I will not be doing that."

"No. But like I told ye, I never suspected ye and Mrs. Prior were so friendly. And when 'e tasked me with wooin' Miss Sutcliffe, things got dark and complicated quickly. And ye know what 'appens if ye go against Walstead . . ."

His voice faded, but Anthony understood his meaning. Going against Walstead would mean the end of his career.

Timmons continued. "I also hear ye are t' be married. Everything seems t' be working out for ye."

"Don't do that," Anthony growled. "Don't you dare speak as if I've had anything handed to me. We've been in the same situation; we only reacted differently."

"Except you are whole," Timmons shot back, his gaze firm and accusatory. "You have your hand."

Anthony would not argue details. He straightened his shoulders. He'd said what needed to be said. He knew better than to expect an apology, so instead, he fixed his eyes on his friend for what could very well be the last time. "I came to bid you farewell, Timmons. And to wish you luck. I hope you are able to find whatever it is you are so desperately seeking."

Anthony did not wait for a response before he turned on the heel of his boot and exited the cramped stone gaol. He nodded at the constable as he stepped through the door and into the bright Yorkshire sunshine.

He would always look back on Timmons's participation in this with a tinge of bitterness, but he could not control the man's actions any more than he could have anticipated Walstead's. As Anthony mounted his horse and headed back toward Hollythorne House, he focused on what he could control—and he would spend every day making sure he made the right decisions.

Chapter 47

CHARLOTTE SHOULD NOT be so nervous to see Silas Prior again. Yet a thread of uneasiness wound its way around her.

He'd sent word that he would arrive this morning. The King's Prize belonged to Roland's estate, and as the executor, Silas would collect the King's Prize and ensure it was sold and that the proceeds were applied appropriately to Roland's debts.

The events of the past month flew past her in unbelievable detail. Despite the horror they'd endured, every moment, every shocking experience had led to the point where they were now: Henry was safe. Slowly but surely, Hollythorne House was becoming whole and welcoming again, and she and Anthony would be married. Freeing themselves from the King's Prize was the last step to freedom.

She glanced up from stoking the fire as Anthony entered.

How handsome he looked. His dark hair was combed back away from his face and curled over his tailcoat's high collar. A bright white cravat was tied neatly at his neck, and his high-topped boots had been recently polished.

But these were not the things that caught her attention.

She smiled and turned as he stepped farther in the room, relishing his scent of sandalwood and soap. "You've shaved!"

He chuckled and ran his hand over his jaw. "I figured it was time. You don't find the scar too unsightly?"

Charlotte lifted her hand to his face and stroked his smooth cheek and jaw. How could anything about him ever be unsightly to her, when he alone was such a tremendous part of not just her past but her future? She let her fingers drift to his hair and trailed them through it. She fixed her eyes on his—intently, intimately, and shook her head. "No. Not at all."

He wrapped his strong arms about her waist and leaned in to kiss her, but noise in the courtyard interrupted them, and she stepped back, quickly reestablishing an appropriate distance and remembering the purpose of the visit.

Outside the window, Silas's carriage, surrounded by several guards, approached in obvious preparation to transport the jewels.

"Do you have them?" she asked, whirling back to Anthony.

He patted his pocket. "Ready?"

She nodded and turned back to the window to see Silas exiting the carriage. She was struck anew by how much the brothers resembled each other. From this distance the man could easily be mistaken for Roland—like a ghost from the grave.

But he was not Roland.

And soon that part of her life would be done, and the new one would begin.

Even so, she braced herself. Conversations with Silas were never easy.

The moorland wind caught the wool folds of Silas's caped

greatcoat, billowing out behind him as he approached the main entrance. At one time the confidence and the intention in his movements would have caused her to buckle under the strength of his presence.

But now she had seen too much.

Yes, she still was fully aware of his power, but Roland's estate had dwindled. And the last few weeks had taught her she was capable of so much more than she had thought. She was capable of managing Hollythorne House. She could raise Henry here. She could keep calm and make decisions. And she could stand up to Silas Prior.

She met Silas at the door to the screens passage and opened it.

"Ah," he said with no other greeting as he swept into the great hall, the day's chill and dampness still clinging to him. He doffed his hat from his head, his white-blond hair disheveled and his complexion ruddy from the cold. "No longer in mourning, I see."

"Good day, Silas." She ignored the comment about her gown.

"You know why I am here," he stated as his face formed with hard lines and he fixed his gaze on Anthony. "We've a great deal to discuss. Alone."

"No, Silas," she countered. "Mr. Welbourne will stay."

"The devil he will."

"Mr. Welbourne saved Henry from the kidnappers. Do not forget it. He will stay." Charlotte took a step forward, summoning her courage. For as much as she did not care for Silas Prior, he needed to know. "Anthony and I are to be married, Silas."

His expression did not change at the news, and his response came out almost in a hiss. "You're a fool then. And you." He shifted his attention to Anthony. "How dare you take advantage of a situation."

Charlotte did not give Anthony the chance to respond. "He is taking advantage of nothing. I am in full control of my life now. And after how you insisted that the Walstead Watchmen come and live with me on my property, you hardly have the right to have an opinion on how things have transpired."

Silas's face reddened, but his voice remained alarmingly low. "How dare you disrespect Roland in this manner."

"How dare I disrespect Roland?" she shot back. "Roland was intolerably cruel, and I dare you to say otherwise, for you bore witness to it. I will not live in the shadow of a man who cared so little for me. I will be happy and productive with the rest of my days, and my decisions will forever be my own from this time forward."

His gaze narrowed. "When you marry you will receive not a single penny from Roland's will."

"I don't need it, nor do I want it," she countered. "Besides, Mr. Walstead told me that the estate is in dire straits. I cannot speak to Henry's inheritance, but I expect nothing more from Roland's estate. In fact, it is time to give you this."

Anthony handed her the pouch, and she stepped past Anthony until she was quite close to Silas. "The King's Prize. It belonged to Roland. Do what you need to do with it to set things right with Roland's estate and settle the necessary debts. From what I understand, once that is done there will be little left of an inheritance for Henry."

Silas snatched the pouch and looked inside.

"As for Henry," she continued, "he will continue to live here at Hollythorne House. Permanently."

Silas's tone remained hardened, but he was losing his argument—and his power over her. "He will still receive an inheritance from me, and he will need to know the business. What sort of mother would not want her son to be prepared for such things?"

"I assure you, Silas, I am a very good mother. And don't you worry—Henry will be prepared to be a gentleman. He will go to school and be educated, but all that will be decided by me, and as for his future career, he will decide that when he is old enough to do so."

"You will regret this," he shot back, face flaming. "I'll make certain of it."

"You have no control here, Silas. You cannot control Henry. And you certainly will not control me."

Silas did not respond. Instead, he turned on his heel, King's Prize in hand, and stormed from the house.

Charlotte stood alone with Anthony in the great hall as they watched the Prior carriage depart the courtyard for what could very well be the last time. At one time the sight of that vehicle would incite fear and uncertainty. But now, as she leaned against Anthony, she felt strength running through her.

Once they were again alone, Anthony pressed a kiss on her cheek and snaked his arms around her waist. "You said you thought my father would be proud of me. But I think your father would be quite proud of you too."

She relaxed against him, relishing the strength she found there, and rested her hand atop his arm. "I hope he would be. But even through all of this, I can't help but feel a measure of pity for Silas. He'd fought so hard for control over Roland. Over Henry. Over me. Now what does he have? A big house. A great deal of power but no family. His legacy had been all that mattered to him. And now . . ."

Anthony shifted, slowly pivoting her to face him. "And now," he picked up where her words faded, "Silas will live with the consequences of his actions. If the last few years have taught me anything, it is that every deed, every decision, has a consequence. Timmons learned that. And I've learned it too."

Anthony's countenance lightened. "Now, Charlotte Prior, where were we before being interrupted?"

She laughed at the playful grin she saw on his face—the happy laugh of a woman content, at peace, and in love.

He pulled her tight and kissed her, and her future spread before her, as vast and as free as the moor itself.

Epilogue

THE VIBRANT SUN shone down on Hollythorne House's budding garden. Purple heather painted the moorland landscape around them, and the azure expanse of shimmering sky spread out overhead. After a long winter, spring was finally arriving, and with it a fresh perspective on all that lay ahead.

Charlotte tucked her hand in that of her husband's as they traversed the brick path she had walked many years ago with her mother. Before them Henry toddled on, then paused, amused, to pick up a stick that had fallen in their way.

Anthony dropped her hand and stepped forward to scoop up Henry.

A little more than a year ago, her life had been bleak, but in a matter of mere months, her world had shifted, and now it began and ended with the two people with her in this garden.

Charlotte took Anthony's arm once again, and they continued their stroll through the blushing hyacinth and brilliant golden daffodils. The sun's yellow warmth reached down, and the soft breeze blew her hair waywardly about her face, but she didn't mind. Overhead, the swallows dipped among the budding branches, and life felt fresh and free. "Do you think that if you had never gone to war and if I had never been married to Roland, we would still be the same people we are now?"

He tilted his head to the side. "Probably, to some extent, but I think we appreciate our blessings now more than we ever would have. It would be easy to take things for granted if we didn't have to endure so much to acquire them."

Charlotte thought about his words, and they sat on the bench at the garden's center. Anthony lowered Henry to the ground to explore.

"Mama, Mama!" Henry toddled up, a piece of grass in his hand, and extended it to her.

"Let's see what you've found." She took the grass and held it up before them. She wrapped her arm around him and drew him close and kissed his cheek. She studied her son, with his fair complexion and blond hair, and every so often, the light would catch his face just right, and memories of Roland would rush back to her. It frightened her at times.

"One day, he'll ask about Roland," she said, growing somber. She lifted the boy onto her lap and brushed his hair from his face. "In spite of everything he will still have a small inheritance when he is of age. It is only right he will be curious about it."

"What will you tell him?" asked Anthony.

Her memories of Roland floated through her mind, but with each passing month and the deeper she sank into her new life, the less vibrant the recollections became, as if they were from a dream passing into nothingness. "I suppose I will tell him that family is who we choose to love and those who love us in return."

Their walk took them from the garden onto the moors, and there they traversed the overgrown paths that ran past the stony crags, past the copse of trees, and past the broad expanse of heather until they reached the small cottage at the foot of Thoms Tor. She would never be able to pass this house and not relive the fear of those moments but also experience the gratitude for the lives they now lived.

"What do you think ever happened to Mr. Timmons?" she asked.

Anthony looked toward the cottage where he and Timmons had fought. "I am not sure we'll ever know."

"I did receive news from Sutcliffe. Did I tell you?" She lifted her hand to still the hair blowing about her face. "She is settled in a situation in Scotland, of all places. She said she was content, and after all she has been through, I hope that is true."

"I'm sure they each have their own story to tell." Anthony hoisted Henry up on his shoulders. "Just as we all do. And while I am sorry for the paths that others have taken in life, I am grateful every day for mine."

She smiled up at him.

"Do you remember? When I asked you to marry me? It is when I knew you would always be mine and I knew my life would forever be better. And it has."

She rose to the tips of her toes and kissed him. "Mine too."

She took his hand, and together they returned to the shelter of Hollythorne House and the life that awaited them there.

Acknowledgments

THE PROCESS OF writing every book is a unique journey, and there are so many lessons to learn along the way! I am grateful to those people who have supported me in every stage of the writing process.

To my family—Each and every day I am so thankful for your unwavering encouragement. I truly am blessed!

To my agent, Rachelle Gardner—Your guidance and friendship are so very valuable to me. What would I do without you?

To my editor, Becky Monds, and my line editor, Julee Schwarzburg—Thank you for diving deep into this story to make it as strong as it can be. To the rest of the HarperCollins Christian Publishing team—I am constantly amazed at your skills!

To KBR and KC—your friendship is a gift!

And last but certainly not least, to my readers—Thank you for sharing the love of story with me.

Discussion Questions

1. Miss Sutcliffe may have been Charlotte's lady's maid, but Charlotte also considered her a friend. Do you think these women were good friends to one another? Why or why not?

2. If you had to describe Charlotte in one sentence, what would that sentence be? How would you describe Anthony?

3. Who is the true villain of this book?

4. The characters in this story grow and change a great deal. In what ways is Charlotte different at the end of the book than she was in the beginning? In what ways does Anthony change?

5. Who is your favorite character in this novel? Who is your least favorite? Why?

6. When Anthony was young, he was so focused on living up to his father's expectations that he did not realize the impact his uncle was having on him. Looking back on your own life, can you think of someone who had a

positive impact on you, even if you didn't realize it until years later?

7. By the end of the story, Charlotte realized she couldn't solve every problem on her own and that sometimes she had to rely on others. Have you ever had a similar realization?

8. It's your turn! If you were the author of this book, what would come next for Anthony and Charlotte?

THE CORNWALL NOVELS

Set in the same time period as *Poldark*
and *Bridgerton*, these stories are rich
with family secrets, lingering danger, and
the captivating allure of new love.

"*Northanger Abbey* meets *Poldark* against the resplendent and beautifully realized landscape of Cornwall. Ladd shines a spotlight on the limitations of women in an era where they were deprived of agency and instead were commodities in transactions of business and land. The thinking-woman's romance, *The Thief of Lanwyn Manor* is an unputdownable escape."

—RACHEL MCMILLAN, AUTHOR OF *THE LONDON RESTORATION*

THOMAS NELSON
Since 1798

About the Author

Photo by Emilie Haney
of EAH Creative

SARAH E. LADD is an award-winning, bestselling author who has always loved the Regency period—the clothes, the music, the literature, and the art. A college trip to England and Scotland confirmed her interest, and she began seriously writing in 2010. Since then, she has released several novels set during the Regency era. Sarah is a graduate of Ball State University and holds degrees in public relations and marketing. She lives in Indiana with her family.

Visit Sarah online at SarahLadd.com
Instagram: @sarahladdauthor
Facebook: @SarahLaddAuthor
Twitter: @SarahLaddAuthor
Pinterest: @SarahLaddAuthor